VERY

BAD

ELITE

Also by Jane S. Wonda:

Kingston University series:
Very Bad Kings

Jane S. Wonda

Very Bad Elite

Second semester

Kingston University series – part 2

Uitgeverij Zomer & Keuning

ISBN 9789020559903
ISBN e-book 9789020559934
ISBN audiobook 9789020559941
NUR 343

© 2025 Uitgeverij Zomer & Keuning
Postbus 13288, 3507 LG Utrecht

© 2021 Jane S. Wonda
Originally published in German as *Very Bad Elite* by Wondaversum,
Germany.

Cover design © Wondaversum
English cover Liesbeth Thomas, t4design

www.zomerenkeuning.nl
www.janeswonda.com

Zomer & Keuning believes it is important to use natural resources in an en-
vironmentally friendly and responsible manner. The paper that was used for
the edition of this title, is guaranteed to have not resulted in deforestation.

For all those who can't decide

They say, "All good boys go to heaven"
But bad boys bring heaven to you
Julia Michaels

SOUNDTRACK

It will always be the wrong one, Belle
The Path of Silence | several artists

Even a pawn can capture a king
Arrival of the Birds | XOMA

The beach house
Filaments | Scott Buckley

Two new allies
In These Dark Times | Aime Simone

The game will never end
Legendary | Welshly Arms
Costello Ave | TRAILS

The Mask of the Kings
Nightmares | Two Feets

I am no longer a character
Jekyll & Hide | Bishop Briggs
Young Minds | Saavan

Full playlist on Spotify at:
Very Bad Kings Soundtrack by Jane S. Wonda

TRIGGER
WARNING

I hope you don't expect it to get *better*, do you?

Very Bad Elite ends in a cliffhanger and may contain triggers, including bullying, mobbing, attempted rape, mentions of suicide, (sexual) harassment, (sexual) violence, psychological torment, (mentions of) death, knife play, and alcohol and drug abuse.

Please take these content notices seriously.
Your mental health matters.

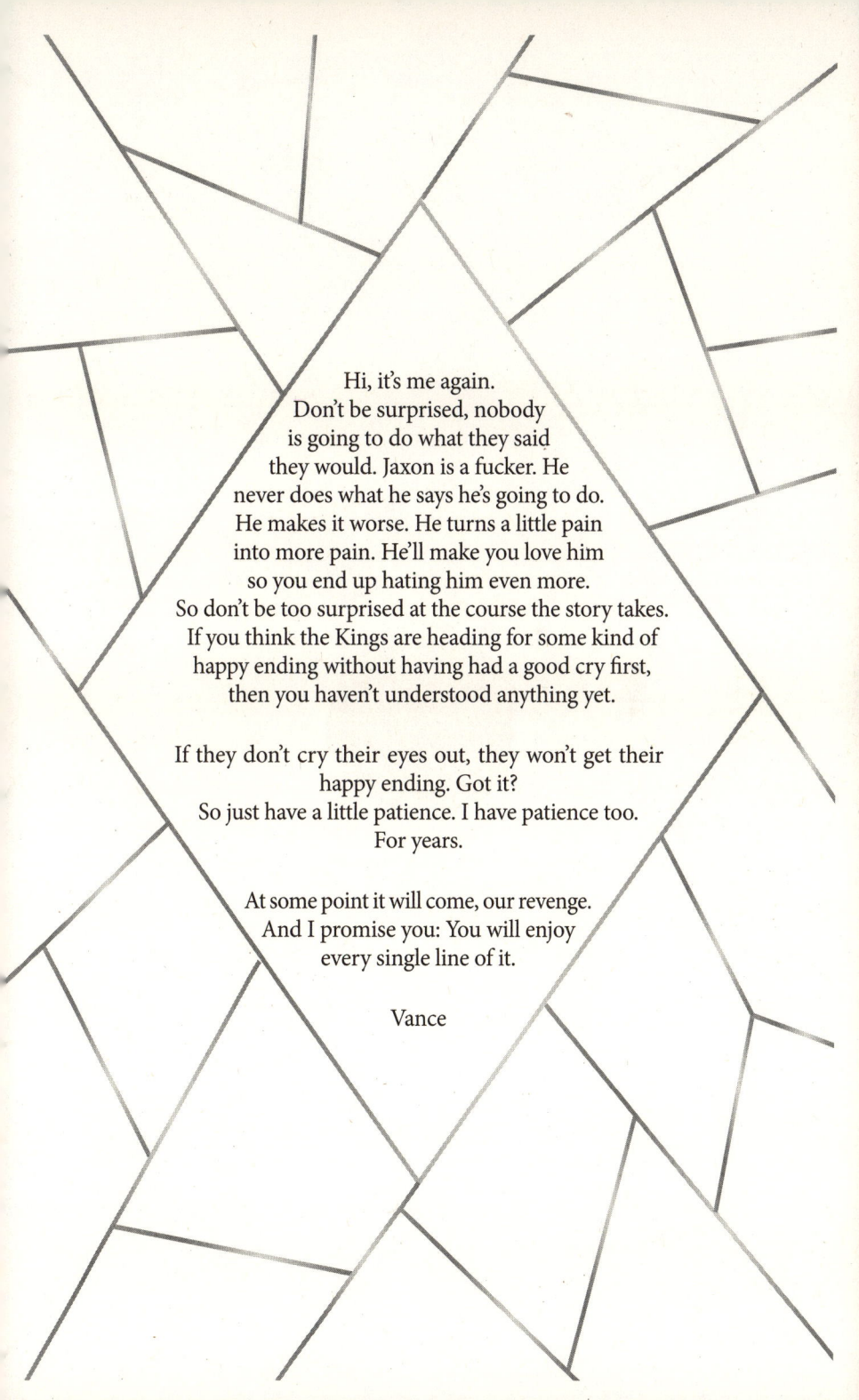

Hi, it's me again.
Don't be surprised, nobody
is going to do what they said
they would. Jaxon is a fucker. He
never does what he says he's going to do.
He makes it worse. He turns a little pain
into more pain. He'll make you love him
so you end up hating him even more.
So don't be too surprised at the course the story takes.
If you think the Kings are heading for some kind of
happy ending without having had a good cry first,
then you haven't understood anything yet.

If they don't cry their eyes out, they won't get their
happy ending. Got it?
So just have a little patience. I have patience too.
For years.

At some point it will come, our revenge.
And I promise you: You will enjoy
every single line of it.

Vance

THE DECISION

Three kings stand before me.

Three dark faces.

This time I'm not tied up and yet I can't move.

Jaxon, Sylvian and Reece take me in, stare me down and demand something from me that I can never give them.

"Which King do you choose?" Jaxon asks with a dark smile. His voice leaves no room for any other choice than for him. There he stands, the King of Kings, challenging me in an even crueler way than last semester.

I should decide.

I should choose.

One of them.

Reece. The friend.

Sylvian. The heart.

And Jaxon. My personal fragment that I'm determined to get hold of so that I finally feel whole.

"You understand the rules of the game, don't you?" Jaxon's eyes flash dangerously. In all his vanity, he must hate me for not choosing *him* long ago. "One of us will save you. Another will let you keep playing. And the last one means… your death. It's a wicked game. Utterly reprehensible, the worst of its kind. You only have this one choice, Belle. Choose the right one or let the campus become your personal hell again."

"That really is a tempting offer," I reply ironically and

the crowd at his back laughs. Are they laughing with me or at me? It seems many of them no longer see me as the victim. No, I'm the one lady that everything revolves around. Should that make me happy? Does the support of the masked students mean anything to me? "But I'd rather choose hell than you."

Silence spreads through the room.

Jaxon narrows his eyes imperceptibly, the others step forward. They approach me as if they crave my blood, my tormented heart. I am completely in their hands, with no prospect of escape as long as they won't let me go.

"You choose hell?" Sylvian asks. It's the first time I've seen him raise his voice in front of the others. So far, only Jaxon and Reece have spoken. "I don't think you have any idea what awaits you there."

"If you don't decide, someone else will do it for you," Reece explains coolly. "Don't waste the opportunity to end it. Now."

I look at him, wondering if he would be the one to save me. I can't imagine it. The Kings are still cruel. They do heinous things. And they won't stop just because I choose one of them.

What I did last semester was daring. I challenged them, provoked them, gave in to their thirst for retribution. But no one could have predicted that the game would take a completely different turn when I came back. Maybe I should have listened to Harper and Vance. Maybe I should have been as cruel to the Kings as they were to me. Would it have done any good?

Can I even win this game?

Or am I forever doomed to be a piece on their stupid chessboard?

"No," I reply nervously, not sure if I can allow myself to

defy them again. "No matter who I choose, it will be the wrong one."

Jaxon smirks, the crowd murmurs, but Sylvian steps forward.

"You don't seem to have understood." Sylvian growls. The green jungle in his eyes devours me. The anger that I defy his will seems endless. "This is not a *request*. It's not an *invitation*. It's an *ultimatum*. You only have one choice. Make it."

"Are you still not afraid of what might happen?" asks Reece impassively. As if he doesn't care about what's happening. As if he's already sure I'd take him if my pride didn't get in the way. The Kings have involved me in a game of lust and desire. It was clear that I wouldn't last long. My pride is the only thing that keeps me from falling for them again.

"There's only one thing I'm afraid of," I whisper.

"Oh yeah?" asks Jaxon, stepping closer. I can feel his breath on my sensitive skin. It's crazy and reprehensible, and most certainly spells my doom, but I can't wait for him to touch me again. I should hate him. I should want to hurt him. But there's something else. Something deeper.

Something completely dark that I can no longer escape.

The reason why I didn't run.

Why I can't leave Kingston.

Although it would be smarter. Definitely. You can't win the game of the elite with just one piece. Even when Sylvian's lips brushed mine for the first time, I should have resisted.

But all I could do was let myself be wrapped further and further in their net.

Like a butterfly that has become addicted to being caught. Something tells me that there are wings waiting for me at the end of its abyss that will propel me back up.

"And what is this thing you're afraid of?" Jaxon murmurs in a quivering voice, with uncontrolled vindictiveness in his words because I will never play along with his stupid game. "If it's not us?"

"That you're taking away the most important thing in my life."

Curiosity flickers in his gaze.

"My studies. I want to stay at Kingston. But not at any price. You want something from me that I'm not prepared to give."

"You just have to give a name. That's all. Sylvian's, Reece's or mine," Jaxon summarizes smugly. "And you won't even do that to save your fucking studies?"

I swallow hard. Again, it seems so easy to end the game. But I'm not strong enough. I can't lie. I can't betray my heart just so I can stay at Kingston. "Maybe you haven't noticed," I whisper, "but you're not exactly guys a woman would willingly choose."

Restrained laughter erupts in the room again. But it dies down as soon as Jaxon laughs.

The other kings also purse their lips. It gives me goosebumps to see Sylvian and Reece like this. Do they long for my downfall more than Jaxon ever did?

"Are you really going to force me?" I ask anxiously.

All the masked students follow our battle of words with interest. How will the Kings react if I don't make up my mind? What consequences am I allowing?

"Of course not, *Belle*," Jaxon whispers back. "No one will *force* you. If you don't choose, be prepared for us to *destroy* you this time. But so much more. Until there is nothing, nothing left of what you once were. Do you really think you know what it means to defy our rules forever? What it means for your *life*?"

"So I have to choose? Come what may?"

"Or you leave. If you leave Kingston, it will save you from what will happen otherwise."

I raise my chin. Although my heart is racing, I feel safe and strong. I lower my voice and look him firmly in the eye. The beauty in Jaxon's flawless face is eclipsed by the shadows of his soul. My life used to be a hell. Compared to Kingston, it's *nothing*. Still, I won't give up. "Never."

Jaxon smiles. "Then choose. Now."

JAXON

You wanted to take us on and we're ready for round two. But this time everything will be different, you realize that, right?

We won't be wankers anymore. We're going to be nice. Each in their own wonderfully destructive way.

We have to spin the web around you until you think the spider threads are silk, wrapping you up like a dress.

We have to make you believe that you can trust us.

You'll fall in love with us, so relentlessly deep that even when our fangs dig into your flesh, you'll still think we want your best.

Flutter, flutter, little butterfly.

Soon I will catch you.

1

MABLE

When the elegant minibus pulls up in front of our trailer and shortly afterwards a massive parcel appears on our snow-covered terrace, I think at first that it's a bomb. Yes, after all the tears, the anger, the despair, I wouldn't be surprised if the Kings simply sent me a huge bomb. As a Christmas present, so to speak, so that I could finally be wiped off the face of the earth.

But when I finally recognize Harper, who picks up the gift again, stands in front of our door and peers out at our windows from under a fat bobble hat, I discard this thought.

At least to a certain extent.

Harper wouldn't be holding a bomb that could go off at any time, would she?

"Who's that?" asks Olive, pulling out her phone. Ever since she got it as a present yesterday, she's been taking pictures with it all the time. Her camera was far too bad for photos before.

"Harper," I mumble, even though I know that's not a satisfactory answer. Harper: the friend whose ex and now fiancé I had a foursome with. And the friend who watched the entire campus bully me to the brink of insanity.

I can no longer stand not knowing what she's doing here and pull open the door of our trailer.

When Harper sees me, the huge package falls out of her hand. She stares at me as if she didn't expect me to live here, and big tears well up in her eyes. "Mable," she whispers. And then she says it, and after all the pain of the last few days, I'm almost too cold to let it get to me. "I'm so sorry!"

Almost. My hands are clawing at our door frame. Even if I wanted to, I couldn't speak.

"I just wanted to… bring you something." She points to the package in the snow.

Will I dare to open it, or should I listen first to check if anything is ticking inside?

"Okay," I reply. I don't have the strength for more. Or the courage. And perhaps because I realize in some intuitive way that Harper feels the same way, we're lying in each other's arms shortly afterwards.

We hug each other so tightly that it hurts. I'm sure she can't tell me how we overcame the distance between us either, but it's not important.

I hug her and press her so tightly against me, as if this could prevent me from losing her again.

"I'm so sorry," I whisper. "I should've listened to you."

"Never mind," she whispers back. She howls even louder than I do. "No one ever listens to anyone when it comes to Jaxon's fucking asshole behavior."

I laugh because I missed her anger at him so much.

She moves away from me, holds me by both shoulders and looks me over. Her make-up is soaked up and she looks like a clown who's had an accident. "I'm the worst person in the world."

"That would be me," I mumble.

"Uh… no."

"I lied to you."

"You said you would never hurt me on purpose, and it wasn't intentional! But I just sat there and watched! And did nothing! It *was* on purpose!" She hugs me tightly again and I allow her touch.

No matter what stands or stood between us, in this one moment I just want to forget it. I want it to become meaningless, because I like her as a person. And the fact that she's here and showing remorse, even though she's the only one whose hatred I deserve, proves that I can't be that wrong. I cheated on her and she took revenge on me. We both hurt each other to the extreme. If she can forgive me, so can I.

"How are you?" she asks anxiously, looking at my face.

I haven't smiled since mid-December. Ever since I had to leave campus in a hurry with nothing more than the knowledge that I would have to return, even if it cost me everything, my heart has been devoid of any joy. I've been empty and hollow inside ever since. Winning Harper back as an ally – or at least as one who *doesn't* want to scare me off campus – raises a glimmer of hope.

Don't be so naive. You can't rely on her never dropping you again.

"I see," she mumbles, "not very well." Shadows move across her pretty face and I try to smile. Or at least chuckle.

It's not working.

"Do you want to open your present?"

"I think it would be great!" Olive hops out of the trailer behind me. She's so much slimmer and shorter than I was at her age.

Whatever Harper has given me, I don't really want to accept it. But I guess I have no choice. Should I reject her, even though she's the only one who's ever apologized?

I take the package – it's light – and place it on our snowy patio table. It's wrapped like one of the decorative gifts in the Target windows and I carefully untie one of the golden bows.

Olive is waiting next to me, shivering. We should put some coats on, but the cold is bearable at the moment. After peeling off the paper, I open the box. Inside is a metal frame. Thin bars, delicately gilded.

"It's a photo collage." Harper helps me get the frame out and holds it out in front of me. Four metal squares are connected to form a photo display. The whole thing is huge and dozens of photos are stuck to the struts. "I wanted to give you something to remind you that there are beautiful things about Kingston."

Tears well up in my eyes as I look at all the pictures Harper took of us last semester. At dinner, watching Netflix, in her apartment, in my dorm room. In the Kingston fall sun, on the stairs to the library. I never realized how many photos she *actually* took with her phone. Between the pictures are doodles we've slipped to each other in the hallways between classes, alongside a few photos of hot actors we like – thouh they don't even come close to the charisma of the Kings.

"Do you like it?" asks Harper.

I don't know what to say. There seems to be nothing left of the quick-witted Mable, who even stood up to Jaxon. With all the money Harper could have used to buy me something, she gave me something priceless instead.

"I can't promise that I won't have another breakdown and become a disgusting bitch," she says quietly. "I may never be able to be as honest as you. But I wanted to show you that I really like you, Mable. And even if my lousy character makes you think otherwise, all you have to do is look at these pictures to know what it's really like."

A knot has tightened my throat and I'm fighting back tears. "I'm not honest," I say, barely audible. "And what lousy character?" I look at her, pretending to be confused, and she laughs.

And then, finally, I laugh too.

We laugh for so long that Olive rolls her eyes in annoyance and disappears back inside.

"I left out one or two photos. Because I wasn't sure what you'd think of them. Especially since I didn't take them and they were actually... taken to expose us. You know. But I honestly love them." Harper reaches into her bag and pulls out more prints.

When I see our happy faces, beaming with joy and laughing as we throw chicken feathers at each other on the stairs to the main building, I am beside myself. I start crying.

"Oh, I'm so sorry!" Harper hugs me tightly and I cry louder. All the pain is suddenly as tangible as a sword. And someone points the blade right at my heart. Jaxon, Reece, Sylvian. I fell in love and trusted and was betrayed like never before in my life. How will I ever find the strength to let anyone get close to me again?

How am I supposed to get through this trauma?

A door of her luxury van is opened and slammed shut again. Harper lets go of me, waving her arms to scare away her driver, who obviously wants to join us, but he approaches anyway. I don't turn around. He probably thinks he could be shot by my neighbors in our trailer park at any time, so he wants to leave as quickly as possible. As I continue to look at the pictures, she gestures at my back.

"Please, just go!" she finally says and I turn around.

That doesn't sound like she's talking to her driver. And

it's not a washed-up guy standing in front of us lighting up a cigarette.

It's Sylvian.

My heart falls deep into the snow and my tears dry up immediately.

He looks at me without a care in the world, as if my tear-stained face couldn't affect him less.

"Hello, Mable." His voice sweeps through me and I think of everything that was between us. Every word, every gesture, every *kiss*... The memories overwhelm me and erase every happy feeling.

"Why aren't you waiting in the car? We agreed!" Harper asks him reproachfully.

"I wanted a smoke." Sylvian raises the glowing cigarette in his hand in reply. He's wearing what he wore in the fall. A leather jacket and white sneakers. Plus a black cap that gives him even more gangster style than usual. *He deals drugs on campus. And he's engaged to Harper.*

I don't know how to breathe for a few seconds. All the dark emotions he has triggered in me come crashing down on me. Sex in the forest. So animalistic and dark. My first real time. And the kiss in my dorm room. Possessive, hungry. Then the night in the frat house. How he was inside me. Just before Reece. How he came in my mouth. I get cold, nauseous, and hot all at the same time, and I wish he was just dead. Yes, dead. Then only my memory of him would survive, and that would be far less painful than knowing that his every word was a lie. Except for the warnings at the beginning at Crowns, maybe. Not those.

"I told you I wanted to be alone with Mable," Harper says.

Sylvian glances at his watch. "You've been alone for fifteen minutes already."

She makes a face at him. Are they having sex? Probably when they're engaged, right? The very idea drives such a deep stake into my heart that I want to vomit.

Harper sighs theatrically and turns to me. "Sylvian came with us so you know he's behind us. Behind me and therefore behind you too."

"Great," I choke out.

I hear Sylvian laughing at my ironic answer and would have liked to throw something at him. With something much harder than a snowball.

"What we did, what we *allowed to happen*, was not right." Harper looks at me seriously. "Shortly after you declared war to Jaxon, I followed you. I was stopped, but… What I'm saying is Sylvian will be on your side because I am. So next semester will be different. I promise you."

"Or else what? You're not marrying him after all?" The cynical comment slipped from my lips unintentionally. "Sorry," I add. "I'm just never going to trust him again, all right? Never. The fact that you do is up to you."

Her mouth opens and she squints at Sylvian, as if hoping he can tell her how to react.

"We've both made mistakes," I implore her quietly, even though Sylvian can hear us either way. "He, on the other hand, is one of the *Kings*. He's *Jaxon's* friend. He would have had several opportunities to stop him. To at least make him regret his actions. Instead, he stands next to Jaxon and lets it all happen."

"You're right," Harper begins haltingly, "but –"

"Does she want to come with us or not?" asks Sylvian impatiently. "Come with you? Where to?" I ask icily.

Harper wrings her fingers. "I wanted to kidnap you, in a way. To my grandparents in the mountains. They own a chalet in the Catskills and it's a fantastic place to enjoy a winter vacation. Surrounded by ski slopes and toboggan runs –"

"With Sylvian?" I ask her, stunned.

"He won't hurt you. Nothing at all. I promise."

"He's already broken that promise to you once," I remind her angrily.

She looks helplessly at him again and my stomach turns over completely. Why is she so submissive to him? Why is she *with him* of all people? How did she come to appear here with him?

"Thanks for the present, Harper," I mumble and roughly wrap up the photo collage. Then I cover the box, leave it on our cheap plastic garden table and turn towards the door.

"Please, Mable, are you sure you don't want to at least think about it? We could certainly have a great time!"

I turn around to her. Stunned and bruised. Has she come to exacerbate all my heartache, all the pain, all the trauma? Is she here to hurt me? Or is Sylvian here to hurt me? Is he here to destroy me? Punish me for good for everything I've done wrong for whatever reason? I blink and decide that while Harper may turn into a stupid cow when it comes to her 'fiancé', Sylvian is even worse.

Much, much, much worse.

I look at him.

He stands there, unmoved, as if I'm not even there.

As if I were nothing.

A speck of dust.

Somewhere on the edge of his vision, where he takes no notice of me.

"You," I hiss.

He raises a brow, holding his cigarette with his forefinger and thumb.

"You only got engaged to her to hurt me." I say it and maybe I'll break Harper's heart. But better it breaks than it continues to be blackened by Sylvian until it can no longer show any beauty. "You've said so many times that you don't care about her! You betrayed me, manipulated me, forced me to say nothing to her! She means absolutely *nothing* to you, I know it! If anything, you love yourself and what you can do to others. You probably stand in front of the mirror all day and jerk off about what a massive fucker you are and that your best friend still trumps you at being an asshole!"

Sylvian has very slowly lowered his cigarette. The jungle in his eyes is unfathomable.

Harper's face turns pale. "Mable, I –"

"This guy is the biggest scumbag I've ever met," I snap at her. "And he's lying. He's lying to you, and he's lied to thousands of other women. If you think so little of yourself that you won't take that stupid engagement ring and shove it up his ass, then I'd rather be friends with Clarisse. At least she openly admits to being incredibly stupid."

Sylvian laughs again, and I know I'd shoot him if I had a gun.

"Just get out," I mumble and leave them standing in the snow. Unfortunately, the door of our trailer isn't suitable for slamming it shut.

As soon as I'm inside, I meet Olive's totally distraught gaze. My mom is off somewhere, probably looking for a job she'll never find, and I throw myself on my bed. Burying my head deep in the pillow, I cry.

I let it all come over me, all the terrible pain, the inescapable truth.

I have no allies. I have no friends.

And I have to do it alone. All fucking alone.

2

JAXON

New York in the snow chaos. I appreciate the thought behind this city and I appreciate it most from afar. New York is loud, restless, stressful and constantly makes you feel tiny. Nothing compared to the skyscrapers that reach the sky.

I sit alone at a table and wait. I play the piano on the table with the Kings' signet ring between my fingers. The ring dips down, pops up, falls down and back up again. The eyes of the other guests are on me and I hate this feeling.

The restaurant is exclusive, probably has a Michelin star, and it's noticeable when someone like me sits at a table all alone for over an hour. Like I've been stood up by my date.

I'm offered a second wine. I haven't even touched the first one.

An hour and a half after the agreed time, a man enters the restaurant. He nods to the waiter as if he owns the place and heads for my table.

I sit up straighter and try to hide my nerves.

The man pulls back the chair opposite me, keeps his coat on and looks at me with a cold, blank stare. "Was anything we asked for unclear?"

Bile shoots into my throat, and I try not to screw up my face. "No, sir."

"But it seems that one of them will still graduate this year."

I know the man. He's been talking to me about the circle's affairs for years. But I've never found out his name. Or what rank he has. Perhaps he's just an errand boy? "That's not going to happen," I counter as politely as possible.

"Really?" he asks impatiently. The mere fact that he belongs to the circle means that he holds incredible power. "None of these lowlifes will ever graduate from Kingston," he reminds me. "That was the order, and it's going to be close if you don't start thinking of something."

"I have a *plan*."

"That would be?"

It's the first time he's asked me what I was thinking during the chess game. I'm not prepared for this and I try to come up with a satisfactory answer in a matter of seconds. "Keeping Vance Buchanan at Kingston is a means to an end. He's the main help in getting rid of the other scholarship players. But he's not going to graduate. I'll see to that."

"Yes? Just like you made sure that a girl from the *trailer park* achieved above average grades?"

I clench my teeth and try not to think about Amabelle. My counterpart's eyes flash knowingly. "You're failing, Tyrell."

"Nobody could have known that she would be so good," I counter coolly. "It won't happen a second time."

"It won't happen *a second time*?" He leans forward. If I didn't know that he belongs to one of the richest thousand families in the world, I wouldn't be able to tell. His hair is gray, his blue eyes are milky and the contours of his face are puffy. Probably from too much alcohol. He's not my role model, definitely not. But he's someone who could stand in my way – and only because he thinks he's better than me. "Not a second time?" he repeats again, his lips twisted ironically. "What do you think we're doing here? Mistakes are unforgivable. Especially when you normally *can't go wrong.* What were you doing when that girl was taking all her exams? Did you sit there twiddling your thumbs? Didn't you realize that she was well on her way to outdoing everyone? How could you have missed something like that? Are *you* even fit for Kingston?"

I try to keep my game face on. *It's so much easier to act when I don't actually have to, Belle. Lies used to be my strength. But since I've met you, I know that the truth can hurt even more.*

"Nothing?" the man asks, smiling at me as if I were a pathetic loser who can't do anything.

"Amabelle Weaver was almost raped."

"Oh, should I feel sorry?"

"I forced her to apologize to her tormentor to make him stop, to demonstrate my power to her. I then gave the entire campus a free pass and she had to hide in her room until the exam period so that nothing would be done to her. She didn't take part in the exam preparation courses. Not a single one. So if she's still the best in her year, maybe Kingston shouldn't allocate places solely on the basis of parents' income, don't you think?"

The man bares his teeth in disgust. "I don't give a shit *what exactly you do,* Tyrell." He knows I'm right. The fact that Amabelle did excellently doesn't mean she's particularly smart. The other business students are just particularly stupid. "And I don't care about what exactly happens at Kingston. Just make sure the result is right."

"Should I kill her?" I ask point-blank, because that seems

30

to be what it will come down to if none of the Kings break Amabelle for good.

The man laughs caustically, and suddenly I can imagine that he wouldn't have any problem with it. *He would kill you. He would let me kill you. He might even demand it.* "Tyrell, you know what will happen if you take the easy way out. The circle won't want you if you act like a gangster. Be fucking smart. Offer the girl something *better.* If she's not impressed by rape, then think about what the hell else it could be. You must realize what's at stake if you fail. The circle isn't looking for members who *want to be* members. It chooses who *must* become a member because their actions show great influence. Without knowing the girl, she just strikes me as someone the circle would love to have in its ranks. While the name Tyrell fades more and more with each passing minute."

My jaw feels like a slab of stone as he stands up, adjusts his coat and leaves the restaurant without another word.

I reach for the wine.

And almost crush the glass in my hand.

3

SYLVIAN

The number one rule of a dealer?

Never take that shit yourself. Never.

Let others taste it, pump them full of it, be there when they push their bodies beyond every conceivable point, *but never take that shit yourself.*

Because being so close at the source, having the entire supply constantly under your nose and *then* becoming addicted to it is a damn expensive business. Besides, drugs suck. Sooner or later they always fuck you up.

Now I'm already fucked up. And actually high since Thanksgiving.

I don't even know *what* I'm taking anymore, but it's getting more and more every day.

Watching Mable awakens many desires in me. I could run after her and hurt her a little more.

I could also just fuck her. But she wouldn't want it.

And then I could take the knife I'm carrying and stop her next breaths all at once. Hers, mine, Harper's, whatever.

But I do nothing. I stand there, continue smoking and watch the expression on my 'fiancée's' face, which is only slowly clearing. For a moment, I leave her in the agonizing belief that Mable might have told the truth. That every word is as true as it is. *In case you haven't figured it out yet, baby, I'm a sadist. But the physical pain my victims feel is not enough for me. Psychological pain goes deeper.*

It opens wounds, hollows out people, gnaws at every bit of existence.

If you really want to hurt someone, don't use weapons. Don't use violence.

Hurt them with words.

Hurt them just by watching.

Because their psyche will do the rest.

Until there is nothing left but pain.

Hurting Harper lost its appeal ages ago. I toss the butt into the snow as I walk towards her. "I told you she hates me. Why does that surprise you? Once we get back to Kingston, she'll see that I've changed and forgive us both little by little."

Hope flutters across Harper's face like a butterfly through a storm.

"Let's go," I murmur and nod towards the van. Harper's driver is probably getting more nervous with every minute he has to wait outside Mable's trailer. Philadelphia and expensive cars? I'd rather do honest work than rely on some jerk not slashing the tires sooner or later.

"I don't know if we should, Sylvian," Harper says quietly.

I have to force myself not to roll my eyes. Who is she kidding? Harper is a little bitch and she knows it. It was so easy to get her to hurt Mable and play along. *To hurt you. To do anything to make you suffer.*

And now she's supposed to be Mable's friend?

I didn't hesitate when she said we had to go to Philly. Of course I'll take any opportunity to find out what I've done to

Mable. But that she would give her a fucking photo collage?

What's wrong with her?

There *must* be a reason why she is really doing all this.

A good reason. One that puts everything in the shade. She would never have turned against me or Jaxon otherwise. Never.

"Then go after her," I suggest, without being serious. "I'm sure she'll be happy if you explain to her what it's really like. I told you it would hurt her. She thinks I've fallen in love with her. Do you really want to do all this to her? On top of what's already happened?"

Harper buckles and shakes her head.

God, she so boring. Why does she trust me? How can she not realize that I'm using her to hurt you?

Because I am good.

That's why.

Because I'm a fucking asshole. *And trust me, baby, when I tell you: Harper deserves an asshole like me. But you don't. It's best for you if I'm with her – or anyone else – instead of getting close to you again.*

"Then let's go." I gently place a hand on Harper's upper arm. I'm good to her, no question. After all, I want her to think our relationship is based on friendship. On mutual respect. She has to trust me, because if she doesn't, she'll never tell me why she wants to help Mable in the first place.

She nervously glances over her shoulder at the trailer one last time as we walk to the van. There is sadness in her eyes, despair. She is constantly experiencing two extremes when she thinks of Mable. On the one hand, there is a certain longing and, at the same time, a great fear.

A fear of what?

I'd kill to know.

"Are you looking forward to our time in the mountains?" I ask, making small talk.

"Of course," she says and smiles at me. A little fiery and also a little doubtful as to whether Mable might be right after all.

So far, Harper doesn't know that there was more between us.

It would have been unwise to tell her about the sex in the forest.

She thinks we had a foursome, and she thinks Mable would go for Reece. Maybe Jaxon too. That's the only reason she came up with the idea of inviting Mable to the Catskills. She doesn't know that's why I want to come, because my sadistic traits have gotten the better of me.

Because I want to punish Mable.

To see her suffer.

Shit, I want to punish you so badly for everything you let happen last semester. And most of all, I want to nip any tender positive feeling you ever had for me in the bud.

I don't know why I want that myself.

But the idea that you could like me is the most unbearable thing ever.

As Harper seems to be unsure about Mable, I'm about to remind her why *she* really wants to go to the mountains when the door behind us opens again.

"I'm coming with you."

Harper and I turn to Mable at the same time.

She's standing there, a jacket in one hand, her laptop and a backpack in the other. Her eyes are red like she smoked a few joints. Her fingers are trembling slightly, her braid is undone, and there's this blush on her cheeks that I just can't forget.

This light red…

Beneath me. Glowing. Your body. Like fireworks.

Slain by your innocence, your unadorned perfection.
The lust on your lips.
The longing in your eyes.
How you fucked Jaxon.
How you lay in my arms.
Everything. Everything is accompanied by the heat in your cheeks.
Your blood is not the only thing I desire.

"You're coming… with us?" Harper asks in surprise, snapping me back to reality.

Mable trudges towards us. She has a fighting spirit in her eyes that will break all of us Kings. I have little doubt about that, unless Jaxon just kills her.

"Yes." She stops in front of us, but doesn't look at me. "You want to invite me to a winter paradise? Fine. I've never been on a real vacation, let alone to the mountains, and if you feel like paying for the whole thing, I'm sure that asshole aka your fiancé won't stop me. Besides, the only way I can prove to you I'm right is by coming along."

Harper stares at her. Shit, what a mess. I can see that Harper is about to decide against me and for Mable, but a warning look from me is enough to make her not do it.

"Okay," Harper says surprisingly bluntly to Mable, "you sound angry. That's a good thing. I think you should be mad. I am, too. Maybe it's really good if we just talk openly about everything. Maybe Sylvian also lies to me all the time?" She turns her head and looks me straight in the eye.

How I hate it when she tries to imitate Mable's strength.

"You know I'm not lying," I say, lying once again. "Let's go."

"What about your sister, Mable? Can you just leave her alone? Or would she like to come along too?"

"She's fourteen," explains Mable, "and she would never go

anywhere without her boyfriend."

Harper makes an unenthusiastic face and I'm glad she doesn't think of inviting Olive's boyfriend.

I get in the front seat and reach for my cell phone. A quick check of what the others are doing to distract me from the fact that Mable is getting into the car behind me.

What the hell are you doing? asks Reece.

I'm just checking how she's doing. If Mable was doing well, I'd be jealous as hell and would do everything I could to make her feel bad again. So I want to make sure that I've lost to the monster inside me. And that I was right to warn Mable about me. That I was right to keep her at a distance. Damn right.

Why? Why the fuck can't y'all just forget about her pussy? Zayn. He's probably on the toilet right now while Reece is staring at his phone the whole time in the next room until I answer.

Jaxon sends a smiley. I bet all but Romeo are waiting for more to come. *Have fun in the mountains, Sy.*

That's all he writes and I'm suddenly sure that we'll only find out what he thinks of this later.

I lean back, close my eyes and then I just imagine it.

I imagine what it would be like if Mable wore one of my rings.

That it would be her friend we were picking up.

How I would look forward to enjoying the winter in a huge chalet for two weeks.

What it would be like to pull her into the snow. To rub her nose in it.

How her eyes would shine.

How her smile would make my cock twitch. And then I would kiss her.

Kiss her and everything would be fine.

37

JAXON

I know that he can hardly stand to be near you. That he can hardly bear not to touch you. I know that he suffers like a small dog whose bone has been taken away. Not that I would compare you to a bone. Or him to a dog.

Rather, we're no longer fooling ourselves.

Sylvian has gone so far with his… fanatical affection for you that he will destroy you simply because he can't stand feeling love.

So all I have to do is sit back and watch.

Sorry, Belle, but you should really think about whether Kingston is still your future. Because the worst thing that could ever happen to you is…

… that a King likes you.

4

MABLE

It was a great decision to ride with Harper. I experience a hundred firsts within twelve hours.

Going on a road trip in a super comfortable luxury van with a driver for the first time.

Seeing the Catskill Mountains in the Appalachians for the first time.

Sledding on a real wooden sled for the first time.

Trying on skis for the first time.

Having a guest room that's more luxurious than any hotel all to myself for the first time.

Waking up at night because Harper is moaning loudly for the first time.

All the joy collapses when I hear it. It hurts so deeply that I want to scream. The huge villa on the edge of a ski slope is practically empty. The staff are only here during the day. So no one can hear her.

Except for me.

I feel a lump in my throat and a knot tightening my stomach as I try to ignore the noise. There are several possibilities. Maybe Sylvian is doing it on purpose. In that case, he's doing it to hurt me, and that means he cares about me. That's not a great option, though, because it'd just prove how mean he really is. Or maybe he really loves Harper. If so, fine. I won't stand in the way of her happiness.

Part of me likes Sylvian and wants him to be happy.

Even if he doesn't deserve happiness because he bullied me into madness.

I decide to tell Harper everything tomorrow and fall asleep with my headphones on.

***

Sylvian doesn't leave Harper's side in the morning, but that's not the reason I barely get a word out around them. It would be so easy to find out how she feels about what happened at the frat house. Or in the woods when Sylvian and I had sex for the first time. But she doesn't ask, and I don't have the heart to tell her. Or maybe I'm too ashamed. After all, I should have been honest from the start.

And so the days go by, and I focus on what I have instead of what was taken from me. I know by now that my youth in the trailer park makes me hardened enough to have a good time with Harper without thinking about who she really is.

That's what it's all based on. Spreading fake facts to make a profit. Apparently, human greed is as much a part of the elite as the underclass. *True friendship? Where do you find it?*

The huge chalet awakens every single one of my girlhood dreams. Apart from any memories of the Kings, I feel incredibly blessed. I am so lucky to be able to enjoy the pure luxury of a huge bathtub, the most delicious food, a heavenly bed and new winter clothes from Harper. These wonderful days dispel all the shadows that haunted me in the trailer park.

It's the nights that wear me down. Whenever I wake up.

Once it's so bad that I flee to the terrace to get away from Harper's bedroom.

I sit there, wrapped up in a thick winter coat, trying to forget. The days are fantastic, especially because Sylvian hasn't joined us on the slopes yet, but just one moan from Harper's mouth in the night is enough to plunge me into a deep hole. Sometimes, the longing slams into my body so blatantly I feel like throwing up all the amazing food that Harper's family's cooks conjure up.

Jaxon, Sylvian, Reece.

Sylvian, Reece and Jaxon.

They and the memory of them still have such a firm grip on me that I sometimes tremble, just like that. Or I stop dead in my tracks, tense up, put a hand on my stomach and fight back the tears.

But it's just little moments. Just brief shocks because I've survived everything so far.

It's basically like it used to be. When my mom had visitors every night.

The patio door next to me opens and I flinch.

A clicking lighter, the smell of cigarettes.

Did he spot me? Should I draw attention to myself?

"Is that what you meant by 'your monster'?" I ask him point-blank. It's the first time we've been alone. The first time I haven't ignored him.

Sylvian turns in my direction and switches on the light, bathing the snow- covered winter terrace in enchanted light. "How long have you been sitting here?"

"Why? Do you want to know if I counted the orgasms?"

His face is shadowy and expressionless. As always, when he's not smiling at Harper. "I didn't know you could hear us."

I raise a right eyebrow. Unfortunately, I have no idea

whether this is true. "Well, now you know."

"Why didn't you say anything?"

"Why would I think for one second that you didn't fully intend for me to hear everything?"

Sylvian comes to me, pulls up one of the snow covered chairs, swipes away the snow and sits down in front of me. The green in his eyes is clear. "Mable, I know it wasn't right of me to watch what Jaxon did to you. When you come back to Kingston, it'll be different."

"Yes? Even better?" I ask ironically.

"I don't want Harper to think I care about you." He smiles warmly at me, a little pained, a genuine apology in his green eyes. "After that night at the frat house, I realized what I really want. I'm tired of sharing women with Tyrell. Women who can't make up their minds. Harper wants me. And it wasn't until Thanksgiving that I realized I want her, too."

Sylvian Silvano sounds like he's reciting a script. Of course everything he says could be true. Every single word. And it hurts. It hurts so much I want to scream. What if I'm just trying to see the monster in him? Because I don't want to admit that everything is completely different? That he never wanted me? That I... fell in love without him ever feeling anything similar?

"Is that the monster inside you?" I ask, a little more desperate than before.

"What do you mean?" he asks unconcernedly, in a way that I have yet to hear.

"The liar," I spit out, even though I'm revealing to him that I hope he's not telling the truth, "trying to manipulate me, trying to make me believe that everything was completely different. But I'm not *stupid*, Sylvian. I was *there*. You told me that sharing wasn't your problem. You were trying to protect me from you, from this very thing."

He chuckles to himself and shakes his head. "Mable, I'm sorry if you think there was more…"

I stand up with a jerk and take a step towards him.

His reaction is quick. He also gets up and then we're face to face.

Our coats touch. His light beard shadow hides part of his face and his lined coat makes him look more like a gangster than ever before.

"Say that again," I whisper. My condensed breath hits his face, that's how close we are.

"What?" he asks. His smile is gone.

"Everything you said just now. That you want Harper. Because she loves you and only you. That you realized it that night. That you stood by just because you were afraid Harper would think you had feelings for me. Are you such a coward? Say it again."

His jaw tightens and then suddenly there's all that jungle in his eyes. All the depth I know from him.

"Tell me what happened in the forest was meaningless to you. That you *felt* nothing. That it was just about some stupid bet. Say it!"

His nicotine breath rattles against me as he grabs my upper arm firmly and pulls me close. Our upper bodies collide and adrenaline rushes through my veins. There he is. The real Sylvian. "I warned you," he growls and I tear myself away from him.

"Yes, for an inner monster!" I shout. "I thought you were a fucking sadist! Someone who needs to see blood during sex or has some kind of sick fetish. That's what I thought!"

"I *am* a fucking sadist!" he snaps at me, the hand holding his cigarette shaking. "All I want, Mable, is for you to stay away from me. Before I hurt you any further."

"Hurt me even *further*? How could that be possible?"

"Believe me. It's possible."

I shake my head vehemently. More pain? No. Impossible.

"Why else would I do all this?" His voice breaks and he looks at the ground. "It's better if I'm with Harper. It's the only way I can protect you from me."

My rage flares up. "That's not true!" I shove him hard but he's unmoved. He's much heavier and more muscular than me. "It can't get any worse than what you're doing to me now, you fucking asshole!" I try to push him again, because physical force might make him understand. But he grabs my forearms and pulls me in.

Tears stream down my face and then I just do it. I lean forward and kiss him. Not to hurt Harper. Or to satisfy my longing. I want to find out the truth. To find out if I've ever been wrong.

He kisses me back as if there had never been anything between us. His tongue searches longingly for mine, his mouth opens wide. When I feel the same feelings overwhelming me as last Thanksgiving, I cry harder.

I love and hate it at the same time. It hurts. Our kiss tastes of despair, of longing and salt. And when I break away, it's not just my face that's wet.

Astonished, I reach out a hand to his cheek and wipe away the tear rolling from his right eye.

"Why?" I just ask and look at him piercingly.

He laughs harshly. His voice sounds strained. "Why am I sad, you mean?"

I stare at him and at that moment something breaks. Not my heart. And certainly not his. But the mask. Whichever one of us was wearing it, it falls to the ground and shatters.

All the air we breathe around us suddenly becomes our shared oxygen and I can feel him.

I feel him like I've never felt a person before.

I feel something I didn't know I could feel at all.

All the pain condenses between us into a dark nothingness, swallows us up like a black hole and we drown.

Drowning in each other, our mouths meet and we inhale the other as if it offered us more than abyss and injury.

Now it's Sylvian who pushes me. He pushes me with all his might towards the house, supporting me but vehemently pushing me forward, and I let him.

There is no other way. In this moment, I'm no longer just myself, but this incredibly deep and infinitely painful connection between us. There is so much *more* that I can hardly bear it. As his hand drops the cigarette, reaches into my hair, grabs it tightly and slides his other one under my coat, I'm even faster.

I don't know how it happens.

I just know that it shouldn't happen.

But my head can't stop me from unbuckling his belt and letting him half undress me.

He moans even before he thrusts into me, and it is certainly the wettest sex I will ever have. Because I'm crying. I'm so convulsively and bitterly and endlessly in love that I can barely see. I have to rely on my feelings. On the longing that tears me down. My hands claw into his back as he pushes me against the wall of the house and fucks me fast and dirty.

I can't think about how he was in Harper shortly before.

The mere thought of it tears my soul apart.

Breath. Kisses. Sylvian. My life. That's what I'm clinging to at this moment. And grief. Grief that throws me into an ocean of desperate tears.

"Don't cry," he implores me, taking one cheek in his hand, pushing himself deep inside me and kissing me again and again. "Not because of me. I'm the last person who deserves your tears."

His words only make it worse. And maybe he knows. Maybe he's just manipulating me. Maybe that's his trick and the monster he warned me about.

"I'm not crying because you're hurting me," I reply tremulously. "I'm crying because you're hurting *someone*. Because you want to hurt someone, because it seems to give you deep satisfaction."

He looks at me. Dark and penetrating. And we remain standing, intertwined. But neither of us moves.

"That someone happens to be me. Or Harper. Or yourself. You have all this hate inside you. It must be eating away at you. No one can do what you do without suffering the most inside of anyone."

His jaw tightens and the green in his eyes becomes dull and empty. "Accept it for what it is, Mable," he says softly, slowly pulling away from me. "From a distance, I'll be able to protect you from Jaxon and not hurt you further."

"Your idea of 'protecting' and 'not hurting' borders on schizophrenia!" I shout at him, grabbing his collar and pulling him back in front of me. My cheeks feel puffy, unnaturally soft. "Nothing you could do could be worse than that." Anger grips me and in this glorious moment of strength I want to prove it to them all. They use the people around them. They mistreat them. The elite are dirty, mendacious and disrespectful and that's exactly how they need to be treated. I claw at Sylvian's coat and move against his stomach. He lets it happen, throbbing hard and demanding inside me as I push myself towards orgasm with every movement against my clit.

When I come, I hate him again.

Perfect.

Hate.

It's all I'm allowed to feel.

As soon as that wave has washed over me in a short, heavy burst, I push him off me, slip back into my jeans and walk back to the house. Before I open the door, I turn around once more.

Sylvian stands there, gloomy and lost, and I still don't know what's true and what's not.

"Either you leave or I'll tell Harper everything."

Sylvian laughs, shaking his head. "She'll never trust you as much as she trusts me."

Dick. "Do you really want to find out if that's true?"

I pull the door shut behind me and deprive him of the opportunity to say anything back.

The next morning he is gone.

5

REECE

When I enter the room, I catch Zayn in my bed. I roll my eyes even before I realize who he's fucking between the sheets.

Rachel's hair is streaked with sweat.

He has spread her legs wide towards the ceiling, rams himself into her like an animal and glances over his shoulder at me. A crazy gleam in his eyes. *Join us.*

No, thank you.

You're missing something.

I doubt that.

Good, that leaves more for me.

He turns back to the front and continues to fuck her while I get my cell phone. When I turn around and Rachel is moaning behind me, my patience finally snaps.

Clenching my jaw, I put my cell phone in my pocket and quickly pull my shirt over my head.

Changed your mind? Zayn asks as I approach the bed. He moves back to make room for me. Rachel is breathing heavily, blindfolded, with a forced smile. Suddenly I'm sure she was faking the orgasm. It's not that Zayn can't make her come. There's just no harmony between the two of them.

He's fucking her to annoy me. He probably has to squeeze his eyes shut and think of someone else to cum.

I wait until Zayn has vacated the space, then I squat down on the bed. One hand on my belt, the other in Rachel's sweaty red hair. I pull off her blindfold and she retreats into the pillow, satisfyingly anxious.

I stare her down. The Kings' look that doesn't even need words to put someone in their place.

"You didn't try hard enough," I snap at her and she flinches. "You think you can fake a fucking orgasm for me? Who do you think I am?"

"I ha-have," she stammers. "How... why..."

With my hand still in her hair, I push her off my mattress. She hits the floor hard and stares at me in panic.

"*Fuck off*," I hiss.

She quickly scrambles to her feet. Even naked, she's ugly. I know what she did for the game, I saw every single challenge last semester. She willingly got involved with us while hoping for her advantage. *The complete opposite of Mable.*

"Why are you like this now?" she nags at me and picks up her clothes. "It's not my fault you can't get it up!"

I laugh hard. "Ah, and who could do anything about it but you?"

She clenches her teeth. "And how am I supposed to get home now? I don't have a car!"

"Take an Uber. The driver will probably pay you in kind. Maybe you'll have better luck with him and convince him with your little performance."

Rachel holds back the expletives that pop into her head without question. "Loser," is all she says. She gets dressed frantically and storms out of my room.

As soon as she's gone, Zayn lets the door to the bathroom

swing open. He stands there, almost more distraught than Rachel. "Was that really necessary?" he asks me, as if I've just sent a drone to a civilian hospital.

"She is ugly. Inside and out."

Zayn laughs, stunned. "The vast majority of women who slide over our dicks are ugly on the inside. And getting one who doesn't go to a salon every day to get her ugliness waxed off her face is a change."

"Never mind. We're on vacation. Do you really like her enough to invite her here?"

"Yes. So what?"

I don't believe a word he says.

"What's wrong with you?" he asks smugly. "The only reason you're not joining me is because Rachel was bad to Dole."

I raise an eyebrow.

"Since when do you care who I fuck in your bed? Come on, someone has really infiltrated your head. Just admit it."

It would be easy to let him think that. I'm the only person who can fool Zayn, but it would also be wrong. Mable showed me that there's a difference between women and *ugly* women. That it's not worth shagging anything and everything if you think highly of yourself and don't want to let everyone have it.

At first it was curiosity. I thought Mable was cute, just like I find girls cute. I wanted to fuck her like I want to fuck girls. And I wanted her like I wanted every girl before her. Until I met her, I had so much sex that I don't even remember individual faces, but hers never slipped my mind. Now all I have left is my imagination.

Zayn is still half naked and reeks of sex. His eyes pierce through mine, and I see the shadow in them that won't go away since I see more in Mable than a lady on our court.

"Why her?" he asks in a murmur. "She's a walking cliché, Reece. Why not Rachel? At least she has red hair. And no snub nose and hazel hair and all that good girl cliché shit. She's spunky. She does what she's told."

"She's a whore," I blurt out.

"And Dole isn't?" Zayn clasps his hands behind his head and stretches. "At least one of us has to stay loyal to the Kings. Rachel is hot and flexible. You can have fun with her. I don't know why you're so against it." Zayn sighs when he realizes I'm serious. "Jax will do anything to get Dole kicked out of Kingston. No matter how hard Sylvian and Harper try to fight it."

"He has no choice but to let them. Mable will come back. What do you want Jaxon to do? Break her neck before she reaches campus?"

Zayn lifts his lips in disgust. He hates that I like her. And that hurts me.

You have to see that she's different, I implore him.

I'm not blind, he replies, annoyed. *I can see that she is normal.*

"Rachel is *normal*," I counter. "She's a dole. She's cheap, only looking for her advantage and fakes her orgasms. It's embarrassing that you don't even realize that." Without waiting for Zayn's reaction, I turn away and leave my room. I'm not just anyone. I am a King. And I can't afford for the entire campus to think I have a soft spot for obnoxious bitches like Rachel.

Above all, I don't want Mable to believe that.

Shit. Of course, before Thanksgiving, she thought I was the nice guy. The one who stays friendly most of the time. Courteous. But then she saw how we treated her. She watched

Zayn, and I did nothing to stop her heart from being torn apart.

I don't have much of what drives Jaxon, Sylvian or Romeo. I lack the tendency to live out abysses. I lack the malice. But I also know the electrifying feeling of power that flows through me because I'm not just anyone.

I'm Reece fucking Crescent.

And Amabelle Weaver is mine.

JAXON

There's more between us. More attraction than I ever dared to hope for. And more hatred than I know what to do with.

Not just because Sylvian wants to protect you from me, not just because Reece pines for you.

It's about me. Only about me.

To my lust, my perverse vengefulness and the ultimate urge to always achieve my goals while having a lot of fun with you, Belle.

6

MABLE

As soon as Sylvian left, I was able to enjoy the days. However, as we make our way back after another wonderful week in pure luxury, I realize that I haven't given a single day's thought to what I'm going to do when I get back to Kingston.

"We need to find allies," Harper says. We sit across from each other in the comfortable luxury minivan that's taking us across the country back to Philadelphia. "Sylvian will only ever stand by us so far as long as he doesn't have to stand up to Jaxon. And we know that's not very far."

She took the stupid ring off, thankfully, even though I think she did it for me and not because she wants to break off the engagement. That's all she was willing to do before we pretended Sylvian never came along. It's the first time she's mentioned his name in over five days.

So much for the fact that we should talk. We're both scared. She's probably afraid of finding out the truth. And I'm deeply ashamed of every single day that I lied to her. For writing to her that night in the frat house that she could trust me.

Can we still pretend that nothing ever happened?

Can't she break up with Sylvian for the obvious reasons?

Do *I* have to tell her everything that speaks against him? Does she really not see it?

"I've come up with lots of ideas, some of which probably work better than others," she babbles on, bringing me back to the here and now. "But what about you?" She looks at me curiously, a gleam in her eye that proves how much she wants to get one over on the Kings.

Am I her weapon? Or am I really the warrior Harper wants to help?

I don't know. Even less do I know how to deal with what awaits me in Kingston. "A woman in South Africa has invented a kind of condom for women."

Harper's ears seem to prick up when I use that word. Is she afraid I might have sex with one of them again?

"You put it up there and it kind of attacks the rapist's dick with barbs. It can only be removed surgically in hospital."

Harper grimaces in disgust.

"I thought I'd get one of those."

"*No one* is going to rape you on campus."

What if she doesn't even know what happened in the lecture hall? What if she doesn't know how much Jaxon tortured me to make me apologize to Hilbredge, who tried to rape me in front of a group of freshmen? Jaxon has threatened me that he won't be there next time it happens. And I'll be able to rely on his word.

"It's more likely you'll slip and break a leg because someone has tipped out soap," says Harper. "Or that someone puts worms in your food or parasites in your bed."

Goose bumps form on my arms. When she lists it like that, I have absolutely no desire to return to Kingston.

"I'll study online," I suggest resignedly. "And only go to the exams."

"That would work anywhere else, Mable. But this is *Kingston*. The first semester was a walk in the park compared to what's to come. You won't be able to do without the labs and lectures."

"I know," I sigh heavily and look out of the window.

"I have an idea." Harper's eyes light up.

"Which is?"

"There is someone we can pay to help us."

"Oh?"

"As long as we pay him more than the Kings, he'll do exactly what we ask."

"And what could we ask for?"

"Well, that he supports us in our revenge. He knows the Kings better than anyone. He really does. I even think he knows who Zayn is."

"Vance Buchanan."

"Oh, you know him? Right, I introduced you at the frat house party."

"He drugged me and took me to the lecture hall," I remind her. "Great idea, let's just ask this asshole."

"We don't have much choice. Actually, all the students at Kingston are assholes, right?"

"Is there any other solution besides you paying Vance Buchanan?"

Harper plays with her handbag and thinks for a long time. "Yes. We could try to get him on our side without paying him. That would be even better."

I roll my eyes and lean my head against the window.

Kingston.

All my life I dreamed of being accepted there. I spent a year doing a social project in the middle of the most impoverished hospital in Philadelphia instead of going to a normal college in order to fulfill the requirements for admission to the elite university. I waited so many months to finally be allowed to start.

To finally learn why things go wrong and how to change them sustainably.

And then the stark reality caught up with me.

A dream turned into a nightmare.

And I'm not even creative enough to come up with a suitable revenge plan against the Kings. In my mind, I pull out a marker. Vandalizing the Kings' cars seems to be their only sore spot.

But there's got to be more.

7

JAXON

My poker face is crumbling. I can feel it in the way I react irritably when my hand is bad, and even more irritably when it's good but someone else's is better. When I play with the Kings, I want to practice not letting even my closest friends know how I feel. What I think. What I *am*.

But it's different when bullshit women are involved.

Clarisse chews my ear off. Her ugly Barbie friend with the dark blonde hair sits next to her and keeps giving me a look when Clarisse doesn't seem to notice. I've been fucking her instead of Clarisse the whole time, simply because it gives me a thrill to fuck with Clarisse. But that's the only reason.

And that makes me angry with myself.

If I lose the next round, I swear I will only have sex when it's really about the sex and not about… distraction.

I don't want to have to buy distractions like a punter. Sex should be fun for fuck's sake. But how is that supposed to work if none of the other Kings show the slightest ambition to share a woman again?

Have I sunk that far? Can I only feel real satisfaction when I'm not the only one pumping my seed into my chosen hole?

"You're losing," Zayn remarks, grinning wryly at me. Rachel is sitting next to him. She's the first scholarship student I really want to *murder*, because everything about her annoys me so much that I forget myself.

"That's because there's nothing worth playing for," I say dismissively, and I'm one hundred percent lying. I don't play to win. On the contrary, I play to influence the game. Like back in October, when I cleverly steered who would win Amabelle's bet. First Sylvian, so he thought he could take her home. Then Amabelle, so she got her points and stayed in the game. Then Reece, so he could lick her in front of us all.

My cock twitches excitedly as I think back on it, and I throw down my hand.

No poker face, period. I don't need to pretend I can do anything if I can't stop thinking about the shiny pussy of a penniless student who has been a pain in the ass from the start with all her feminist bullshit.

"Oh, are you thinking about me?" Clarisse asks, stroking my upper arm when she notices my boner. "Jaxon, you know our deal."

I'm very nice to her, Belle. That's mainly because I can make very good use of her. As king, you only control the majority of your people. A small part longs for the leadership of a woman. Clarisse does as I say and is as I need her to be, and so she fills the void at my side to be a role model.

People need a role model. A hero they can look up to. Whether it's the fucking newsreader or the American president or just some ridiculous scrubs wearer who has a PhD. They want to follow. They want to worship someone. I am their god, and Clarisse is their sainted mother Mary. So she can stay, no matter how many stupid things she says.

"Our deal… right," I reply half-heartedly. The deal that

saves me from having to touch her at all if I don't want to. An open relationship in the broadest sense. Well, that's very, very broad. We fuck everything and everyone. Only my Kings are off-limits to her. And her girlfriends – or rather all Alpha Regina students – are off-limits to me.

But I've never cared about following the rules. Where would the thrill be in that?

"Have you started without us?" Sylvian has come in, closely followed by Harper. He pretends to be in a good mood, but he's not fooling me.

Firstly, he's pumped to the brim with pills.

Secondly, Harper reeks of sex.

I'm starting to hate him for constantly fucking Harper just to hurt you. Can't any of us at least act somewhat manly? If he likes you, let him stand by it and not mark the motherfucker.

The whole thing is just so fucking pathetic that I can't even look at Harper.

"Sit down," I order.

"I'm not staying," Harper informs him, her voice shaking, taking great care not to look at Clarisse and – oh shit, I forgot her friend's name.

"Great," says Zayn. He likes Harper even less than Amabelle, but I've never tried to find out why.

"Well, then…" For a moment she seems to hope that Sylvian will follow her, but he sits down. His eyes are red, his sweat reeks of cocaine and his cheeks look like he's got a damn vitamin deficiency. "Ciao."

"The way she runs away from us," comments Clarisse Harper's hasty exit. "As if she were a dole."

"She's *becoming* a dole," her friend adds smugly. "She's well on the way to destroying herself socially."

"Excuse me?" Sylvian asks the two women.

They fall silent immediately.

"I mean…" Clarisse's friend dodges, "she should just apologize to Clarisse and –"

"For what?" Sylvian asks her point-blank. "For Clarisse telling me in the summer that Harper still fancied me? Who betrayed who here?"

"It wasn't like that," Clarisse hisses. "I know exactly why you're with her. You need her family's contacts. It's pathetic to watch Harper get involved with you when it's so obvious you're just messing with her."

"Stop talking to me like that," Sylvian replies quietly and threateningly.

Clarisse tisks and reaches for her drink. She really does think she's the untouchable queen. "I know you're still into Dole. Everyone knows that. Only Harper doesn't want to admit it."

Sylvian straightens up, puts his hands on the table, but Clarisse looks at him unconcernedly. *She hasn't yet understood that I would always choose Sylvian, Belle. She's just so much stupider than you.*

Before Sylvian can put a damper on Clarisse, my patience breaks. "Get out."

"What?" Zayn asks me, flabbergasted, as he's about to deal the next round.

"Not you, you asshole. Everyone else is."

The women stare at me, perplexed.

"Out!"

They jump up.

I love the effect my words have when I raise my voice a little. Clarisse gives me a bitter look, but I decide at that moment that hell will freeze over before I fuck her again.

"What's up, dude?" Zayn asks as Clarisse, her friend and

Rachel walk outside, whispering, tossing me angry looks over their shoulders.

I bend over the table, swipe all the money, chips and cards off the mat with one arm and lean on the wood with both elbows.

Reece comes in. He must have seen the women leave. "What is it?" he asks, hesitantly joining us. As if he's afraid a bomb might go off at any moment.

"You are my friends," I begin pathetically. Bomb isn't quite right. It's more like a crash from the high we haven't been able to maintain for weeks. "And you all look like little sons of bitches whose asses haven't been properly powdered."

"Oh yeah?" asks Zayn dismissively.

"But I don't hold it against you. I feel the same way. If I see Silvano injecting himself one more time because of Amabelle, I'm going to give him the next shot myself. And Reece, I can't stand your grumpy face for another day. Zayn." I catch his eye. "Rachel's fucking ass is hairy, I bet you. Red, ugly, stubbly hair. Stop fucking it."

He grinds his teeth, but I keep on kicking.

"You're just as scared as the rest of us. We are afraid of losing. Of losing *something*. My whole fucking life is at stake. And whatever you're scared of, I don't really care. Because we*'re the fucking Kings at this fucking university and we're about to enter the circle. If we want something, we'll get it.*"

"And what do we want?" asks Zayn, annoyed.

I just laugh at him. He wants her just like the rest of us. I know it. I just know it. "We want *her*, don't we?"

Silence envelops our table like sound absorbers in a recording studio.

"What if she were here now?" I ask the others. The silence thickens. "What would we do if she came in? Sit down at the table? Gamble with us again? Whose cock doesn't stir at the thought of what it would be like if she lay down on the table? Naked? And each of us... touching her?"

"Stop it," growls Sylvian. Reece's expression has darkened. And Zayn looks like he's going to be sick.

"We need it," I say softly. "We need a girl like her. We're the most fucked up motherfuckers I know, and I'm slowly accepting that I can't fully exist or breathe properly without you. I love you, my brothers. The semester hasn't even really started, and I can already barely stand to just sit here instead of waiting for Amabelle in her dorm room."

Reece contorts his face in such an ugly way that for the first time he doesn't look like something out of a shower gel commercial. *"You did all this to her, Jaxon,"* he says quietly. Quietly, wounded and... grieving? "And Sylvian had a chance to stop it because of your stupid bet, but he didn't. If anyone in this world doesn't deserve a second chance with Amabelle, it's you. It's *us*. Just thinking about how you can manipulate her into looking at you again with more than her backside disgusts me. You'll be lucky if she doesn't take revenge on us. And if any of what you just said is true, then let that girl study in peace and stay the hell away."

"I can't." The two words leave my lips unplanned and completely unexpectedly and I clench my jaw tightly. Am I severely disabled? Why am I revealing my most sore spot to them of all people? "I can't let them win the game," I whisper. Now without a voice and enduring their attentive gazes on me. "Not the scholarship, at least."

Reece shakes his head uncomprehendingly.

"Believe me, I *can't*." Okay, I'm about to sit naked in front of them. The other Kings don't know anything about the circle assignment I've been given. They think we want to qualify for the circle of our own free will by doing what we do. But there's actually more to it than that. A much bigger secret. Not a single scholarship student will graduate, that's the order. Especially not Amabelle, as the stranger in New York made clear to me again. One of the few rules he told me is that I won't tell anyone about this job. Not even my closest friends. And what am I doing? I've kept my mouth shut for three and a half years, but now it's bursting out of me in front of all the Kings? How I hate it when my poker face doesn't work perfectly. I try hard to remember what the coven member said to me. *Offer her something better if she's not impressed by your usual strategy.* "Why don't we show her... something better?"

"Better than what?" asks Reece coldly.

"What if..." I struggle to get it over my lips because what I'm suggesting is closer to the truth than anything I usually reveal to the Kings. "If she gets us?"

Reece raises his eyebrows, Sylvian's eyes widen and Zayn's jaw drops.

"Would she even care about studying anymore?"

My friends look at each other, not sure if I've just seriously suggested bringing Amabelle into our midst. To share her. To... do right by her. As long as she learns to listen to me and leaves Kingston before the end of the second semester.

"We all want her, don't we?" I make sure.

Reece and Sylvian don't get upset, but Zayn groans in annoyance. "No. Romeo and I are immune."

"As if," Romeo hisses from a dark corner to which he retreated over an hour ago. Reading a book on nuclear physics and completely unmoved by our conversation. "The only one who's really immune is me."

"You see," I say smugly. "Listen to Romeo, Zayn."

"What's your real goal?" Reece asks, crossing his arms in front of his chest. "You care about more than Mable, Jax. What is it?"

"Like I said, she's not allowed to stay at Kingston. But she could be with us anywhere else."

A second or two passes and then they laugh at me. Annoyed, I roll my eyes and empty my glass of whiskey.

"What the hell do you mean by 'with us'?" Sylvian asks me, grinning wryly.

"What you're doing with Harper," I reply cynically, "only without using drugs to endure it. Of our own free will and with pure pleasure and all that."

He grimaces.

"Another round in the game?" asks Reece. "I don't feel like playing anymore."

"Me neither," I reply in surprise. "That's exactly what I just said."

"As if anyone believes you," Reece says coolly. Or should I say 'boldly'? I've never felt like Reece would turn on me the way he's doing right now. "Sylvian was right when he asked us to leave Mable alone at the beginning of last semester. We've had our reasons so far, each to our own, as to why he weeded out the scholarship girls. But Mable is different. She *deserves* to study at Kingston. She *deserves* us to leave her alone. And you will do that. Sylvian will do it because Harper demands it of him and he needs Harper. Zayn will do it because I want him to, and I want it. And Romeo –"

"Will still be able to destroy them if I ask him to," I reply cynically. "But right now, I find the idea of not asking him to do it more appealing."

Sylvian leans forward, a killer's look on his face, and in that moment I realize again how much I love him and how much he hates me. I have to get him to stop being such an asshole.

But do I really have enough power over him?

Or is his inner monster worse than I ever realized?

"You. Drove. Her. Away," Sylvian growls. "Why do you want to *save* her now?"

"Wrong. We *all* drove her away," I correct him nonchalantly. "Besides, it was your suggestion to buy her off with a thousand dollars after that night at the frat house."

"Because it's better for her if she disappears."

"But she won't leave," I reply, shrugging my shoulders. "I agree with you, Silvian. If Amabelle was smart, she wouldn't be on her way back to Kingston. But she's not smart. She's perverted. She longs for what we will do with her. And we all want her equally. We can't *wait* for her to be back on campus. So instead of torturing ourselves and her by breaking her, we might as well just suggest an alternative to her. All that matters is that she no longer studies at Kingston. Because *no* scholarship student will ever graduate. But why should she? If she gets us, she'll own half the world. I can't imagine her not agreeing."

My words float in the room for a few moments. Then Reece sits down and is completely relaxed again. "Let's say I believe you," he begins. "That you really care about her. Then you'll have to give her the choice."

"What choice?" I ask.

"Amabelle will choose one of us at the end of the semester."

"Choose who gets to kill her particularly slowly?" asks Sylvian Reece.

I give Sylvian a brittle smile. "Still in love, huh, Sylvian? Why don't you stop fucking Harper all day and own up to who you really want?"

"I thought we were going to work out how to destroy them

for good," says Zayn. "And now you want to extend the bet from last semester? What's it about this time? What will the winner get to do with Mable?"

"No bet," replies Reece.

"Then what?" asks Sylvian.

"I'm serious," says Reece. "I'm not sharing with you. You'll always hurt her. And that's why I want her to choose one of us. So that *one* of us does what we think is right, but the others don't interfere."

Even Romeo's jaw drops as he watches Reece from his corner.

"Excuse me?" Sylvian hisses possessively. "Suddenly you want to protect her from *us*? After you didn't help me with that at all last semester?"

"You weren't convincing enough." Reece twists one corner of his mouth. What's wrong with him? Since when has he been trying to expand his influence? And what the hell does he have in mind? "Mable will choose one of us – or against us. I'm certainly not going to ask her to leave Kingston. But if she wants to because she wants *you*, Jax, I'd accept it. Sylvian is the last of us who deserves Mable. But he loves her, and if she chooses him because she thinks she can endure that love, I'd accept it. We're changing the rules of the game. There will be no more arena. We'll all fight to make sure she chooses the right one."

Sylvian's gaze is absolutely cold, but no one addresses what Reece just said about him. It's actually too obvious that Sylvian is hurting Mable because he's hurting everyone around him that he cares about. Trying to keep everyone at a distance who might recognize the good in him. Except us. He accepts us Kings as his family. Maybe because we're worse than him in some ways.

"What for?" Zayn snaps at Reece. "Why should she even decide? And for which one of us? She doesn't want to share. She wants all of you. You, on the other hand, want to share her. So what's the fucking problem?"

Silence descends over the table, and for a moment I'm sure we all wonder how we can get Zayn's words out of our heads. The image that arises in my mind...

Fuck.

Amabelle. Between all of us. Why does this shit excite me so much?

"I understand why you want her to make up her mind." I clear my throat.

Zayn rolls his eyes, annoyed. "Now I'm curious."

"If she chooses, there will be no miserable competition between us." Besides, that would give the Kings a power I don't give them. Amabelle is mine – or nobody's.

"Ah yes." Zayn shuffles the cards for the hundredth time, as if he's no longer interested in what we're talking about.

"If you don't want to drive Mable off campus, Jax," Sylvian interjects tonelessly, "your position will be called into question. The pawns and Clarisse won't accept that we don't make good on our threat to Mable. We promised a spectacle, a second round. And if we come up with the idea of ending the game abruptly, Mable's life will be in danger. Clarisse, at least, will want to behead her."

I wipe my mouth. He's right. And that's a fucking problem.

"If anyone out there even gets the idea," Sylvian says urgently, "that we want her – not want to *use* her, but honestly *want* her..."

Zayn runs his index finger across his throat to tell us what will happen to Amabelle. "I'm for it, then Romeo and I are rid of her."

Reece mutters something, Sylvian growls and I clench my fist.

"No, honestly?" Zayn stares at us in turn, stunned, as he interprets our reaction. None of us want Amabelle to die. Shit. It's tragic, but true. "Who the hell are you and where did you leave the biggest fuckers on this campus? You fucking *abused* them*! You *paraded* them in front of everyone*! And I went along with it because from the beginning I didn't understand why this stupid girl wouldn't *just leave*. And now you suddenly agree that it was all a mistake? And you want her to choose one of you? What are you going to do at the end of the semester? Marry her? Tell me, are you all insane?"

"And how will you prevent the campus from finding out what's going on?" Romeo asks tonelessly from the shadows, lowering his book. "Or are you putting your reputation on the line?"

"Romeo." I turn to him. My shadow. And the shield of us all when it comes to who has the most cruelty. "You'll be our wild card."

Romeo shifts in his chair. "So a game after all?"

"Yes," says Reece meaningfully. "We're going to play chess again." Reece smoothly ignores Zayn's words, folding his hands in his lap in a relaxed manner. "But this time there are no pawns involved. Just three black kings and the white queen. Shall we set the rules?"

JAXON

Welcome back to Kingston.

I know you can't wait to face the thunderous applause of the crowd that will greet you for daring to return. They will welcome you into the arena and enjoy every second of your suffering.

But I don't care about the others.

I care about us.

About you and me.

Last time I fucked your little heart, but this time I will devote myself to your head.

You will feel me in every single brain cell and your whole body will scream "Take me, Jaxon!" And I will be there to give your body what it needs.

You thought you could stay away from us?

Oh, Dole, how wrong you always are about yourself...

8

MABLE

When I enter my dormitory, it's like coming home and entering a familiar hell at the same time. It reminds me of the trailer park. A home and a deep hole from which there is no way out.

Harper did offer to help me move my few things to my room, but then she stood me up for a date with Sylvian.

I try not to think about what the two of them are doing together and concentrate on not setting off a trap that the students may have placed outside my dorm room.

The hallway is just as deserted and empty as it was on my first day. A glance into the kitchen reveals that not all the scholarship holders have been away for the vacations. The garbage can is full, cutlery is in the sink.

I take a deep breath, carry my bags outside my room and take out my key. No one has stopped me yet. Or thrown tampons at me. Or even raped me.

It's actually an okay start, right?

I immediately discard this thought when the door opens without turning my key. Goose bumps spread across my arms. Whatever awaits me in my room, it won't be anything good.

Without stepping over the threshold, I push the door open. It opens to reveal a man sitting on my second bed, one knee drawn up to his chest, as if he were completely relaxed and waiting for me.

"Romeo," I whisper. I quickly look around the room to see if Jaxon has come with me.

"I'm alone," he says. His voice is somewhere between smooth and cutting edge. He looks unpolished, like a rough diamond, and yet he also radiates the dignity that a King always possesses. His black pupils are accentuated by the dark circles under his eyes. His face is set, giving it a grim appearance, but at the same time it has an almost delicate touch. His dark hair makes him look a bit like Sylvian, but his skin is much lighter, almost milky, and the edges of his face are chiseled rather than curved.

He wears a black sweater with a white shirt underneath, and plain chinos and shoes. The only piece of jewelry on his body is the Kings' ring.

"You don't need to bother checking me out." His gaze is blank and cold.

"Why?" I ask challengingly. "Aren't you one of those Kings who want to get each of us laid once before she has to leave?"

His face hardens, like it's cast in steel. "I have nothing to do with that."

"Yes, you do, they're your friends. What were you doing here in my room?"

"Waiting for you."

"You haven't hidden some toads by any chance? Or bed-bugs? Or removed my bed base?"

Amusement briefly pulls on his lips before he becomes serious again. "Certainly not."

"Because you're too fine for that?"

72

Romeo straightens up with a flourish and I back away from him. "Definitely. We wouldn't even touch a toad." Although he's a little shorter than Jaxon and Reece, he's still taller than me. His body tension reveals he can pack a serious punch when he wants to, and I have no desire to feel his hands on my body, of all things. "I'm here as an ally."

I back away even further, but he remains standing in the room and doesn't come after me. "Sure," I reply sarcastically. That's all I can manage.

"Jaxon and the others want a second round of the game. But I think they should accept that you won't be playing."

"Why?" I whisper. "Why would you even *think* that?"

He takes a step towards me. Relaxed, he puts his hands in the pockets of his chinos. "Everyone here on campus can tell you who I am. But no one really knows. No one knows what I actually do. I'm part of it and yet I'm on the outside. They whisper my name, but no one recognizes me. I'm a bit like what Jaxon will make of you if you stay." He reaches into the air, closes his hand into a fist and then opens it. "Do you see?"

I shake my head.

"Nothing. You will be *nothing*."

"He won't succeed."

"Yes, he will." His smile is almost warm, as if he's telling me that Jaxon likes to catch butterflies because he thinks they're so pretty. "He achieves everything he wants. If not on his own, then through the others. He will always direct it in such a way that you will end up broken if you don't listen to him. And he only has one goal."

"That would be?"

"That you're leaving Kingston."

"I wouldn't have come back if I didn't think I could take him on."

"No. You came back because you have no other *choice*. Kingston means everything to you. You've been told that all your life, haven't you?"

I swallow hard.

"You know, mystery surrounds you, Weaver. Maybe there's more to find out about you than which of the Kings you like best."

"I hate them all," I hiss.

He flashes a crooked grin. But it's a cold grin, one that I can't imagine could ever express inner joy. "Of course."

"What do you really want from me?" I ask dismissively.

He takes another smooth step towards me. He's like a snake trying to lull me, to ensnare me. "You and I are similar. We belong and yet we don't. You're an outsider among five outsiders, who simply refuses to play the game. And an outsider among the five most powerful students. I've had enough of watching Tyrell wear down women like you. Rubbing them out and throwing them away like used merchandise. I'm tired of being *something* and *nothing* at the same time. And you can be something and everything at the same time. That's why I'm going to help you."

"I didn't understand a word you said," I mumble, not sure what to say. Is he trying to be nice? Or is this just another one of the Kings' tactics?

"If anyone deserves the money from the Tyrell Foundation, it's you. Tyrell, Crescent and Silvano will realize that too. But until then, I'm standing up to them." Romeo's eyes fix on me lustfully before he takes another step back and stretches his back. "You won't even notice me. I'll pick you up and take you to the lectures. And sit near you in the canteen. That'll be enough to make sure *no one touches a hair on your head*. They know what happens otherwise."

"Which is?" I swallow.

A smile appears on his thin lips. "Very bad things. Do you want your job at Crowns back?"

"No, thank you," I reply simply and cross my arms in front of my chest.

"Derby was fired. I'm taking his place. We can do the shift together on Thursday. You earn money and I stay in the background."

"You want to… work there?" I ask mockingly.

"Trying to distract yourself from exam stress is not a luxury that only applies to poor students. See you around, Weaver."

He calls me by my surname, which irritates me more than anything else. He gives me a curt nod and rushes past me through the door.

I look after him and at the same time feel that it is not his presence that fills me with fear, but his departure. As if he had left a mark on the room that slowly creeps into my limbs and makes me shiver. What the hell does it all mean?

JAXON

The fact is, Belle, we don't give a shit about your social status. Are you fuckable and will you break like a glass that's too thin?

Then you are our choice.

We are not social, nor do we care about poverty in this country. Anyone can get to the point we have reached. Sometimes it takes a couple generations, but it's possible. America is not a fucking monarchy, even you could become a queen if you put your mind to it.

So don't give me that shit about social inequality and all that filth.

There is no difference. All people are the same. Whether they are black or white, stupid or clever, they all have the same choice. To work hard for their success or not to. I'll tell you a secret that you may not like to hear: Most people rest on the fact that they can't do it, instead of first trying and then realizing that they really can't do it. True winners don't let setbacks or societal expectations stop them.

Are you a winner?

9

MABLE

"You can't trust Romeo *under any circumstances*." Harper stands in front of me, gesticulating wildly.

When I told her Romeo had sat exactly where she was sitting now, she jumped up from the bed as if he'd left toxic chemicals behind. "He's a puppet. Everything he does is controlled by Jaxon. He *breathes* for Tyrell. He *exists* for him."

"May I ask how you know all this so well?" Maybe I need to find out more about the Kings so I can finally figure out how to get revenge on them.

"I'm engaged to Sylvian?" she says surprised, only then realizing that this is neither an argument nor particularly tactful. "Sorry." She closes her eyes and a moment of awkward silence falls between us. "Sylvian doesn't tell me everything, but he did tell me about Romeo. He hates him. Because Romeo has no character. He doesn't actually exist. He's really Jaxon's shadow. Nothing more."

I picture Harper and Sylvian lying in bed and him telling her all about the one King he says he can't stand, and again the heartbreak hits me like it's the trunk of a tree being cut down right above me. "I never intended to trust him."

That's all I can come up with. To busy my hands, I continue unpacking my things.

"Mable, I'm really sorry..."

"No, it's fine." *She's not your friend. She's nice and you can enjoy your time with her. But she's not your friend. She's not going to break up with Sylvian. She's sticking by him – despite everything.*

"You should go to Vance."

I just laugh.

"Please, Mable. If your first classes start tomorrow and you don't have anyone to look after you... What could happen?"

"And you think *Vance*, of all people, would 'look after me'? That fucking asshole?"

She looks like she really thinks it's possible. "You could just ask him..."

I shut my eyes and feel anger rising in my chest. I'm so mad at her, at the Kings, her stupid fiancé and the huge hole in my chest that just won't close, no matter how hard I try. "Okay," I hiss, throwing my unpacked things onto the bed and heading for the door.

"Now?" Harper asks me in surprise.

I just shrug and step out into the hallway. Rachel and Brittany are in the kitchen. Rachel calls after me, but I'm already in the stairwell.

One floor up and the whole hall of residence looks different.

There are posters on the walls and shoes are strewn across the hallway. It's livelier and the way I've always imagined student housing to be, even if there's no one around.

I'm not going to talk to Vance. I don't even know if he still lives here. But Harper has given me another idea.

Last semester, I tried to convince the other 'queens' in the

Kings' chess game, their arena, to work together so everyone could stay. Rachel laughed at me. But it's not just us five girls – now down to four – with a scholarship.

There are also five male scholarship students studying at Kingston in their first year. Why don't I try to get them on my side?

The very first room I try is unlocked. When I find no one in the room, I scurry in, close the door behind me and look around. A normal room. Notes on the desk, an unmade bed. A small TV on the windowsill, packs of cigarettes and porn strewn around.

I have no idea which of the five men live here. I'm a little annoyed that I didn't think of asking them if we wanted to get together much sooner. However, if one of them catches me snooping around in their room, they probably won't trust me blindly.

But now that I'm here, I might as well take a look. Figure out if I can trust these guys. I fear they might fuck with me too, because that's what the Kings want.

I run my fingers carefully over the notes, looking for a clue. Maybe I'm hoping to find a contract to sell their souls to Jaxon Tyrell or something.

Sighing, I sink into the chair. It's ridiculous. I'm not going to find anything. I kind of like Romeo's tactic of simply waiting in the room for the occupant to come back. Why not just get straight to the point?

I *have* to break down the walls of my fellow students and force them to pick a side.

The easy side or the good side.

Will they help me?

Or will they allow me to remain a pawn in Jaxon's sick psyche forever?

It takes less than ten minutes for the door to open.

I brace myself for a conversation, but shrink away in my chair as a huge figure enters the room.

Vance.

I swallow hard, and not just because his upper body fills the entire doorframe and he stares down at me like he has more hate for me than all the Kings put together.

"What are you doing here?" he asks in his deep, melodious voice, which doesn't match his dismissive expression. He catches my eye. "What are you looking for in Sid's things?"

"I wanted to… talk to him." I try to sound confident.

"About what?" growls Vance. Now that I know he wouldn't hesitate to grab me, drug me, and tie me up, I'm not as brave as I was the last time I ran into him.

"Do I have to… tell you?"

"Yes." He comes in and closes the door behind him. *What if he drugs me again?* "You have no business up here. But you don't like to play by the rules, eh?"

He sounds so rough and deep that it makes me dizzy. I shake my head, clasp my hands nervously and decide to take a direct approach. If I could gain him as an ally, he would help me much more than this Sid guy ever could.

"Is this *your* floor?" I ask him.

"More than you do."

Okay. "Harper talked me into it," I explain quickly. "She thinks I should ask you for help. She thinks you'd take my side if we… well, if she pays you to. If the Kings make good on their promises, I probably won't even be able to attend a class without being attacked. Please… I can't do it alone."

"None of you can do it *alone*."

"I just want to study. I want to be able to stay at Kingston and…"

"It's not gonna happen," he grumbles, standing in front of me like a football player waiting for his turn. "I've watched every single year as the people from this dormitory have been burned, as if they were a pack that deserved to be punished. There were people like you as well as much weaker ones. What do you think is supposed to be different for you when twenty-four people before you didn't make it either?"

I clench my teeth. Why am I even trying to justify myself to this guy? "Can you please just name your price?"

Vance laughs bitterly. "No! You annoy me! You should have left long ago! Besides, I hate you for letting those idiots... touch you. Just *leave*."

I open my mouth. "Excuse me?" I breathe. "What does that have to do with whether I –"

"Fucking the Kings, who invented this game in the first place, is... I mean... my *God*." He runs his fingers through his short black hair. "Never thought I'd meet a woman whose pussy messes with her head as much as a dick would."

"Yes, well, *I* thought I was living in the twenty-first century and no longer had to justify my sexual choices. But apparently, I was –"

"Wrong," he interrupts me. "Why these assholes?" He sounds almost desperate. "Wasn't there anyone out of the other thousand students on this campus you could think of having a fiver with?"

"It wasn't a fucking fiver! There were four of us!"

"Then you still haven't figured out who Zayn is, have you?" he snaps at me. His voice boils over and he tenses up, barely restraining himself from jumping up at me and shaking me.

"Who's Zayn?" I ask calmly, trying to remain brave. Vance won't hurt me. I follow my instincts and Harper's advice.

Something that has gone wrong before. But it's the only weapon I have. My intuition.

Vance ignores my question, shakes his head and looks past me as if the wall is more interesting than me. As if there was something there that would give him an answer. An *instruction*. Is he someone who always listens to orders? And no longer makes his *own* decisions?

"You know what?" I stand up and walk towards him. "I'm glad you don't want to help me. And I'm glad I don't know any more about the 'Kings.'" I practically spit the word. "You seem to take huge pleasure in being their pawn. Congratulations. You rightly won in your first year. You're just like them. Just pathetic."

His face has darkened even more, but I've once again reached that one black spot inside me where I think it can't get any worse anyway. No matter what he does, I can't feel more empty and meaningless. More abandoned or lonely. I can't. There's not even pain in my chest anymore. I'm on a battlefield, and the only allies by my side are midfielders, of all people, who are either screwing one of the Kings or just obeying them. And Vance isn't someone who would help me because it's the right thing to do. There is no right thing. Especially not in Kingston.

"Do you hate me?" I ask, stopping right in front of him. "You hate me of all people, the only one who seems to have ever stood up to the Kings? What's wrong with you? Did you play in their game or how did you make it to the football team and senior year? Unlike you, I didn't sell out. I didn't let them get to me because I wanted something from them. I'm not a whore or getting paid for cruelty like you. You probably only fuck women if it brings you something, don't you? You're just like them. You think like them. You're pathetic like them. You want to let them win. Against me, against you, against all of us. I stand before you and ask for your help. And all you can think of is to beat me up for being a normal person and falling for three men. I'm not the first. Anyone who lets a setback like that get them down only made it to Kingston with money. That's why it takes a game to get rid of us scholarship students, isn't it? We're not giving up. But you did give up. And that's just... despicable."

I want to walk past him, but he stands in my way. His breathing is rushed, but it's not anger that has taken hold of him. It's something deeper. Something much darker.

"It's not three men against you," he murmurs. "It's the elite against us. You won't be able to change this balance of power. Never."

"So I should just accept it?"

His brown eyes are troubled, and I can feel an energy emanating from him that knocks me back. If he were to grab me now, I wouldn't be surprised, but I have no idea what would happen. We remain reproachfully silent and the air around us becomes more and more charged.

"Why them?" he asks, sounding agonized. "Why did you let them get close to you of all people?"

"Why them and not an asshole like you, you mean?" I ask challengingly. "What's the difference?"

His jaw grinds and the anger in him returns. As if I hurt or even rejected him with these words, he backs away and looks at me disparagingly. "I'm not risking everything for a thoughtless, naïve thing who only proves her intelligence by doing homework and studying for exams," he growls. "And no, I've never slept with a woman I wasn't serious about. If you really want to win their game, you only have one chance."

"And what's that?"

"You have to make sure that nobody *wants* to see you lose."

"How am I supposed to manage that?"

"First of, I would stop scribbling dicks on their cars."

I burst out laughing. It sounds too good. If I lose, then I lose with pride. It wasn't *me* who brought the level down to this subterranean level. It was the Kings themselves, with their stupid being-around, their not helping with all the bullying, the horrible masks so no one can see their faces when they're acting like freaks…

Vance also laughs. "You have a sense of humor. And balls. But nothing more. So go now."

I have to accept that I can't break down his walls for now, and I nod. "Thank you for trying. You said to me last semester that you'd held back your pawns. Whatever that meant. But maybe that was already more help than I deserved."

I walk to the door, but he clasps my wrist. His amber eyes pierce me, and something in his gaze makes me feel warmth where his hand touches my arm. "Go before it gets any worse, Mable."

Of course he knows my name.

He lets go of me and I leave. And I feel even more defeated than before.

JAXON

Vance, Vance, Vance. What are we going to do with him? He's like an annoying, fat blowfly that you just can't get rid of. But if you catch it and put it on your enemies' food, it's quite useful. Maybe I should remind him who he's beholden to. He's not going to help you.

But he doesn't have to, does he?

You have Romeo.

Romeo, Oh Romeo.

We want to feel the dark poison of his affection.

It will corrode you, Belle.

But don't worry. I'll be there to save you.

After all, that's the plan, isn't it?

10

MABLE

On the day of my first lecture of the second semester, I am overcome by three feelings at once. Excitement because of all the new content. Fear of the other students on campus. And hopelessness, which hangs around my neck like a millstone.

When I more or less drag myself into the kitchen, a surprise awaits me. Romeo is sitting at one of the two tables, an espresso cup in his hand, reading something on his tablet.

Rachel and Brittany stare alternately at him and at me while I make myself breakfast, but finally Rachel raises her voice.

"Have you seen the plan yet, *Dole*?"

'Plan' can only mean one thing, and even though I want to feign disinterest, I turn around. Our semester schedule is hanging on the board next to Romeo. And a notice next to it.

I step closer.

Second round
As long as Dole doesn't play, nobody plays.

A shiver runs down my neck and I feel Rachel's greedy gaze on my back. In one fell swoop, the other scholarship girls are no longer just my rivals. They are my opponents.

"Please do us all a favor and finally accept that you've lost," Rachel hisses sharply. "Why are you making life difficult for the rest of us? We'll all have to go in the end! Not just you! What exactly do you get out of it, eh?"

"Ignore the note, Weaver," Romeo says without looking up from his tablet. "It's just a dramatic way of saying 'The arena is suspended.'"

"What!" Rachel jumps up, and I unconsciously take a step back towards the fridge, as if I'm suddenly afraid of her. "Are you here for *her*?"

Romeo lets his empty gaze slide over Rachel and clearly shows her that he couldn't be more indifferent to her.

"*You're* not the one who decides whether the game goes on!" she yells at him.

He has a much gentler manner about him as he puts his cup on the table and switches off his iPad. Gentler than all the other Kings. I'm sure his gestures are deceptive. Inside, he's probably even tougher than Jaxon. "I'm absolutely the one who decides. After all, *we* invented the game in the first place."

"But Reece said…" Rachel's voice goes up an octave.

"Reece?" Romeo asks, the corners of his mouth tinged with mockery and malice. "What did Reece say? That you're going to win?"

Rachel's face grimaced. "You're just one of their sidekicks!"

"Their sidekick, huh?" I love Romeo a little for showing Rachel up like this. "Would be news to me, really. But surely a whore like you will know my role better than I do. Are you done, Weaver? Let's go."

I just nod.

Romeo stands up, lithe, sinuous. He would be a Slytherin, for sure.

"You want to help *her* of all people?" Rachel asks, stunned, and she gives me a look that could kill if I were a little less strong.

"Her of all people?" asks Romeo. "I'd actually be happy to watch *you of all people* lose. Let's go."

I don't need to be asked twice to leave the kitchen.

Shortly afterwards, we are standing outside my dorm and I look back with unease. Suddenly I fear that Rachel will run after me and hit me. So much hatred in her voice, so much disgust...

"What was that about?" I ask Romeo, crossing my arms in front of my chest. "Do you want to make them hate me even more?"

For a tiny moment – it's only a second, half a breath, but I can see it clearly – something like compassion flits across his face. His black eyes are warm, then full of anguish and finally ice-cold and empty again. "No," he replies calmly. "I can't take care of that, only you can."

"I never did anything to Rachel!" I shout angrily at him, not caring who hears me. "You made them ostracize and hate me with your ridiculous game!"

"Did we?" he asks. "Or would they have done it sooner or later anyway?"

I shake my head, as if to drive his words out of it, turn away and make my way towards the main building.

He walks a few steps behind me and I still don't know what to make of it. It seems as if all the glances I normally attract are now glued to him. I feel almost invisible because I'm accompanied by one of the Kings. Do people wonder what will happen next? Are they hoping Romeo will expose me to everyone?

But none of that happens.

JAXON

I know what those little bitches want. My money, my name, my honor and my promise. They're prepared to do anything for that. They would kill each other to be by my side in the end.

That's boring. They're all too easy.

You, on the other hand, are different, aren't you?

You came to college to really study. You want to be independent. Emancipated. And all the shit I'm going to talk you out of.

11

MABLE

The first week of lectures starts uneventfully. Although I expect Romeo to suddenly show his true colors and stun me, drag me out of my dorm or a lecture and tie me up somewhere, I am left completely alone. Not a chicken feather in sight.

Even though people still stare at me whenever Romeo isn't around, they leave me alone and I have time to soak up every lecture and exercise like a sponge. Nobody disturbs me or comes closer to me than I want.

In the first few days, I'm so happy about this development I wrote Romeo a thank you letter several times in my mind, but by the end of the week, I start to fear that it's the familiar calm before the storm.

I sit up until just before midnight every night doing the follow-up work for the lectures and switch on my phone every ten minutes to check whether Harper has texted me.

She makes herself scarce throughout the week and by Thursday it's like she's disappeared from the face of the earth. I start to worry. What if she's been snatched up by the Kings again to answer to them like last semester? Or is she just spending time with Sylvian?

Luckily, I see her walking through the park from a distance in the morning. She looks stressed but healthy, so I decide to leave her alone. I have no idea how challenging the sophomore year at Kingston University is and don't want to be a burden to her when she has a lot on her plate.

The storm is brewing for the first time on Thursday afternoon. I am engrossed in my notes on business accounting, trying to ignore Romeo, who has taken a seat near me, and wait for my order.

Yes, at one of the most expensive elite colleges in the world, the food in the canteen is freshly prepared to order. All you have to do is pick it up.

When I hear an affected laugh, I involuntarily look up.

Clarisse and her friends have taken a seat one bench over. The canteen right next to the main building looks like a museum from the inside, and only the many salt shakers on the dark wooden tables show that this is a dining hall. Clarisse pretends to ignore me, but as soon as I read a sentence, I feel her eyes on me.

Sighing, I get up, get my food and try not to get irritated. For the fact that I was almost raped last semester and tied to a chair in front of a crowd of sensationalist students, surprisingly little has happened so far. I was bound to meet a Clarisse sooner or later.

I turn back to my notes, blindly push my fork into the pasta and am suddenly bumped brutally by Romeo.

"Don't eat that!" he shouts, suddenly right next to me, and pushes the tray across the table away from me with such force that the noodles spill over, spread with all the sauce and crawl over my notes....

Yes, crawl.

I jump up in panic, back away and try not to scream. Larvae are wriggling across my notes. Worms. Maggots. I don't know what they are. But they look incredibly disgusting.

I feel nauseous and cringe as I quickly pull my bag out from under the table so no maggots fall into it. The laughter around me is evidence that I've been deliberately tricked. It's *nothing* compared to what's already happened, and yet I probably would have put the noodles in my mouth if it hadn't been for Romeo.

One look at him and there's that expression of compassion in his face again. For a brief moment at least – then he straightens his face, takes a knife and pushes the maggots off my notes.

"Why are you helping her?" Clarisse has stopped with her entourage of blonde sorority girls. The only one who stands out from their group is a brunette who punishes me with a scathing look, as if it's *my* fault there's maggots crawling around on the floor.

Romeo ignores Clarisse.

"I'm talking to you, Romeo."

He raises his head. The cold that emanates from him even reaches my body, even though he's not even looking at me. Everything about him has fallen into an attack posture. Like a snake about to pounce on its coiled victim. "I couldn't care less what you say."

Clarisse raises her voice. "You're helping her, even though she shouldn't be here anymore!" By now, everyone in the room is looking at us. Another show for the students. Another time for them to watch me get my ass kicked. "She has *embarrassed* us all. Punished us with her *contempt* and *arrogance*. She's *ungrateful* and an *embarrassment* for this university and everyone who studies here. And you of all people are helping this little whore?"

Romeo slowly straightens up. The threatening thing about this movement is not his height, but his body tension. I would never want to meet him at night. I really wouldn't.

"You can keep trying to get back at her for those missteps by using maggots," Romeo replies coldly. "Or you can accept that you'll never be on her level."

"What?" hisses Clarisse. The room holds its breath.

One of the Kings against the Queen.

I would love to take my things and leave. But something is holding me back. I feel like I have to stand by Romeo's side, even though that's nonsense.

"You're *nothing* here," hisses the brunette at Clarisse's side. "No one can be on your level because you have none, Romeo. The only purpose in your life is to do what Jaxon says. Why don't you just keep doing it?"

For a moment, I wonder if that isn't exactly why Romeo is helping me: that Jaxon told him to. But I dismiss this thought again. Why would Jaxon do something like that? It goes against everything he did last semester.

"Do you know how I've been playing this game for the last few years?" asks Romeo. Every pair of eyes in the room lands on him. His voice is cool and biting and the slight, amused tug around his lips makes him one of the Kings. By now, I no longer doubt that he's as much one of them as the others. "Not by revealing to you and your little bitches what I do and why. You know *nothing* about me. And that's what crowned me. So fuck off. Because even if Jaxon doesn't approve of me helping Weaver, he'd probably rather lead you to the scaffold than me, right?"

Clarisse looks as if Romeo has pulled her by the hair and dragged her across the room. "You'll regret this!"

He no longer answers.

So she turns to me. "What did you have to do, you little slut, to make Romeo of all people stand in front of you? Fuck him just like the others?"

"Be nice?" I suggest, causing her mouth to widen into an ugly smile. "You should give it a try."

Clarisse takes a step towards me, but Romeo stands protectively at my side. This gesture is so heroic that I feel really empowered for a moment, but Clarisse has nothing but contempt for Romeo's behavior.

"If the Kings, for whatever reason, think you belong at this university and allow Romeo to help you, sit out the game because they know you'll never play, and want you to win, then that's not what everyone else wants. If Jaxon is too *fine* for that, *I* will destroy you, Dole. You won't spend a single day at Kingston not realizing how little you belong here. You're living off our families' money, taking advantage of what we've spent centuries building, and sucking the dicks of men who see you as nothing more than an ugly whore in the most disgusting way. If you stay on campus for even a single day, *you'll regret it.*"

Clarisse grins shabbily at me before taking another step back. I don't deign to reply – in fact, I don't know what to say – and silently take the sheets from Romeo, stow them in my bag and leave the table.

"You forgot something else, Dole!" shouts the brunette.

I stupidly turn towards her and get a load of maggot covered noodles on my chin, which I brush off as quickly as possible. She's not too shy to throw a second spoonful at me straight away.

"Come on," Romeo hisses, grabs my upper arm and pulls me out of the line of fire. As soon as I take a step into the corridor, a student steps in front of me and tips his Coke cup towards me. Cheers erupt around me as the liquid soaks my clothes. Romeo drags me on, but he can't protect me from everyone in the room suddenly jumping up and throwing their food at me.

"Get out of here, Dole!"

"You're too ugly for the game!"

"Eat shit and die!"

Laughter, bawling and tens of portions of food land on me. Some of it on Romeo too. The staff are aware of what's happening, but in the commotion they can't do much more than wave their arms around wildly and ask people to stop.

When we finally reach the door, I'm covered in sticky stuff from top to bottom.

"Mable!" Harper comes towards me, snatches my arm from Romeo and pulls me outside. "Why the hell are you eating alone in the cafeteria?"

She drags me further across the square to the snow-covered meadow. There she tries to wipe the worst of it off my clothes. "You have to put on a coat, otherwise you' ll catch a cold." She anxiously picks a slice of banana out of my hair. "And you, Romeo, just get out of here."

"He helped me," I defend him.

"Yeah, and we'd rather not find out what his plan is behind this. Go to Jaxon or whoever, but leave Mable alone!"

"Without me, neither she nor you have a chance."

Harper wheels around to face him, puts her hands on her hips and juts her graceful chin. "And if Mable flunks out of college; *you*'re the last person she can trust! What were you doing a year ago? Made sure Eliza set fire to the physics lab just before finals and then went to jail for several months? I know for a fact that you manipulated her to do that! She was Reece's lady and you turned her into a criminal!"

The satisfied look in Romeo's eyes, which flashes just as briefly as the compassion earlier, confirms every one of Harper's words. "It wasn't me who made her a criminal. She did that herself. I'll stick around. If you try to shake me off, Clarisse and her horde will probably slaughter Amabelle tonight. But whatever you say, Mitchell."

As he moves away from us, his gait could be described as an easy stroll if it weren't for his snake-like quality.

"Great," Harper mumbles in frustration. "I hope you don't fall in love with him."

I stare at her. "Who ever said anything about being in love?"

She shrugs. "Let's go to your place. You need new clothes."

12

SYLVIAN

I've never seen the King so angry before. It's as if I've slipped into a parallel world in which a Jaxon Tyrell can feel something other than indifference and gloating.

I look around the throne room uneasily. No one else is present. Just the five of us. Although I hate Romeo, I give him a questioning look.

What happened in the canteen, Mable?

Romeo looks back darkly.

The others sit there and look at Jaxon as if he were a pendulum, hypnotizing us all with his constant pacing up and down the room.

"Where's Vance?" he asks irritably and stops abruptly.

"He hasn't come yet, Jax," Reece replies.

"Why is he late?"

Zayn lifts his shoulders helplessly. "How are we supposed to know?"

"Find. It. Out," growls Jaxon and keeps pacing in front of the five chairs standing in front of the floor-to-ceiling stained glass windows.

I take a deep breath and light a cigarette.

Romeo has made himself comfortable on the chair next

to Jaxon's and swings his leg, which he has placed over the backrest, back and forth in time with Jaxon's steps.

I'm starting to get impatient.

"Where's Vance?" asks Jaxon again, giving Reece and Zayn a death stare.

"Man, I have no idea! Are we his babysitters?" asks Zayn.

Jaxon takes a step towards him. He gives him a look that could kill. "Well, now you are. It's important. I want to talk to him before he does any shit. Before he allows himself to be taken in by *Clarisse*."

Zayn rolls his eyes and reaches for his cell phone again. "He says he'll be there in a minute."

At that very moment, the door opens.

We all raise our heads and look at the pawn who enters the throne room as if he were as much a part of us as we are.

"What is it?" Vance asks disinterestedly. His arrogance towards us makes me crack the knuckles of my hand.

Jaxon growls again.

Have I ever heard him growl so many times in a row?

"Sit down," he snaps, waiting exactly one second for Vance to sit down on one of the three chairs closest to ours. "Everything you ever thought you knew about us, you'll forget."

"I never wanted to remember any of it anyway. Is that why I'm here?"

Zayn purses his lips. If anyone hates the athlete, who is in his fourth year as a scholarship holder, it's him.

"No." Jaxon stops in front of Vance. "You're here because you're a fucking little loser that I don't trust. I want to make sure *no one* buys your fucking loyalty. That's why..." Jaxon nods to his right. There's a single suitcase on one of the tables. I hadn't noticed it before.

We all notice how Vance hesitates before standing up and approaching the table. He opens the clasp and flips open the case. A miniature version of a gold ingot lies inside.

"Fine," he finally grumbles after taking a good look at him. "What should I do this time?"

"Nothing." Jaxon sat down in his chair. Finally relaxed and at ease.

"Nothing?" asks Vance with extreme suspicion.

"You will do absolutely *nothing*. And if I find out that someone else is offering you more and you accept it, all your offenses of the last few years will come crashing down on you in one fell swoop. I will *crush* your fucking insignificant life if you betray us." Jaxon looks up, smiling kindly at him. "Any questions?"

Vance raised a brow and looked at us in turn. "How exactly do you define 'nothing'?"

"What have you been doing at college for the last three and a half years, Vance, that you don't even know the definition of 'nothing'?" Jaxon asks snidely.

"Very funny," grumbles Vance.

"You'll be there when we need you. But the rest of the time, you keep a low profile."

"Great."

I know that he would love to give us all the finger.

"Then just get in touch. You have my number, I think."

None of the Kings laugh, but he curls his lips into a condescending smile.

"Fuck off," growls Jaxon, which Vance doesn't need to be told twice. He is gone as quickly as he arrived.

"Ooookay," drawls Zayn. "Are you sure you got it through his thick skull what you want from him, Jax?"

"Of course," mumbles Reece. "We have to make sure he

doesn't let Clarisse pay him. Otherwise we'll have one more problem on campus that will make Mable's life hell."

"Yeah, right. The cute little Dole you're suddenly determined to protect," Zayn replies mockingly. "What's this really about?"

"We need to be more strategic." Jaxon stands up agilely, walks across the room and fetches one of the old-fashioned blackboards on wheels. With a piece of chalk, he draws three crowns, a pawn and a queen on the board.

Reece and I don't get upset, but Zayn groans in annoyance. "Why don't you just draw Amabelle as a pussy?"

I have to smile and for a moment I feel nothing but deep relief. Jaxon has finally realized that Mable is not just any dole. *You are more. Every day that I can't be around you is twenty-four hours of loss. I never thought I could do more than be there when Jaxon attacks you and try to deflect those attacks.*

No.

He even takes our side.

My side.

It gives the monster inside me the support it needs not to break out again.

I can't quite believe it yet that *all of* us Kings seem to have suddenly changed our minds, but that's what's happening.

Jaxon is no longer planning Mable's downfall.

He is planning her rescue.

Never before has a realization felt so damn relieving.

"Did I expect you to just tell us how hard you fucked Clarisse for the nonsense that she slammed into Romeo's head?" asks Zayn. "Why the blackboard? The stupid crowns?"

"I'm not going to fuck her anymore. I don't care about Clarisse." Jaxon stands next to the blackboard and smiles serenely at us. Romeo stops bobbing his leg, and we all probably ponder what the hell is going on with Tyrell at this very second.

"Okay." Zayn stands up. "Since no one else dares to ask, are you sure you're okay, Jax?"

Jaxon laughs openly. "You're afraid of her coming between you and Reece, Zayn. But that won't happen if you stop fighting it."

"You've all got a massive hit to the head!" Zayn exclaims, looking at us in turn. His gaze lands on Romeo last, as if he's hoping for help from Jaxon's shadow of all people. "Please!" he shouts. "Say something about it!"

Romeo straightens his clothes and stands up. He's the quiet type. The one who never says anything unless he has to. So I'm all the more surprised that he gets involved. "First of all, I can guarantee you that I will manage to protect Amabelle Weaver. I'll be even more vigilant, and everyone will think I've secretly fallen in love with her and that's why you're letting me have my way."

"Of course," Zayn scoffs, "that's probably what *everyone's* thinking."

"Whatever." He clears his throat. "Everything we've ever done has been against the Tyrell Foundation. We thought it was appropriate and logical to drive the scholarship students out of Kingston so that no more money would flow to them. But we never asked ourselves what was *actually* behind it."

"My father," Jaxon reminds him. "He's pursuing some insane agenda to jeopardize our places in the circle…"

"Really?" Romeo interrupts him. I've never seen him do that before, and Jaxon is also perplexed. "Or is it something *more*? Is there something those scholarship students have that could be a threat to the *circle*? Why is the circle, of all things, not a big supporter of the Tyrell Foundation? What is behind this? Who is waging whose war here and which side are *we* on? We have behaved like college students who want to make it big and have no plan. But we have one now. I'm in favor of Amabelle Weaver staying. There's a mystery surrounding her. Weaver could be a significant pawn in the game for the best spots among the elite. It would be foolish and short-sighted to expel her without discovering the key to her secret."

"I'm impressed, Portcharles," replies Reece appreciatively. "You, of all people, are the first of us to take a look behind the curtain."

"Unfortunately, you have massively destroyed her trust." Romeo smiles tightly. Something like reproach flashes in his eyes and I feel harshly judged, and rightly so. Shit, I never thought he could become sympathetic to me again after what he did last year. "I've been watching Amabelle. She's strong and confident. If she doesn't hear every single one of you say you're sorry for what happened last semester, you don't need a strategy. Then you can just forget about it."

Silence spreads between us. Are we all really *that* stupid? Have we fallen out with the girl we desire in the darkest way? In the *deepest* way?

Romeo holds out his open hand and Jaxon, completely perplexed, puts the piece of chalk in it. The fact that he lets Romeo take the lead shows how much the last semester has changed him. Tyrell is no longer just a piece, the king who moves across the board and beats everyone. He becomes a player. *And me? What am I?*

"Each of us has a good reason to stay away from her," Romeo begins, stepping in front of the table. "Crescent is a psycho, Silvano is engaged and Tyrell can't afford any of this. But I know you. If she lets anyone else get close to her but one of you, you really will kill her."

"Then we'd be rid of her," Zayn interjects. "That's the idea. Let's get Vance to shag her, Romeo. Are you in?"

Romeo laughs coldly. His eyes wander deep into Zayn's, causing him to stare back, unpleasantly touched. "You'd do anything for Reece, wouldn't you? And Reece has made up his mind. Live with it." Romeo turns back to the table. "By now, even the last fool on this campus understands you won't take revenge on Weaver. You're not going to *punish* her for coming back. That means we have all those against us who were just waiting for a sign of the Kings' weakness. We could pretend we don't care and all start protecting Amabelle from the attacks that will come. But that would just lead to Clarisse targetting her. She will never accept that Jaxon cares for Amabelle or even helps her."

"How clever you are, my friend," Jaxon praises him.

"That means the campus must think it's a game. While only Weaver knows it's not. But if we tell her, she won't believe us because you are complete idiots. I wouldn't believe you either, and especially not me. That's why we need a better plan." He draws an arrow pointing from Vance's pawn to Mable's queen. "I don't care which one of you she chooses. But that decision will be this year's game. Amabelle Weaver will have to choose. And you will live with her choice." He winks mockingly.

None of us know whether the fascination we have felt for Mable since Thanksgiving will last for a long time. But it will remain until we own her again.

Jaxon will never accept that she chooses someone else. But he'll probably tolerate it for the game's sake. He believes in his own rules. He sticks to them.

Reece wants her for himself. He made up his mind long ago, and maybe he's hoping she's the one for him. Someone who doesn't crave his fortune and who is up for a threesome now and again.

And what about me?

Would I be able to handle it if you chose me?

No. I will teach you that you don't have to choose. Because your true revenge will be that none *of us get you.*

JAXON

The fact is, Belle, you can't stay at Kingston.

Anywhere else in the world you could be by my side.

Maybe that's what we want?

What we all want?

I just have to convince you to get involved with us a second time. Trust us. And I know that's going to be damn hard. Not only because your life is in danger the moment four out of five Kings choose you as their lady.

Believe me.

As soon as that happens, everything up until now is a shadow.

Our hatred is not the danger.

The danger is even the slightest bit of affection.

13

MABLE

"You have to imagine your heads like vessels. Deep, hollow vessels. These vessels have been filled with all sorts of things for years, since birth. Let me assure you of one thing: there's a hell of a lot of garbage in your heads."

Some students in the front rows laugh.

It is good to see that the elitist heirs of huge companies and political hierarchies react to a professor's bad joke in the same way that everyone would.

I have to smile and make a note. *Head = garbage.*

"He didn't say that," Harper whispers, tapping the equal sign with her pen. She's taken an extra course as a minor in philosophy so we have a lecture together. "Garbage *in the* head does not equal garbage head."

She makes me giggle, which earns me a look from professor Goldman. But I'm not too embarrassed. He's the friendliest and most normal teacher I've met on campus so far.

His light hair does not disguise the fact that he is actually still quite young. Perhaps in his early forties? His energetic gait in the auditorium makes him look athletic, but his clothes are comfortable and inconspicuous. I can imagine how high his salary must be if he teaches at Kingston. Unlike his colleagues, he doesn't flaunt it.

"If you think you're here so that I can put more garbage in these vessels, then you're mistaken."

"Well, I can't really do anything with garbage," I whisper to Harper, who also giggles.

This morning she appeared at my side, pressed an extra large latte in my hand, gave me a kiss on the cheek and revealed to me that she had taken Reality and Knowledge I as an elective so she could spend Friday afternoon with me. I can't tell you how much better it feels to have her by my side. With all the stares, I would have gone crazy otherwise.

Then there's Vance and Reece and then Vance again… My head is already spinning from all the testosterone around me.

Harper gave me a very long monologue in which she listed various reasons why she has hardly any time for me at the moment. She mentioned the death of one of her sister's cats as well as the misplacement of her cell phone. And, of course, the stress of grades. If I understood her correctly, she only passed one exam last semester. I pretended to believe every word.

Basically, she could be as dangerous as the Kings or Vance. I don't know her true intentions and I'm not naive enough to think that everything will be okay between us. She watched me get bullied and she's still with Sylvian.

But it doesn't matter.

For the moment, I'm enjoying the informal interaction with her as I did during the vacations.

"This semester," Goldman explains, "we are going to focus exclusively on the question of how you can recognize that there is nothing but garbage in your heads and that you have no –"

The door at the back of the lecture hall swings open.

Three figures enter the hall and it is as if everyone is holding their breath. Jaxon, Reece and Romeo.

"Excuse me?" Goldman asks the three of them tensely. "What is it?"

"Oh, nothing to worry about, professor," Jaxon replies nonchalantly and he sits down in the front row between Reece and Romeo. "We're still missing credits in a pointless course. And since, thankfully, there are no gender studies at this university…"

The entire lecture hall laughs. Much more uninhibited and amused than with professor Goldman before.

"You thought you'd honor us with your endless intellectual wealth," Goldman finishes the sentence in Jaxon's place.

The lecture hall suddenly falls silent.

"Indeed," Jaxon returns coolly.

"Excellent, then first of all let me tell you something about the component of time for supposedly pointless things. Your attendance will only be assessed in this course if you are punctual. And unfortunately, you are not in a position to discuss the importance and value of punctuality in social life without my teaching."

Jaxon is silent, but Harper huffs into my side. "Brilliant! Goldman hates Tyrell! This is going to be entertaining."

"Why did he choose this course?" I ask worriedly. Reece, Romeo and Jaxon.

"Don't worry, professor." Jaxon's voice has taken on a cutting undertone. "I bet you can teach me a lot about punctuality. After all, it's a privilege of those who have nothing more important to do."

The air in the lecture hall has become a lot thinner and I don't see anyone even *moving*.

Goldman has both eyebrows raised and doesn't counter Jaxon's attack. Part of me hopes that he doesn't want to get involved in Jaxon's games because he's far too wise for that. Another part of me is fascinated by Jaxon's behavior.

Is it because he has an answer for everything?

And I want that for myself?

"Before I was interrupted, I wanted to use a typical anecdote for a philosophy professor to illustrate to you the need to internalize the profound truth about your existence immediately and regardless of all consequences, which will not just make you a *different* person, but a person *at all*."

I hold my breath so as not to miss any of his words as he goes to the blackboard, pushes the bottom one up and reveals the word written in capital letters on the back board.

"You know absolutely *nothing*." Goldman pauses for effect. There is a murmur. Presumably everyone – myself included – was expecting a more interesting revelation than the word 'nothing'.

"Let me explain." He raises his voice and paces up and down in front of the students again. "The basic principle of philosophy is to find your *own* principles. Nobody is going to put something in front of you and expect you to just swallow it. What good would that do? No, philosophy is a tool, just like all other sciences. And it is only useful for those who have created this tool themselves. Otherwise you remain a parroter. A copy of a much more brilliant thinker and therefore unworthy of Kingston. If you do not learn this lesson, you will not be able to attend any further courses at this faculty."

I give Harper a look, but she just shrugs her shoulders.

Jaxon raises his hand casually in the front row.

"Yes, Mr. Tyrell?" Goldman says coolly.

"If I supposedly know nothing, are you saying I spent the

last three and a half years at college for nothing, professor?"

Mocking laughter fills the room, but Goldman remains calm. "Absolutely right. Except for the advantage that these three and a half years seem to have led to the development of a passable perceptive faculty."

I can hear Reece laughing and Jaxon also twists a corner of his mouth in amusement.

The lecture hall falls silent again. I get the feeling that those present are either not used to it or don't particularly appreciate it when their King is exposed.

When I raise my hand, Harper pulls it down in a flash, but Goldman has already noticed me.

"Yes?" he asks in my direction.

"Professor…" As soon as I raise my voice, all heads turn to look at me. Jaxon and Reece are also staring at me. Shocked by the reaction of the audience, I almost lose my temper. "Professor Goldman," I try again, "when you talk about knowledge, do you also mean memories?"

Goldman looks at me as if he can't believe I've asked a question. He can't help but notice how the lecture hall has reacted to me. All the students are slow to look forward again. But Jaxon's gaze remains fixed on me.

"That's a very good question, Miss…"

"Weaver," I mumble.

"Miss Weaver has asked an interesting question." Goldman clears his throat and turns back to the lecture hall. "If you attend this lecture and the accompanying lab, you will – should you be able to – end up filled with a deep doubt. And yes, if you *can* accept it, this doubt itself will gnaw at your memories. Only when you understand that you know *nothing, absolutely nothing* with one hundred percent certainty, are you ready to begin to deal with philosophical questions that revolve around *truth* and how to attain it. If this doubt never completely fills you, and you continue to believe that your memories cannot deceive you, then do humanity a favor and give up the study of philosophy. It would be a waste of time. And we've already learned from Mr. Tyrell today, that time is one of our most priceless resources." Goldman goes to the blackboard and jots down three names. "I would like you to study the works of these three authors, insignificant and absolutely brilliant minds whose vessels, however, have never been empty enough. They all deal with the same subject and none of them has yet been successful. Next week, we will discuss what they lacked to break through. *Or what they had too much of.*" Goldman nods to us and sorts through the papers lying on the podium. "You may go," he informs us, as if surprised that we are still here.

He finishes the lecture an hour earlier than planned.

"Wow," Harper whispers, stunned, staring at the names on the board as the MacBooks, iPhones, watches and Vuitton bags flash around us as they're packed up. "This is absolute psycho shit. I knew Goldman was quirky, but for him to turn on Tyrell? And what made you think to ask something? What was that about?"

I roll my eyes, pack my bag and tuck it under my arm.

"Oh, Miss Weaver?" Completely astonished, I hear my name coming from the direction of the desk. "I'd like to have a word with you," says Goldman and he waves me over.

I glance at Harper, who gives me an encouraging nod. "See you later!" she calls.

I break away from the stream of students and go to the desk.

"Some advice," Goldman begins kindly but firmly, "don't let Tyrell get to you. He's asking questions he doesn't want to hear the answers to. But you, you should know that it's wiser to come to me after the lecture and ask me your questions in person."

"I'm sorry if my question…"

"Your question was clever. But you're studying with a bunch of brutes who are just waiting for you to make a mistake. And because the parents of these children pay my salary, my hands are tied. I'm not allowed to reprimand the auditorium, as much as I'd like to. Just come up to me next time you have a question. I'm sure we can have a much better conversation undisturbed. And may I give you another tip?"

I'm not sure I'll like what he has to say.

"You're friends with Harper Mitchell, aren't you? Her father was my brother's best man. Ask her to buy you a matching wardrobe. You're not a student at Brown or NYU. There's a dress code here." He smiles wryly, but looks like an ally who's putting a knife in my hand. "I know colleagues who judge by it. And I'm irritated that no one has told you this before. Welcome to Kingston University, Miss Weaver."

He takes a step back and turns to the student who has been waiting some distance behind me. "Yes, Tyrell? Do you want to put my debating skills to the test again?"

"No, professor."

The back of my neck is burning up. Why did Jaxon of all people stay? Alone? I stand rooted to the spot. For so many days I've managed to convince myself that he doesn't exist, and now he's only a few steps away.

"I want to talk to Amabelle."

"Ah, Amabelle." Goldman looks at me thoughtfully. "Leave the girl whole, will you?" He shoulders his bag and heads for the door.

I don't know why I'm not following him. Am I interested in

what Jaxon has to say to me? Do I want to voluntarily listen to him having fun with his game? The last time I heard him speak near me was when he made my chair fall over with a mask on his head. Since then I've been dreaming of scratching his face. Or kicking him in the balls. Or laughing at him.

All three seem possible.

I turn around to him.

My heart falters the moment his smile infiltrates me like sweet poison. Jaxon's eyes gleam blue, his teeth flash, and his entire appearance crashes down on me in its perfection, as if a storm were sweeping over me.

I try not to let on, but it's impossible. It seems like there are three Jaxons at the same time. The asshole who can't be too mean and who wanted to have me raped. The arrogant student who walks around campus, fucks a different girl every day, kisses Clarisse in front of me and acts like a King. And… this one. A young man who smiles like a god and is as beautiful as a chiseled statue.

"If you think…" I start to speak, but forget what I wanted to say as he leans casually against the desk, his hands hidden in the pockets of his light chinos and his muscular chest relaxed. He stands next to me as if for a chat. As if we were friends. "What do you want?" I ask him coolly.

"Remind you that you're not supposed to be here."

Not impressed. "So?"

"And tell you that I'm glad you are after all."

"Why? So that your miserable game isn't over yet?"

His blue eyes flash. "That's one of the reasons, yes."

My hands clench into fists on their own accord. What would it be like if this arrogant pretty boy's nose bled? The red blood dripping onto his white cashmere sweater? Along his prominent chin?

Just thinking about it draws my attention back to his body. It's outrageous that Jaxon, of all people, is one of the most attractive students on campus. Why him?

"You specifically intercepted me to tell me *that*?"

"Yes." Jaxon stands calmly beside me. For him, this seems to be just another conversation. "I can't stop thinking about you. Thinking about what was between us… all of us. Maybe I was wrong to want to lose you. No one deserves to stay more than you."

I bite my tongue. All the nausea takes hold of me again, makes me stagger. I clutch at the desk, trying to stay clear. But in this clarity, nothing but sadness washes over me. "I can't stop thinking about you either," I whisper.

"Really?" he asks, satisfied.

"About what it was like to be humiliated by you. That you behaved towards me like some immature teenager who watched too much 13 *Reasons Why*. I remember exactly what it was like to wake up tied up in a chair. All those eyes around me, staring down at me."

A shadow flits across Jaxon's face. A shadow that I can't place.

Shouldn't he be happy? My suffering is his elixir of life!

"You didn't play along, Belle. What else could we have done but make an example of you?"

"You're justifying yourself?" I ask, choking. "You still find words of justification for all the cruelty you've done to me?"

"You're not even playing along *now*," he continues unperturbed. "It would be so easy, all you'd have to do is shag a few guys. I'm sure they'd be lining up for you. Especially after what happened between us, there's no doubt about it."

"Is that supposed to be a compliment?"

He realizes that I'm about to throw up on his shoes and

115

takes a tiny step back. "Listen…" he begins and puts his hand next to mine on the desk. Our fingers almost touch, making me flinch nervously. "I'm an asshole, Belle, yes. My ego fills the entire lecture hall and more. But you were right to resist. You didn't listen to us for a reason. I predicted that you would become a whore, but you're not. You are stronger than we thought. That's why we want you to stay. And if you let us… we'll *all* make sure that happens."

Mixed feelings fight against each other in my chest. Hatred and gratitude. Relief and despair. "So what happens? That it gets even worse for me?" I whisper.

"You're trying to convince yourself that I haven't changed my mind, aren't you?" Jaxon suddenly asks with a laugh, running his fingers through his hair. "We've stopped playing in the arena. What the peasants do is not our business."

"You're still firing them up! You reward them with recognition when they're particularly nasty! The fact that you shift the blame is even more disgusting than the game itself!"

Jaxon becomes serious. For a moment he says nothing, then he leans forward and casts his long shadow over me. "Without this game," he murmurs, his pleasant breath hitting me, "it would be far worse. You're clever. You know when I'm playing. I had to drive you away because otherwise *they* would have driven you away. When I told you that I wouldn't be there the next time someone like Hilbredge tried to hurt you, it wasn't a threat. It's a *fact*. We may be the rulers, but even we can't always do anything against the perversion of the mob."

I look at him like he suggested reading me a fairy tale. "And why should I believe you?"

"Well." Jaxon tilts his head. "Did Harper tell you about how far we usually go?" He shows no remorse at all. How rich are these guys? What do their parents do? Is being cold-blooded in their genes? Someone has to decide whether to bomb a civilian hospital in Iraq with drones. Is that it? The reason why Jaxon passes over death as if it didn't exist? Because his parents are like that too? "So ask yourself what's different this semester," he continues. "Why would we leave you alone if we didn't want it to be exactly the same?"

"Because Sylvian, Harper and Romeo are against you?" I guess into the blue, but I don't mean anything I say. Jaxon can come up with the most beautiful words, but I won't forget how he stood in front of me wearing a mask and said all those things about the underclass and about me. You don't just come up with stuff like that. You *are* like that.

"You think we're changing any rules of the game because of… *Harper*?" He seems to doubt my sanity. "No. Believe it or not, but I've decided I'm going to make this very easy for you."

"Earlier, when the whole lecture hall stared in my direction because I dared to ask something as a scholarship student?"

"No, yesterday, when Romeo told me about the incident in the canteen." Jaxon looks deadly serious.

"Oh, didn't Clarisse rave about it to you at dinner?"

His expression closes. "I use Clarisse like a chess piece. I'd never listen to her talk about anything. So, do you want to know what the game is about this time?"

I shake my head. Jaxon's whole demeanor disgusts me so much. Even if it was just shining his shoes, I couldn't do it. I couldn't put my dignity in his hands.

"Never mind," I reply resignedly and turn away. "That I'm even talking to you is a mistake. Either way, I won't end up with enough points in your game. No matter what you offer me. I won't trust you a second time."

A quick movement behind me and Jaxon is suddenly so close that his chest is touching my back. From behind, he carefully embraces my shoulder, holding back.

Curiosity gives me pause. Why would he suddenly play the nice guy? What's behind it all?

"Belle, there's only one way you can stay on campus without getting ripped apart by those people out there," he murmurs, and goosebumps rush down my spine. "They must believe that we're playing with you."

"Believe it?" I repeat mockingly. "What else could it be?"

"Well, it's no longer a game for us." His eyes sink into mine. "Kiss me," he whispers.

"Excuse me?" I ask, stunned, and back away.

"You want it too, don't you?" he asks gently, grabbing one of my strands that has slipped out of my plait.

I slap his hand aside. "Fuck off, Jaxon," I hiss. As I take a step to the side, he wedges me against the desk with both arms without touching me.

"You're clever, fearless and beautiful," he whispers in my ear. "And you want something from us. From all of us. I can't let the others already know what you *taste like*... when you and I are meant to be together."

I open my eyes and my mouth. He's a megalomaniac. Yes, that must be it. He has a brain defect and is babbling completely insane things.

"Just one kiss," he demands again. His ice-blue eyes look warm and friendly and his otherwise hard features are relaxed. "Look, we have to offer people something. If they think you're going to let us reel you in again, that we're just messing with you, then they'll be happy to watch us and leave you alone. But I don't care about the game. I really want it. I took this class just for you, even though Goldman fucked my mom and I should kill him for it. Doesn't that mean anything? I want to be near you. You must realize how much we *desire* you."

"You wanted to watch me being raped," I remind him angrily. "What's wrong with you, Tyrell?"

"Call me Jaxon."

"I'll call you whatever I want, asshole!"

"About the rape…" When I pull away from him again, he follows me. "I didn't really want to. But I had to do it to maintain my position, and I knew you could have made a stupid excuse to anyone. This isn't about you or me. Your fate or mine is not being decided in the halls of this university. There are a thousand things in favor of you just disappearing, but none of us really want that. Neither you nor us."

I reach the door, but he puts his hand against it.

"Belle…" he begins. I silence him with a look.

"Don't call me that. Kiss one of the hundred other girls on this campus, who don't realize that your personality is garbage. Let me go!"

"Kiss me and you'll play along without being our opponent. You are our ally." His eyes light up with excitement.

"Is this a trap?"

"No trap."

"Why should I believe you?"

"Even if I were lying, it would only be one kiss. How prudish are you?"

"Why does it mean something to you?"

He hisses. "Touché. It means something to me because I'm jealous and want to know why the others can't stop talking about you. Since I'm the only one who hasn't gotten more than a fleeting kiss so far, your lips must be magical in a way."

I think back to the sex. The *magical* sex. "That will make me win?" I whisper, trying to control my voice. "'Kiss one of the Kings and you're through to the next round'?"

"Not quite. The whole campus must think we're still after you. But we're about more than that."

"More?" I ask in a shrill voice.

Jaxon shakes his head so his dark blond hair falls onto his forehead and he smiles warmly at me. "Nothing like you're thinking. We have two ways we can make this look for the outside world. We should actually make your life hell and tear apart every last shred of your self-confidence. But then you'd never fuck us again, would you?"

I feel hot and cold at the same time. "I would never do that anyway –"

He interrupts me. "The second possibility is that we're making everyone out there think we're playing with your heart. With your innermost being. To destroy you *even more deeply*. But since you're smart, that won't happen and we'll just pretend. In the end, you can win because we'll set it up. All I ask in return is that you refresh your memory that it's worth it. That you're not like one of the thousand other bitches."

"Everything you just said goes against everything I know about you. Why are you even bothering to lie to me? Do you think I'm *that* stupid?"

"Stupid enough that you can't even do a few simple assignments to save your studies." Jaxon lets go of the door handle. Now he looks resigned. "Please, if you want to, go. It was just a well-intentioned suggestion."

"Are you *stoned* or something?" I ask, perplexed.

"Maybe I've realized that I want you?" he asks seriously.

"It's not reciprocated."

Jaxon raises his shoulders. "That's better. It was nice meeting you, Belle." He opens the door for me and wants to see me out, but I brace my elbow against it and push it shut again.

If I let him go, one of my greatest opportunities goes with him. To tell him what I think while we are alone and have no spectators, and to hurt him. Verbally. Because words are my only weapon.

"If anything you just said is true," I mumble under my breath, "and you're not on drugs, then I seriously wonder how you made it to senior year in the first place."

Jaxon smiles. "I wonder the same thing about your scholarship –"

"I'm serious," I interject. "Do you know that I saw through your tactics long ago? The magic that emanates from you and infiltrates everything around you? You're always *half true. Half real.* You lie and tell the truth at the same time, you're nice and nasty at the same time, you show affection and disgust at the same time. That's your shtick. You always reveal enough about yourself that others think you're a super honest guy, and then you're the mask again. The black mask with the gold emblems to hide how ugly you are on the inside. You want to kiss me? If that really is a demand from the real Jaxon, then I feel nothing but pity. And the other part of you? What could he be trying to achieve? Does it really satisfy you to force me into a situation that I would simply never accept if it weren't for my studies? Are you looking for a reason to finally be able to rightfully call me a whore? Damn it! What is it?"

He has been listening to me in silence, but now he sighs. "Goldman is right. You don't know *anything.* No one here knows anything. Why we do things. Why *I* do things. The fact is, we could still destroy you with ease. Ask yourself why

121

we don't. What would be the point other than that we don't want you to leave anymore?"

I catch my breath, but I can't think of a suitable retort. "You want to hurt me." I don't like how desperate my voice sounds. "You just want to entangle me in the web of lies again…"

"Amabelle." He sounds stern, like my father, whom I barely remember. "Normally, you'd already be *dead*. You wouldn't even remember your former self. My hatred is boundless, and combined with the Kings, it has the explosive power of a nuclear bomb. But we can't destroy what we all desire. *You* are the true winner. *You* fucked our brains. We can't forget you. We…"

Before I can think about it and my sense of honor holds me back, I stand on my tiptoes and press my lips to his mouth.

Fortunately, the moment passes before I can even really feel it, and I'm glad that I can get through the whole thing without any conflicting feelings.

"Is that enough?" I ask him straight out.

Jaxon stands there frozen. Slowly, he puts his fingers to his lips, touches them and looks at me darkly. "No."

That was kind of obvious, wasn't it? But something inside me isn't happy with what happened. I wonder what it feels like to taste him properly. *Damn. Why am I thinking this?*

"Do you want to try again?" he asks calmly.

Two extremes are fighting with each other in my chest. Of course I don't want it, but on the other hand it's just a kiss… A kiss with an attractive fellow student who could have anyone, but really wants me.

No, he doesn't want you, Mable. He's using you for his games.

But what kind of game is a kiss?

I nod. This time I let him come. As if in slow motion, he leans forward, his eyelids sensually closed. But instead of kissing me, he leans past my face to my ear. "Sit on the lectern."

No! scream all my instincts, and *yes!* begs my curiosity. What Jaxon is offering me is roughly equivalent to an obnoxious but beautiful woman undressing in front of a man and luring him into bed with her.

Who says only men think with their genitals?

Of course, it's kind of depraved… or perverted… But it's still better than anything I've ever experienced in the trailer park. Women are beaten there. They don't ask for a kiss, they demand hard sex that only satisfies one side. It's almost always the male side.

"Your mind has really drifted off, hasn't it?" Jaxon asks me attentively.

As if of my own accord, I walked back to the lectern. "It must be the influence of this lecture hall," I quip weakly. "I'm philosophizing."

"That's what I like about you. You're the first scholarship student with philosophy as a second major." Jaxon stops in front of me and watches me sit down on the desk next to the lectern, where Goldman can spread out his notes.

"I don't believe a word you say. You don't like anything about me," I reply, "but I like that it's hard to tell how boldly you're lying."

Jaxon's eyes light up. I can't tell from his expression whether I'm right or whether it's something completely different. "We should stop talking," he says quietly and steps between my legs.

I immediately slide further back so that his crotch doesn't touch mine, but he grabs my thighs and fixes me. It should disgust me to be this close to him, I should hate him, but right now every bad feeling is wiped away.

With one hand on my thigh, he slowly extends the other towards my head. He places it tenderly on my neck. My breathing quickens and I try to ignore the tingling sensation that passes from his warm fingers to the back of my neck.

Jaxon hesitantly lowers his head. His lips are open and everything about him is gorgeous and beautiful. In the seconds it takes for him to approach me, I don't care if this is about a challenge. Or any points. I don't care if he's just using me. I want to believe for a tiny moment that he's not. To taste the feeling that everything is completely different. He would have met me on campus. We would have flirted with each other a few times. Now we're kissing for the first time. As a couple.

I smile because it would suit us. In a parallel universe, I would have a crush on him and maybe he would have a crush on me too, because I'm not like the others.

Or whatever.

"Don't think so damn much," he murmurs, grabbing my hair. "It's exhausting watching your facial expressions change all the time."

"I'm sorry," I say a little too breathlessly.

Jaxon hisses, and then I think for a split second that he was just messing with me. That he's about to tell me he'd never kiss me. That I'm filth, unworthy, a *whore*. The moment passes as quickly as it came and his lips are on mine.

I can't say for sure whether it comes from me or from him, but our tongues touch from the very first moment. A feverish rush runs through me as he takes his distance again, comes back. He touches me tenderly with his lips, seeks out my tongue and leaves again.

Kissing Jaxon Tyrell is like kissing the man of my dreams.

It's so much more intense than the fleeting kiss in the frat house. Because it's not about sex. It's about so much more.

He touches me again, opens his mouth a little wider and pulls back.

Careful, attentive, reverent.

I imagined all sorts of things, but not this.

Not that it could be good.

Not that I would enjoy it this much.

Jaxon's grip on my hair gets a little tighter, his lips open a little further and I'm already craving more. Panic fills me that it might be enough for him. That he is withdrawing, saying that my 'task' has been fulfilled. I don't dare to pull him towards me, but I would like to. I would like to hold him. Hold him captive in front of my body until I've tasted enough of him.

"Can you please breathe a little less excitedly," he demands ironically, cupping my face with both hands.

"I thought I was supposed to offer something?" I whisper back, trying to suppress the shame that arises in me. I have nothing to be ashamed of. Especially not in front of this guy. "After all, this is about my studies."

"Ah, so you're trying hard?" he asks, the charming smile returning to his features. "God, I thought you actually enjoyed it."

I clench my hands into fists in despair. Even when we kiss, he manages to keep me down and humiliate me. "I do enjoy it," I reply, my voice quivering. "I wouldn't do it otherwise, Tyrell. You can call me a whore all you want. It won't make me one."

Recognition flickers in his gaze. "You're a mystery." Slowly, he lowers his hands, causing me to overreact violently.

His kiss – his kisses – were, if anything, a foretaste, and I'm not ready to end it just yet. At least the physical part of me that is driven by lust, not rationality.

I grip Jaxon's sweater and hold him tight. If I could, I would have pulled him back for more kisses, but his body is too strong.

He looks at me in amazement. Questioning and scrutinizing and with a hint of doubt. "I think that's enough."

"Oh," I say stupidly and now I feel really ashamed. Being rejected by Jaxon Tyrell when I'm trying to tempt him into more doesn't feel good. "Sure, that's enough."

I awkwardly slide forward to get off the desk and bump into his crotch again. He still standing between my legs and I can feel that he's… hard.

His excited dick between my thighs is one thing. Much more exciting is the thought that I have created this pleasure in him.

My breathing becomes unsteady. Jaxon looks down at me, his blue eyes transfigured and his expression impenetrable.

But then he moves, and it switches off my thinking.

I groan as he presses himself against me. He grips my ass, pulls me in front of his hips and kisses me again.

His reticence has disappeared. As if it had never been there. He pushes his tongue into my mouth with dominant force. I open myself up to him willingly, I surround his lips, searching for his tongue. I claw at his neck for support and moan again.

He moves rhythmically against my crotch. His clear hardness excites me, rubbing against my most sensitive spot under my jeans.

With every thrust, I curse the fabric between us and want to feel him completely. To feel more. I want him to penetrate me.

God, I want him everywhere in me.

"Jaxon!" I didn't want to shout his name, but the impulse was just there.

He grabs me, never stops kissing me, conquering my mouth with his tongue. His hands pull my thighs around his hips, then he suddenly lifts me up. I don't notice anything else around us until my back hits the blackboard.

With firm thrusts between my thighs, he presses me against it. Our mouths get lost in each other. It's more like breathing into each other's faces, always interrupted by the longing search of our tongues. I claw at his shoulders, clutch his hips with my legs, breathe headlessly, and then scream.

Damn.

An enchanting tingling sensation fills my entire body. In this one second, when every feeling intensifies and builds up to an explosion in my center, I perceive so much.

I am happy.

I have done something forbidden.

Jaxon braces me against the blackboard in the lecture hall where my philosophy lecture is taking place.

I feel desired.

A bit like being liberated and reborn.

And I don't want it to ever end.

My intoxication fades, but the deep feelings remain.

Jaxon lets me down slowly, but continues to hold me tight. His eyes are on me, inflamed. Magic fills the space between us. I want to say something, but the right words would have to be invented first. How easy would it be to say 'I like you' if everything between us was normal?

At least now I know what Harper has been warning me about for months. Everything is clear to me. It's absolutely impossible to get close to Jaxon Tyrell without falling in love.

And I've already done that, haven't I?

I fell in love.

The snap of a lighter interrupts the silence between us.

Jaxon immediately takes a step back and turns his head in the same direction as me.

My heart, which was already suffering, skips a beat.

The other Kings are in the room with us.

Sylvian, leaning against the wall next to the door and lighting a cigarette.

Reece, sitting relaxed on a chair in the front row, his legs stretched out as if it were a comfortable sofa. And Romeo. He's sitting in the corner by the window on the stairs.

No one says a word until Jaxon puts on a rock-hard face and raises his voice. "Don't you have anything better to do, you perverted voyeurs?"

Reece looks boredly at his fingernails, Romeo doesn't move and Sylvian ashes his cigarette on the floor.

My feelings are going round in circles. I don't have a guilty conscience towards Reece. But it's different with Sylvian. I don't want him to think I'm pathetic for starting something with Jaxon, nor do I even want him to think I've 'started' something with Jaxon. And besides, he's Harper's.

Oh boy.

You can be happy without a college degree, right?

Maybe I should *hope* I lose the Kings game before my conflicted feelings drive me insane.

I smooth out my shirt, shoulder my bag, which I left on the desk, and head for the door. The few steps across the room feel like I'm walking on burning coals. Four pairs of eyes following me are one thing. But I've had sex with three of them and…

I have finally reached the door. There's only Sylvian, who stands in my way. I expected it.

I could ask him to step aside. To let me through, to let me go, and my mouth opens, in preparation to say something. But then the smoke from his cigarette suddenly envelops me and his lips rest on mine.

He kisses me.

The fire inside me flares up like an inferno and I lose control of myself for a tiny moment.

Sylvian's tongue tastes of smoke, but underneath is the taste of him. It's absolutely impossible to resist him. I want it far too much. So much so that I willingly open my mouth.

It is not a simple kiss. Not a quick one without meaning. His hand has slid down my neck, holding me close to run his tongue over mine.

An intense tingling sensation fills my stomach all the way to my chest. I get so hot that I think I'm burning up inside. His dominance is different from Jaxon's, darker and more driven, and I absolutely love it.

I could stand there like that forever. Bewitched by his intense energy. But a clearing of the throat from behind interrupts us.

The distinct snap of a folding chair fills the room. Reece stands up, steps. He grabs me by the upper arm and pulls me around to face him.

A surprised sound leaves my lips, which he smothers with his mouth. His teeth gnaw at me, his kiss is much more passionate and wet than Sylvian's. Dirtier, more perverted and full of desire.

He pins me against the wall next to the door and runs his right hand under my shirt. His warm hand touches the base of my bra and I flinch.

My mental strength sails away. I just react, enjoy it, because I don't have time to judge what is happening.

Reece kisses at least as well as Sylvian. Just as good as Jaxon.

If I could decide, if I was *allowed* to decide, I would choose this one. Never leave the room again.

But that's stupid.

They are my tormentors. They hate my guts.

It's a game.

Even if it's just a game of the senses, I can't lose myself in it.

Reece lets go of me and looks at me with a clear gaze.

I purse my lips because I don't know what to say. Whether I should say something or even have to say something. It seems easiest to take a step to the side, open the door and scurry through.

As soon as I stand in the atrium, I can breathe again.

With every step I take away from the lecture hall, the voice that wants to send me back grows louder.

No. Just because you like the lions, their den is not a place where you should stay.

Especially not alone.

JAXON

B elle, Belle, Belle.
Why are you so clever and yet so weak?
It's too easy to get you around.

I'm already a bit shit so that we don't fuck again immediately, but even that doesn't seem to work. Is it because you look under my hundred layers and think you see something there that I don't even know exists?

Or are you just as addicted to my body as I am to yours?

14

MABLE

As I try to escape from the Kings as quickly as possible, I get lost in a part of the university I hadn't seen before. Rounded archways rise up in front of me and I find myself unintentionally standing in the middle of an covered courtyard. Glazed windows on one side, open wall outlets on the other. The scene is gloomy and I have no idea in which direction the part of the outbuilding that I thought offered me a shortcut home is located.

Not wanting to go back to avoid another encounter with the Kings, I cross the courtyard and take the opposite door.

"Oh, look who's lost there."

I stumble into the middle of a group of waiting students. And Clarisse is among them.

"Isn't your Romeo on your heels today, Juliet?" she asks me with a wry smile. All eyes immediately turn to me. Just as I'm about to walk back through the door, a couple of burlier guys get up and block my way. "How cute," Clarisse whispers, "our little Cinderella all alone and unguarded."

My pulse quickens. Last time they threw food at me until I was covered from top to bottom. Last semester, some of them even tried to rape me. What are they doing this time?

A few of those present laugh, the others are obviously waiting with bated breath to see what Clarisse is up to. She approaches me, dressed in the typical outfit of her fraternity. Winter boots, knee-high socks, beige shorts, a white blouse and a checked sweater over it. Even if it makes her look classy, her whole demeanor screams arrogant bitch. Judging from her glare, she thinks the same of me. "At last we can talk to each other in peace and quiet," she says sweetly and she stops right in front of me. "You've come back and you're still here. You must have a death wish. But not only that, you won't stop offering yourself to the Kings like cheap merchandise. That's what you do to get them to let you be, isn't it?"

"No," I reply tonelessly. "Unlike you, I'm not selling my soul to achieve my goals."

Clarisse turns a corner of her mouth and her friends laugh derisively. "No, because you're *too stupid* even for that. You let yourself get fucked even though you get nothing out of it, right? While anyone else would have approached Jaxon just because they were hoping to get something out of it, you think he *really likes* you."

Everyone laughs, and her words make me wonder again why I can't keep him at a distance. Why did it feel like he cared when we had sex? Why did I feel the same just now when we kissed? I am stupid. Stupid and naive, and Clarisse is almost right in what she says.

"You know, Dole, we can't fight that kind of blindness. Unfortunately, we have to make it clear to you that you don't belong here and that *everyone* hates you. Even Jaxon. It will dawn on you sooner or later." She grins shabbily at me, then glances at her wristwatch. "We've got five minutes before the lab starts. But five minutes should be enough to show the little whore who she'd better not mess with."

It's as if she's given an order that everyone understands immediately. I'm grabbed from behind, held down while they snatch my bag.

"Don't!" I shout in panic as they scramble to get my notes. Some of the girls tear up my sheets and throw them in the nearest wastepaper bin, others spill my juice all over the book I've borrowed from the library, but when Clarisse opens my laptop, I'm lost.

One of the guys pulls out my cell phone and holds it in front of my face to unlock it. With just a few clicks, Clarisse has also bypassed my laptop password with the help of the cell phone, and then I stand there cursing the damn security loopholes of the modern age.

I don't have anything on the computer that would make me uncomfortable or that someone could use against me, but that doesn't seem to be Clarisse's point. She's typing something on my laptop, not letting me see it, while the others continue to tear apart my entire bag.

Clarisse's radiance becomes more and more enraptured until she finally closes the laptop and stows it back in my now tattered bag. "You could almost make others feel sorry for you, little Dole." Her batting eyelashes makes me feel nauseous. "But if you don't want to listen…" She straightens her blouse and the others let go of me just as the door to the lab room opens. The group of students goes in and leaves me behind.

The instructor doesn't even look in my direction. I grab my bag from the floor. My cell phone fell out when one of the students threw it roughly into my bag, but when I go to pick it up, a big boot lands on it.

"Whoops," says the guy who is the last to enter the room. "Sorry, Dole."

I try to hold back my tears and don't move until everyone has disappeared into the lab. Then I pick up my cell phone. The display has been completely crushed, but it still works.

I frantically open my laptop to find out what Clarisse has done.

At first glance, everything seems to be fine until I realize that my cloud is empty. Clarisse has deleted my data. Irrevocably. And she has changed my password using my open mailbox. Damn. Maybe I can recover the data, but only with the necessary IT skills... Stunned, I go through my folders. Everything important is simply gone.

Desperate, I just sit on the floor. Five minutes. I was alone for *five minutes*. Got lost once. Wanted to escape from Jaxon and the other Kings.

And this is the result.

This is my life.

The realization of how lucky I've been so far because the Kings have changed any rules makes me feel pure trepidation. If this is what they would actually do, why are they holding back?

Why are they letting Romeo accompany me?

They should want me to experience such attacks every day. Because at some point I would have to give up. I have no doubt about that.

"Mable?"

I look up.

At the end of the corridor, someone has stopped in mid-pass and is now coming towards me.

"What are you doing here?" Vance asks me, running his eyes over the poured- over book on the floor, my tattered bag and the scraps of paper around the garbage can. Then he turns his gaze to the lab door, behind which Clarisse has disappeared. "What were you doing here alone?"

"I'm lost," I mumble and straighten up. "Would you like to kick me while I'm down? Maybe you'd like to destroy my laptop like they destroyed my phone?"

Vance's lower jaw tenses and he picks up the book from the floor. "I'll get you a new one."

I laugh mirthlessly. "A new phone or a new book?"

Compassion arises in his gaze. At least some humanity. "Both, if you like."

"No, thanks. I still have the money Sylvian gave me for sex from last semester, you know? That should be enough." I take the book from his hand, stow it in my half torn bag and walk past him.

"Mable…" He stands in my way. He's wearing the typical outfit of a sportsman. Sweatpants, sneakers, a bulky plain jacket with white stripes on the collar and sleeves and the Kingston logo on the chest, a sweater underneath. In the dark, narrow hallway, his massive stature looks like an explosive device.

"What do you want?" I ask demandingly.

His expression is shadowy and he seems to hesitate before continuing. "It was wrong of me to treat you like that."

"Oh yeah?"

"I did exactly what I hate about everyone here on campus. I was an ass. It…" His voice is dark and rough, and I find genuine remorse in his eyes. "I'm sorry."

I swallow hard. "So are you… going to help me?"

He shakes his head. "I can't."

"Why doesn't that surprise me?"

"It's not about me," he growls. "Or about you. Or about anyone on this campus. I can't help you because –"

"You know what?" I interrupt him because I'm too exhausted to stand another rejection. He doesn't want to help me? Fine. He doesn't have to explain himself. I can't take another excuse or justification for not helping a victim. "I don't even want to hear your excuses. Just get out of my way, please."

"Mable," he says deeply. His voice is really fucking engaging. "At least I can tell you what helped me back when –"

"Really, and what was that? Other than the fact that you're an asshole who likes to play stooge?"

He grinds his jaw and his gaze darkens. He scares me and I know that I can't physically do anything against him. But he stops some distance away from me, exhaling in frustration. "You have to make the campus start to love you. And once they want you to win, there's little even the Kings or Clarisse can do about it."

"Is that how you won?"

"More or less."

"You've collected fans?"

"I'm still doing it now. It works."

Yes, he's damn popular as a sportsman. "Who was your player?"

"You mean which of the Kings I was assigned to in their chess match?"

"Yes."

"Zayn."

"God, who the hell is Zayn?" I ask, annoyed.

"Find out," is all he says.

"So 'Zayn' won in the first year, Sylvian in the third. Who was the winner in the second?"

"Romeo."

"Jaxon has never won before?"

"He loses interest in his ladies quite quickly and prefers to watch the others. Last year it was neck-and-neck between

Reece, Jaxon and Sylvian, but it wasn't about the women themselves, I don't think. They were fighting about something else."

"Harper said Reece lost his 'lady' at the very beginning."

"Well, she'd know better than me, won't she?"

Now I'm clenching my teeth. He's being dismissive again. And I don't want him to dare treat me as badly as everyone else. He of all people should know better.

"Thanks for the tip," I say coolly and I step around him. "It will definitely help me the next time someone tries to rape me."

Vance lets me walk past him, but then he yanks me back by my shoulder. I react quickly, and I want to push him away hard, but I stop dead in my tracks when I notice the desperation in his eyes.

"I'll be there," he says tightly. "I can't take on those asshole Kings. But I can take on everyone else who would go that far."

"*You're* going too far," I hiss, and he immediately lets go of me when he realizes he's gone too far.

Nevertheless, he comes closer and lowers his voice once more. His masculine scent hits my nose, and I wonder why the hell almost only attractive men surround me at this college. "Let me take you to the dorm."

I take a deep breath. Vance is not someone I should trust. But he's not as bad as Clarisse. "Okay," I mumble. "But only because I can't afford for them to destroy my laptop, too. Not that I imagine you'd even hesitate to just hand it over to the Kings if they demanded it."

"I won't."

"Well, I'll just have to take your word for it, won't I?"

Frustrated, I walk alongside him. He holds doors for me when there are doors in our way and gives me an irritating feeling of security that I shouldn't feel. He really is like a bodyguard. In stature alone.

We don't say a word the whole way back to the dormitory either. More and more questions are burning on my lips. About Clarisse, about Zayn, about the chess game of the last few years.

But I'm glad that Vance is silent and leaves me alone with my thoughts. I need to sort myself out. I need peace and order, I need to save my cloud data somehow and…

"I'll come in and see if everything's okay in your room," Vance suggests and I don't argue. If he was one of the pawns, then he certainly knows the nasty tricks used to bully the scholarship students. He's probably done some of them himself.

I pause in front of my dorm room. I was so absorbed in my thoughts that I didn't pay any attention to how the people outside reacted to us. What do they say to a dole accompanied by Vance? But now I notice Rachel leaning against the door to her room, watching us.

"Did you choose Vance, of all people, to *protect* you?" she asks me cynically. "You do realize he's Jaxon's lapdog?"

"My first week of lectures was great, how was yours?" I ask as calmly as possible.

She tisks and raises her right shoulder disparagingly.

"Ignore her," Vance grumbles at my side.

I listen to him. It's no use talking to Rachel. She watched Jaxon show me off to everyone. She smiled when I went down. She wants to get rid of me just like everyone else. She's just another plaything of the elite, I'm sure of it.

Thinking about how Reece slept with her doesn't help, though…

I rush into my dorm room and in that moment everything

comes crashing down on me. Jaxon's kiss, the kiss with Sylvian and Reece, then the encounter with Clarisse. Rachel. I let the Kings get to me, even though they're involved with these... *women*. How incredibly blind and stupid am I? Vance has followed me, closing the door behind us and watching my legs buckle.

"Whoa there," he grumbles, catching me. I'm too weak to resist his grip. "What's wrong?"

I try with all my might to scrape together the strength within me. Not to let on how the mind game on this campus is wearing me down. But I can't.

"Mable..." he murmurs in my ear and at that moment it feels good. So good that I hate myself even more. What is wrong with me? Does my psyche like guys who are shitty to me?

But if I were to push him away from me now, I would dispel the feeling that suddenly arose in me when he embraced me. This tender feeling of protection. His arms are powerful and the skin of his hands incredibly warm. As if he were a sun warming me from the cold moon. I close my eyes for a moment, grasp his bare forearms and just hold on tight.

Vance has an effect on me that no King has ever had. There's something about him that tells me he'll always catch me. Even if he's acted differently so far. It's more a kind of... wishful thinking, I suppose.

"You're right." His voice is low and deep. "I'm a fucking coward. If I could explain to you why I –"

"Let go of me!" I demand weakly, in an incredibly thin voice, and wriggle out of his arms. I almost fall to the floor. I have a breakdown. That's it. And Vance, of all people, catches it. "Whatever Harper thinks, you're the *last* person I'd trust!"

His dark face is impenetrable as he stops in front of me. "I'm leaving. After I've checked out your room."

"What?" I snap at him.

"Trust me. It's better this way."

"No! Leave my things alone!" I shout as he steps in front of my wardrobe.

He looks at me calmly and. He radiates a strength that I would like to have in me. "Clarisse goes far. Yesterday and today. It wouldn't surprise me if she left something in your room. I know all the possible hiding places. Are you sure you don't want me to check?"

I cross my arms in front of my chest, trembling. "What if you actually check that the traps are all set correctly?" I ask critically.

He laughs harshly. "You'd notice." Then he pays me no further attention and starts to search my wardrobe. He reaches into every single drawer, runs over the shelves and looks under my shoes.

Since the students cut up my clothes, the closet has been practically empty. Vance pats it down, then turns his attention to my bed.

"Hey, stop that!" I shout in panic as he lifts the mattress.

A pack of condoms slips down through the slatted frame onto the floor, which I had hidden between the bed frame and the mattress.

Vance checks all slats. "At least you're not trying to get knocked up," he grumbles on the side, searching the entire bed for whatever.

"Why the hell would I?" I ask, desperately trying to hold back my tears, and quickly bend down for the condom packet. I tuck it away in the closet, which I know Vance won't open again.

"Everyone does." Vance straightens up and looks at me seriously. "I don't know any scholarship girls who haven't thought about getting knocked up by one of these guys."

"Do you know the others that well?" I ask suspiciously.

"Well enough to see how they try to persuade the guys to skip the condom because they're supposedly on birth control." He turns the corners of his mouth into a wry smile. "There's a battle for the best sperm on campus. I can only be glad I'm not rich enough for them."

I try to keep a neutral expression on my face, cross my arms in front of my chest and forbid myself to ask questions. I'm not interested in what he means. How he knows all these things. Or who he has sex with. Besides, I'm not *at all* interested in who he has sex with.

Taking a deep breath, I watch him examine every single inch of my room. His upper arms are stronger than my thighs and he lifts my desk, second bed and dresser with ease. He's definitely eye candy, and I'm a little too busy secretly watching him instead of being annoyed that he's trying to play the protector when he's been as much of my tormentor as the Kings last semester.

"I didn't find anything." Vance slams my desk drawer shut. "Apparently no one expected Romeo to let you out of his sight."

"And you? How did you find out? Or did you just happen to be nearby to protect me from Clarisse?"

"No."

"No?"

"I saw you walking alone in the wrong direction."

"How did you know it was wrong?"

"I know your schedule," he replies curtly.

I'm waiting for a further explanation, but that seems to

be it. Great. He knows my schedule . "Why? Why are you even interested in me?"

He runs his hands over his dark face, tense. "If Romeo isn't there, what happened earlier will happen again. It's better if I look after you too."

"But you said you didn't want to help me!"

"I don't want to!" he snaps. "You're fucking those bastards and I shouldn't give a damn about you, but I do! So I'm trying to do everything in my power to be around when something happens. I spent the whole fucking last semester making sure nothing worse happened. Only with fucking Hilbredge was I too far away."

I stare at him. "What does it all mean?" I whisper helplessly. "You – you! – drugged me, dragged me off and tied me to a chair and handed me over to a horde of onlookers!"

"And I made sure you were able to leave campus unscathed in the first place, because usually after you leave…" He clenches his jaw and looks at me with such anger in his eyes, as if I've done something wrong. "After you left the lecture hall, Harper told everyone off. She risked her entire position to stand up for you. She went after you and I followed her. They were already waiting for you at your dorm, but Harper stood up to them."

"Who?" *The Kings had stayed in the auditorium, hadn't they?*

"Those who take this game even more seriously than the Kings themselves. The extended arms of Clarisse. The lunatics who hate your guts and would never allow you to behave the way you did last semester. Not to play along. To hold up a mirror to you…"

"And Harper stood up to them?"

"Yes. Quite impressive, if you ask me. A little too… brave.

143

I wouldn't be surprised if she's also pursuing her own plan. But at least she's helping you in the interests of her own plan – for now. Harper betrayed the entire elite that night, and it was only because I was able to step up to her side as the Kings' arm and Sylvian joined shortly afterwards that they didn't do anything to her... and you were able to escape unmolested because everyone was distracted."

"What is your role in this game?" I ask challengingly.

His gaze darkens. "I'm just trying to survive. Just like you."

"And you're prepared to do some pretty nasty things for it."

"I have my reasons for that. You would probably do the same as me."

Do I want to hear these reasons? "Do they have anything to do with the fact that you care about me?"

His lips open as if he wants to say something back, but he remains silent.

"You... like me?" I guess.

He snorts contemptuously and the thought vanishes. Of course he doesn't like me. Whatever it is, it can't have anything to do with me as a person. Does anyone who isn't a psycho and wants to see me suffer even like me?

"You should stay away from the Kings, Mable," he implores me.

"Why? Obviously they're helping me to ensure that something like Clarisse did remains an isolated incident."

"They'll only do that until they get what they want."

"And what could they want?"

"Are you really that stupid?" he growls.

I cross my arms in front of my chest and he takes a step closer.

"They want their *revenge.* But if you learned anything from last semester, you know they eat their victims slowly.

They savor it. Every single move they use to corner their opponent. Don't be so naive. They still want to destroy you. It will just be different. Worse. Much. Worse."

I swallow hard and look up at him impassively, and then suddenly he does. He reaches out a hand to my cheek, gently brushes a strand of hair back behind my ear, and I try to discern what his true aim behind everything might be.

But there is nothing. Nothing but compassion and warmth in his gaze.

It's like I can still taste Jaxon's lips on mine as he leans in slowly. What would the Kings say if they saw me kissing Vance Buchanan?

Anyone on campus could rightly label me a stupid brat. If nothing else, it would make me look like a nymphomaniac and masochist. I curl my lips into a cool smile and step back. "Get out of here, Vance."

Vance starts to say something back, but I yank open my door to show I won't tolerate him in my room for a second longer. Promptly my heart sinks into my boots.

Reece is at the door. His fist raised like he was about to knock. A smile on his face that dies instantly as his gaze slides to Vance.

"What the hell are you doing in here, fucker," hisses Reece. Everything about him suddenly turns hostile and dark. I've never seen him like this before. In a completely different way to Jaxon, the blond beauty in front of me is as menacing as the night.

"I could ask you the same," growls Vance and he remains standing demonstratively in the room.

A storm plays out in Reece's eyes until he looks into mine. A kind of panic strikes his flawless features. "If you start something with him, you might as well fuck Jaxon a second

145

time!" he accuses me harshly, pointing at Vance like he's a clown at the circus. "This guy is the absolute *bottom* of the starving food chain of assholes. He'll do anything you ask of him for a single dollar. Don't ever talk to him again like he's worth more than the shit he's been causing for the last few years."

I slowly raise an eyebrow. His words show so much arrogance and hubris that I want to throw up. "Get out," I hiss.

Reece steps aside.

"I mean you, Crescent!"

For a tiny second, he looks at me in confusion, then he straightens his face. He doesn't even make an effort to leave.

That makes me explode. "How dare you blame anyone for doing things for money that you – *you and your super arrogant fucking friends!* – do without any pressure or need for money! Vance at least has *some* pathetic reason to suck. But you guys! You don't have a single one! You're monsters with no balls who think the world is a playing field! Who gamble with *my* future like it's any of your business for nothing but fun! Who *sleep* with me and betray my fucking trust just because it gives you one more check mark on your list of *virgins*." I mimic the way they say that last word. "It's you who's worth nothing! You and everyone who has anything to do with you! Get out of my room, Reece, and don't you *dare* come near me again!"

He stares at me.

My pulse hammers in my throat, and I'm not sure what's going to happen now. Reece's gaze flits to Vance, but then it fixes on me again.

"You're right," he says quietly, and the remorse in his voice almost knocks me over. "Every word you say is true, and it doesn't say enough about us. But Vance, Mable, Vance would *kill* you if someone paid him a tidy sum."

"So what? You said the same thing about Jaxon. And Jaxon doesn't even have a reason, does he? I think I'd rather die at the hands of a hitman than a pompous dick who thinks he can murder because the police will never be investigate him anyway."

It seems like I've ripped Reece's guts out with my words, which creates a really deep satisfaction in me. What's he doing here anyway? Why doesn't he go over to Rachel? Does he really think I wouldn't have slammed the door right back in his face if Vance wasn't here, who I want to get rid of as much as him? Just because of the kiss earlier? I was weak, okay? These idiots must realize that.

My body is weak, but my spirit is strong.

My body may be 'easy', but I am not.

"Why is he here?" asks Reece.

"It's none of your fucking business," I mumble.

Reece raises his eyes. "Buchanan?" he asks, as if he's used to Vance answering his questions.

Vance remains silent. The two are the same height, but that is the only similarity between them. White and black, blond and dark, blue eyes, brown eyes, tanned, athletic build, muscular chests. Both attractive in their own way. If this were a fairy tale and I were the princess who got to choose between the princes, I wouldn't know which one I'd pick.

Although, yes. I would pick Vance. Out of principle. So the white and supposedly 'flawless' prince doesn't win.

"Whatever it is, we'll find out anyway." Reece turns to me again. "I came here to tell you –"

"I don't give a shit!"

"I'll be there," he cuts his sentence short. "You don't just have to rely on Romeo. The next time Clarisse attacks, I'll be there too. On time. You'll be safe on campus. I promise you that."

I try to reconcile his words with the Reece who has approached me in the lecture hall, masked and greedy, as if he thirsts for my suffering, but I can't quite manage it. "Fine, if it helps your non-existent conscience to do a little penance, then stand up to Clarisse and everyone else, I don't care. I'm certainly not going to rely on you. And I don't need your help either."

"You don't know what you're talking about," Reece murmurs, trying to capture me with his clear gaze.

He almost makes me think back to the moment when he lay beneath me. My crotch on his angelic face and his tongue deep inside me. Almost. But I push the memory of his hot body aside as if it never happened. "And you still won't stop underestimating me. Will you leave now?"

Reece shakes his head, pushes himself away from the doorframe and disappears. Not without giving Vance a disparaging look.

His footsteps fade into the corridor and silence falls over the room.

Vance clears his throat because I'm still holding the door open, unmoving. My thoughts turn to Reece and what he was trying to do by showing up here.

"Should I go?" Vance asks me, but his voice sounds different. Like he needs to control himself. Probably because, like me, he'd like to beat Reece up. *What's actually going on between the Kings and Vance?*

"Yes, go."

Vance only takes two steps and then he's at the door. But as his massive shoulders fill the frame, he turns back to me.

"I know you don't want to hear it…"

I purse my lips.

"But if you want them to lose interest in you," he murmurs, and there's a gleam in his eye that irritates me, "then it's best to be a little less… adorable."

"Excuse me?" I ask him, puzzled.

"What you said just now… I understand why the Kings are fighting over you. You're fueling their interest when you talk to one of them like that."

I narrow my eyes. "I don't care –"

"Not because they hate you even more for it," he interrupts me harshly. "But because it makes you the most interesting girl on this campus. And if being a pawn in their sick game is dangerous, then maybe you can imagine how many out there really want you *dead* when the Kings stop playing. And still not drop you."

Because my face probably reflects how little I understand of what he is saying, he becomes clearer.

"What I mean is that you're fucking *fuckable* when you talk like that. Men always want what they can't get. They'll leave all the other women to fight over you. Maybe not even just the fucking kings. But also other guys from campus. You make yourself *desirable*. And you *never* want to compete with the women who study here. Trust me."

"I don't intend to," I say with a tremble in my voice.

He laughs emotionlessly. "Then be obnoxious, act stupid outside lectures and ignore people like Reece when he's at your door. Ignore everyone. Ignore *me*. You only have one goal: your degree. Crescent can only insult you when you give him ammunition."

I can feel heat rising in my cheeks. Is Vance trying to give me a twisted compliment about the way I talked to Reece?

"Believe me." His eyes are dark as night. "I'm sure your

words just now didn't just make *my* dick hard."

Then he leaves my room and I slam the door behind him.

Gosh!

15

SYLVIAN

I breathe cocaine the whole week. At the weekend, Harper persuades Mable to go shopping and I have to go with her. I *have to*. The whole time I'm thrilled that I can effectively punish Mable for not listening to me. On the other hand, I know that she doesn't even understand this punishment. That she doesn't realize the extent of my sadism. Accompanying the two women like a friend has only one appeal.

I can see the red rising in your cheeks.

Give myself over to this delicate color.

I can see you looking nervously in my direction. How you hate me and… miss me at the same time.

I have to think back to our sex. When I took her against the wall in the chalet, hungry and greedy because I had been waiting all these weeks for this moment. I can feel her wet pussy around my cock just looking at her.

Why do you have this effect on me?

"Six thousand three hundred fifty-five dollars."

Mable's mouth falls open and she shakes her head vehemently. "I can never accept that."

"Oh, of course you can." Harper hands her dad's credit

card over the counter and has the new shoes, scarf, hat and jacket bagged for Mable. "I owe it to you because your other clothes got cut up."

"Yeah, I'm really happy to accept your generosity too, but can't we just go shopping at H&M or something?" asks Mable, her cheeks glowing and trying to ignore my look. "It's cheap, but not shabby!"

The sales clerk tisks snidely and looks at Mable with pity. *How dare that employee listen to our conversation at all.*

"H&M is shabby," Harper disagrees. "You don't have to pay for it, Mable. I'm happy to do it."

Mable looks as if she would like to give a lecture about unnecessary spending and overconsumption, but decides against it. Harper wouldn't listed anyway. I take the bags and follow them into the next store.

The shopping mall in Baltimore can probably only survive thanks to the Kingston students who shop here every weekend. It's one exclusive store after the next and I've seen half of the clientele on campus before. I sit down in an chair to give the women some time and let my gaze wander. Then I suddenly see her.

She stands like a ghost on the opposite side of the mall behind the balustrade of the top floor. Staring at me.

Eleanore.

I type a quick message to Jaxon, then leave the bags and exit the store. Eleanore stands still like a statue and lets me walk towards her. Only when I'm a few steps away does she turn around and disappears into the corridor leading to the elevators.

I follow her, even if it might be a trap.

There, between the elevators and the door to the stairwell, she leans against the wall. One knee drawn up, her sneaker on the expensive marble. She is nothing compared to what she once was. The result of our game, unfiltered, unadorned and so ugly that I would never have recognized her if she hadn't been following us for months.

Her emaciated face bears witness to an eating disorder coupled with an addiction to pills. She wears a winter jacket, but I know that the scars on her wrists extend down her arms. Her hair looks thin and unwashed, and the little make-up she has applied is smudged, making me wonder why she hasn't been thrown out by security yet.

"What do you want?" I ask her, closing in.

"That you fuck me, Sylvian. What else would I want?" She spreads her legs. Her jeans are full of holes. "Do you remember what it was like with me? Remember what it was like to fuck me?"

I try not to let it show how much her words have affected me and take out my wallet. "Is that enough?" I ask, holding out six hundred dollars to her.

She jumps forward, snatches the money out of my hand and immediately distances herself again. Her eyes are glowing, as if I've put the next shot in her hand. "See you later, Silvano," she whispers, pulls open the door to the stairwell and vanishes.

Maybe we should end this, I text to Jaxon.

He answers immediately. Sure, kill her when you've been accepted into the circle.

And until then?

Until then, we continue to hope that she will do it herself.

There we have it, in black and white. We are murderers. Does that bother me?

Not really.

As I re-enter the store, I head for the changing rooms, lost in thought. I want to be distracted, even if it's just the conversation between Harper and Mable about their latest favorite show.

But when I turn the corner, all changing rooms are unoccupied and Mable is standing alone in front of one of the huge mirrors. She notices me and freezes. A hot blush rises in her cheeks. She is wearing nothing more than a short black skirt and a smart white blouse.

"Harper's at Starbucks," she informs me coolly, focusing on her new outfit again.

"You won't be wearing that."

"Excuse me?" she asks me tightly.

"The skirt is too short and the blouse screams 'fuck me.'" If she were my girlfriend, I wouldn't even let her go to a party dressed like that.

"Oh, so I've finally found the right outfit for me." She turns to me, her expression cold, the tug around her lips challenging. "Maybe I should just wear skirts. Like a easy girl should." She pulls the waistband even higher and moves her hips so, almost exposing her panties.

A storm is brewing inside me.

Desire, which I have been holding back with all my might, comes over me like a monster.

She can't save herself.

I can't save myself.

As if her body attracts me like a magnet, I approach her, grasp her hips and push the waistband of her skirt lower. She tries to slap my hands away, but I hold her tight. *Her fingers, her hips, herself. Everything is close.* I hesitate for a second, but then I pull her to me. One ringed hand at her back, the other slips under her skirt.

Mable's eyes widen, but she stops resisting.

Maybe she's hoping Harper will come in. *Yes, that would suit you. You're clever enough to set a trap for me.*

But I don't care about Harper. I'm not really the type for affairs. Cheating is repulsive to me. Why should I get into a relationship if I'm not serious? I want everyone to think I'm faithful to Harper. I want *Mable* to think so. That's why I'm in a relationship with Harper.

I want Mable to firmly believe that I love Harper and… not her.

But it seems that not even my principles can stop me from approaching Mable.

I slide my hand higher and grip Mable's firm, round ass. My dick gets hard just from touching her ass, and I know I have to have her.

Now.

"How does it feel to know that you'll never have me again?" she asks me sweetly. I can tell from the look in her eyes that she's as hard as a rock inside, and she's right. It does feel like shit.

It's not because I can never get her anymore.

But because I forbid myself to.

She's. So. Damn. Forbidden.

"Or are you touching me because you think I'm going to get involved with you? To prove to me that I'm weak?"

"You're not weak," I murmur, looking deep into her eyes. And then I feel it again. All the storm of compassion. The mistakes I've made, every single one. Eleanore looms before me like a shadow, blending with Mable's stare, and for a tiny moment, she becomes her.

I flinch, but don't let go of Mable.

Nevertheless, the hallucination was deceptively real for that one second.

Take less drugs, Sy.

Mable will become an Eleanore if I don't leave her alone. If the Kings don't leave her alone. I swallow hard and my grip on Mable's body tightens all the more. My job is no longer to warn her. To punish her. To force her to realize that we're going to destroy her life.

I have to harden her. That's what I can do. She is the fire and I am her gasoline. If I don't intervene, Reece or Jaxon will manage to manipulate her again. That *can't* happen. *I have to finally protect you. And if you refuse to run, if you won't listen to me, then I'll just have to teach you to fight.*

"When I pulled you close to me in the chalet –" *and came incredibly hard* "– why did you go along with it?"

Shadows flit across Mable's face, and she doesn't quite manage to stay cool. "I wanted to use you like you used me."

I smile. "Good girl. And that's exactly what you're going to do again."

"What?" she snaps at me.

"Go into the changing room," I order darkly.

Mable laughs at me quietly, but her hardened expression crumbles. "Forget it."

"I'll do what you want as long as you're quiet," I murmur against her ear and gently kiss her neck. My lips taste her sweet flavor. The best drug I know, and the most expensive too. "Forget about Harper. She screwed you like we all did. She watched Clarisse trip you up and did nothing. She let Jaxon have his way. She's pursuing her own agenda, like all of us. You're doing the right thing. Take advantage of her, take what you can get from people like us. Even if it's sex." Mable shudders in my grip. "Take what you need."

"I don't need you," she stutters and looks at me in panic as I slide my hand between her legs. Her panties are wet.

"Are you sure?" I ask.

I see fear flashing in her eyes, but boundless lust as well. Her crumbling resistance is enough to push her into the next changing room. I close the curtain behind us. It reaches down to the floor and is made of thick material. If Harper caught us, I wouldn't mind for a second. Actually, I want the whole fucking world to know.

Amabelle Weaver gets fucked.

By me.

I pull her panties down and push her skirt up further. I grab her throat with one hand and press her against the wooden partition so she is wedged in sideways in front of me. As soon as I have a firm grip on her, I give her a hard slap on her bare ass with the flat of my hand.

Her eyes narrow to slits, but I hold her mouth shut.

"You deserve so many more slaps for not listening to me," I whisper and hit her a second time. Her white skin turns red, which is a dreamlike sight and makes my dick twitch greedily. "For even thinking of putting on a fucking skirt when I'm around."

"I…" she begins angrily, but I cover her mouth with my right hand and hit her again. I don't care if any staff members can hear us.

"Be a good girl and just let it wash over you." I speak as quietly as I can and hit her as softly as I can. The bad thing is that she clearly likes it. I followed an inner impulse without knowing how she would react. But if she's into being chastised on top of everything else, she's our downfall. Not the other way around.

After five strokes, the skin on her ass is glowing just like the skin on her cheeks and her lust is already running down her legs. I decide not to wait any longer and taste her. I lift her left leg, place it on the bench in the changing room, hold the other firmly and then sink to my knees in front of her.

Her hissing breath tells me everything and I get rock hard as soon as I smell her scent. I run my nose over her wet, heated skin and finally dip my tongue into her.

I lick her deeply, barely paying attention to her. The addiction to her overcomes me and for a moment I'm busy taking in her entire pussy. Images flash in my head.

Pictures of that one damn, lost night. The first time I tasted her. How we fucked her. One after the other and in turns. How she first sucked my dick, then the others. I think of her body, how it rose between us, and now I'm tasting all of it again.

How could I refuse you?

It's absolutely beyond me why I didn't trust Reece. Or even Jaxon. I should never have persuaded them to expel you. What had gotten into me? Why didn't I see the diamond in the rough when it was in front of me?

My tongue movements become more urgent, and when I come back to myself, I don't know how many times Mable has already come. Her hands claw at my hair. Again and again I push my tongue deep into her forbidden slit and suck on her clit until her whole body twitches.

It's a waste.

It's a waste to lick her here secretly, alone and in silence, when it could be between us.

If we could control her.

If she belonged *to us*.

"Mable, I'm back!"

I immediately take my distance and look up at Mable, a question in my eyes.

She stares at me, out of breath, her face a deep red.

"Answer," I formulate with my lips.

Mable could just pull back the curtain. She could show Harper what we were doing. She could expose everything in one fell swoop. Instead, she looks like she's even more scared than before.

"I still need a bit," she says in a normal tone of voice. "I think I've fallen in love with a few outfits."

"All right, I'll wait outside, I'm not allowed to drink my latte in here."

"Okay!" shouts Mable, squeezing her eyes shut in despair.

"You did a wonderful job," I whisper as Harper's footsteps move away.

"I'm a bitch," she whispers.

I straighten up. Instead of my tongue, I slide my hand through her swollen pussy. "Do you think so? You're still better than us. One little offense won't put you on the same level as some other scheming Kingston students."

"But she might suffer as much as I do when she finds out." Mable opens her eyes. She doesn't cry, but her voice sounds muffled.

"No, she won't." *You have no idea how incapable she is of truly suffering. She is also incapable of truly loving. But you are capable, aren't you?* "You have to stop feeling bad for me," I implore her, unbuckling my belt at the same time. "Take what you can get. None of us deserve your fucking consideration. If you want, we'll all fall to our knees in front of you. Be aware of this shit. You wanted to have meaningless sex, didn't you? Then just let it happen."

Now her tears are really coming. "It's never been meaningless to me," she confesses quietly.

I rest my forehead against hers, free my dick, put on a condom and push her legs apart. "Not for me either, baby. Not one of your smiles could ever not matter to me."

With these words I start to fuck her, and it is hard, quiet and fast.

I thrust myself so deeply into her that her unprepared tightness envelops me immediately. She claws at my back, tears streaming down her face, and I know I love those tears for so many reasons.

I want to see her cry because my spanking is so hard that she thinks I hate her.

I want to taste her tears because she's not allowed to love me and yet she does.

I want to see the despair on her face every time she opens up to me and breaks a little more.

And I want her to cry with happiness.

That her tears mean that she is the happiest person in the world. Because I am with her.

I press her hard against the wooden wall and pump my seed into her. My lips find her neck and I kiss her rough and demanding as her tight pussy squeezes my dick. My breath is slow to return, and I find it hard to leave the warmth of her womb.

Before she has taken off her blouse completely to reach for her shirt, I reach into her hair.

"Don't even *think* about wearing a skirt on campus."

Her chocolate-colored eyes flash and she widens her smile into a lascivious grin. "Or what?"

JAXON

Friendship is complicated. You always have to rely on the fact that others want to rely on you. Up to a certain point, it's always a risk. But with me and the Kings, it was easy. I felt it. Right from the start.

Romeo, Reece, Zayn. I felt them and knew it from the beginning.

And then Sylvian came along. My sweet, dear, good Sylvian, who does such bad things…

There was less emotion there. I wanted him to join us.

That he would reveal his soul in our ranks.

And so far I've been spot on with my assessment.

At least until you came along.

Should I be worried that you might be the reason why everything is falling apart?

16

MABLE

Over the next few days, I'm torn between feeling guilty and believing Sylvian. He's probably right: I can only survive at Kingston for as long as I stay away from the Kings or at least ignore my feelings for them. On the other hand, Harper has shown remorse and apologized…

Nevertheless, she is still with him.

While it makes even less sense to sleep with Sylvian instead of getting revenge on him, at least he's *my* tormentor. If he had treated Harper the way he treated me, I wouldn't even touch him until he apologized to her.

That is loyalty.

With Romeo by my side, I'm spared any further attacks, which is partly because I no longer go anywhere except to my classes. But the laughter gets all the louder as soon as a professor calls on me and I'm just a tiny bit off with my answer. Notes are thrown at me when the lab instructor turns to the blackboard, and the words 'scum', 'whore' and 'dole' are shouted after me everywhere.

Two weeks after our shopping trip, I decide to take the power back. I was an American teenager just like everyone else and I've seen all kinds of movies about bullying and the consequences of it. So on Friday, I put on my new boots, my extreme classy and expensive open coat, a pair of chaste tights, a blouse and a short skirt, and I step into the sunny February morning.

Romeo completely overlooks me as I walk towards him. Only when I'm almost past him does he recognize me.

"So?" I ask him teasingly. "Do you think I'm hot?"

He doesn't look like a man who thinks I'm hot. But the shock is still written all over his face. "Your hair."

"Huh?"

He clears his throat. "At least undo the braids."

"But they complete the look, don't they?" I ask, wrapping my right braid around my forefinger.

He closes in on me as I stride briskly ahead. It feels good to provoke my entire environment. Much better than I would have expected.

"And what should I do if another Hilbredge or someone else from his pack takes a liking to you?" he asks with a murmur.

"People like that won't wait until I'm dressed like a slut. They didn't before either."

"You're not dressed like a slut," he murmurs in my ear from behind. "You look like you came straight out of some college porn."

"Really?" I ask, embarrassed, and turn to him. The first glances of the day are on us. But maybe for now they're just wondering who the stranger is who's talking to Romeo in hushed tones. "I don't watch enough porn. Is it really that bad?"

Romeo shakes his head in bewilderment. "Since almost everyone here is dressed like that, you'll only stand out because you always stand out anyway."

"So too much porn or not?"

He grinds his jaw. "What's your goal? If it is to get one over on people, then it probably doesn't matter what you wear. If you're trying to get Tyrell to –"

"What would I want him to do?"

Romeo doesn't answer.

"I want to collect fans," I explain and wonder why I'm confiding in Romeo at all. "Someone told me that it's good to have people on your side."

"Fans who want to get into your pants? Did Buchanan give you that tip?"

"So what?"

"If you continue to behave so stupidly, it will be difficult even for me to protect you."

I stick my tongue out at him and produce a rare laugh on his face. I've actually never seen him laugh before. His laugh is so bright and innocent that it makes me like him a lot more. His closeness is a bit like how I imagine closeness to a brother would be. Asexual, but pleasant. I never thought I would ever feel this way about *Romeo*.

***

As he waits outside my lab in the late afternoon, the feeling is even more intense. I don't want to start relying on him being there all the time, but I can't get his friendly laugh from this morning out of my head.

There must be more to Romeo than the smooth, cold, snake-like shell he tries to show everyone.

"Will you buy me a coffee?" I ask him straightforwardly and I adjust my skirt. I feel much more comfortable in this outfit than I thought. Firstly, most of the women here actually walk around like this, so in a way I blend in more easily than before with my cheap clothes from the supermarket. And secondly, I have the feeling that a few of the snappy 'unfuckable' comments have subsided. But now I hear the word 'whore' all the more often. But I can deal with that. I like the fact that I can influence the people around me. Even if it's just the kind of swear words they shout after me.

Romeo frowns. "Coffee?"

"I would never think of buying myself a coffee on this campus. But you could invite me, couldn't you?" I beam at him and immediately stop when he looks at me like he'd rather grind me than a coffee bean. "Stupid idea, forget it."

"Are you trying to hit on me?" he asks into my ear from behind as he follows me.

"No, of course not! Do I hit on Harper when I let her invite me for coffee?"

Romeo narrows his eyes, but then he nods. "If you want to bum something off me, ask me directly next time. I wouldn't even notice if I bought you ten coffees a day."

"God no," I mumble. Why does everyone always think I'm taking advantage of them because I don't have much money? "I thought we could talk…"

"Like the last time we wanted to eat something in public?" he asks cynically.

"Like I said, stupid idea." We reach the stairs of the main building. The one where I was pelted with chicken feathers. The snow has now melted, but the park is covered in frost. It is bitterly cold.

"Twenty minutes," Romeo says suddenly. "Is that enough?"

"Sure." I don't want to be pleased that he took me up on my suggestion, but I am anyway. Why is it so hard for me to dislike at least one of the Kings? What is it about them that makes me forget everything I know about them and want to get to know them?

"What do you want?" he asks uncharmingly as we enter the café where Harper and I always meet.

"Something with almond milk. I don't care about the rest." Romeo rolls his eyes, goes to the counter and orders.

I wait for him, not sure where he wants to sit as there are only four seats left. Two by the window and two at the far back, at a narrow wooden table.

Romeo comes back with the receipt in his hand and stops next to one of the comfortable two-seater groups occupied by two freshmen from my accounting course.

"Get up," he orders coldly and whistles.

The boys notice him and immediately pack up their things. They even wipe the table clean.

"All right," I mumble, half impressed, half unpleasantly touched, and sit down while Romeo fetches the coffee.

He places an iced coffee overflowing with pink sprinkles in front of me. He has an espresso himself. "To go with your new outfit."

I can't help but notice that he's smiling to himself, and I wonder if it's all for show or if he's really starting to open up.

"Why aren't the Kings playing anymore?" I ask, shoving a load of foam and sprinkles into my mouth.

His expression closes immediately. "An interrogation?" he returns curtly.

I swallow. "Curiosity."

"We're still playing. But as long as you don't collect any points, the game is suspended."

"Almost as if someone wants the game to be suspended..." I think aloud.

His lips remain thin. "Almost."

"A year ago, when the game was different… Why didn't you just protect your queen then? Like you're doing with me now? Then you could have won, right?"

"I can 'protect' you from anything and everything… but not from the game. Until last semester, there was only one real rule." He reaches for his espresso and looks outside. "Well, two."

"And what are they?"

"No deaths."

I almost choke when he looks in my direction again.

"And the queens weren't allowed to know about the game. Reece took the easy route and got together with his queen."

I listen up. "The one who set fire to the physics lab?"

Romeo grinds his teeth. "Yes."

"Then she still didn't stay long, did she?"

"No."

"What aren't you telling me?"

He laughs, coldly this time. "Everything. I make small talk, nothing more. What else do you want to know? Why I have nothing better to do than drink coffee with *you* of all people?"

I lean back and cross my arms. "Doesn't Jaxon mind that you're helping me? Or is that his plan?"

"And if it is? Do you think I would tell you?" His brow furrowed arrogantly.

"Why does everyone think you're just his sidekick? Do you care about it?"

"Why don't you hand me a questionnaire to fill out for you, Weaver."

"Why do you risk them hating you too? For me of all people?"

"Who's supposed to hate me?" he asks in astonishment. "Them?" He points around us and laughs mirthlessly. "They're happy when they can breathe my air. Anything else?"

He's starting to frustrate me. "What's your favorite color?" I ask just as brashly as before.

Something changes in his body tension. "Blue," he answers emotionlessly.

"Have I hit a nerve with this question? Is this the first time people have wanted to know more about your personality?"

His eyes regain their usual coldness. "You completely underestimate my relationship with the other Kings. They know *everything* about me. They know every single corner of my psyche. We're more than friends. I'm more than Jaxon's shadow. We are *one*."

"So you're helping Jaxon by protecting me? Because surely you're not only disagreeing because of me, are you?"

The movement of his lips shows the anger he feels at my words. "I'm protecting you because I think it's the right thing to do. Only with me by your side can you survive reasonably safely on campus. What *exactly* the others have in mind for you remains to be seen."

A shiver runs down my spine. I can feel all the furtive glances on me from the other customers, brimming with undisguised hatred. "What did I do to these people?" I whisper. "Why can't they just leave me alone?"

"The Kings?"

"All of them."

"Do you want them to leave you alone?" Romeo asks smoothly.

"I..."

His eyes light up knowingly. "Of course you don't want

that, Weaver. And that's the biggest problem. You come here, live off their families' money and attract the attention of three prime bachelors. I'm surprised you're not dead yet."

"You mean they would… Clarisse would…"

Romeo shrugs one shoulder barely noticeably. "They all hate your guts because you've never accomplished anything in their eyes and yet you're well on your way to getting everything. Jaxon's restraint alone is such an expensive commodity that you can't even comprehend how valuable it really is. He lets you study undisturbed. That's never happened to a scholarship student before."

"And what's he up to with that?" I ask worriedly. There must be a reason, right? A… cruel reason?

Romeo lets his gaze wander around the room. It's loud enough that no one can overhear us, and yet he doesn't answer.

"Maybe we'll just keep making small talk," I whisper, stirring my milk foam. "So blue is your favorite color, eh? What's your favorite movie?"

"I'm not going to expose my *preferences* to you. How about you?" Suddenly he grins crudely, and I dread what's to come. "Who's your favorite?"

My mouth opens in surprise. "Who's my *favorite*?" I breathe. "I hate every single one of the Kings."

"Which is why you're asking one of them out."

"This isn't a date," I murmur. "If you think you can get girls this way –"

He shows me his open hand to keep me silent. "It's okay, Weaver. The others can take you on dates."

"What fucking dates?"

He shrugs. "Are you finished? I've got a poker date."

JAXON

I'm sure you sometimes wonder what I feel. Whether I feel anything at all. Or whether I can feel anything. It shouldn't be about how I answer that question. You should have learned by now that you can't trust my words.

It's about what *you* feel.

What *you* experience.

And I have no doubt that your heart has long since sensed what words could never express between us.

Will you allow all the pain again?

Or will common sense stop you from falling deep this time?

17

MABLE

Even though our conversation didn't go particularly deep, I'm developing something like trust in Romeo. I've already gotten used to his presence and I even enjoy it a little. Because with him, everything is quiet around me. I can walk along the corridors without having to listen to nasty remarks, and when he brings me to my dorm room, I know for certain that nothing is waiting for me in my room that could surprise me.

"Hello Harper," Romeo says in his typically smooth manner when we find her waiting outside my room on a Thursday evening.

"Weren't we supposed to meet tomorrow at philosophy?" I ask her.

"Get lost, Romeo," she greets him. She waits until he has turned on his heels, shrugging his shoulders, and then she beams at me. "Vance texted me that he'll help you," she breathes expectantly. "He's waiting in your room. He's going to help us, I know it! Our plan is working and you can finally give Romeo the boot. Trust me."

My mouth almost falls open in astonishment. What makes her think I can trust anyone on this campus? I don't even trust her. "You just let him into my room?"

"He was already inside."

I shake my head in bewilderment. "Where did he get a key?"

"That's the good thing! Vance has keys to everything. Has contacts. Relationships. He's the perfect protector when it comes to the Kings. And he's *not* Romeo."

At this point I could reveal to her that I find the idea of Vance accompanying me instead of Romeo quite unbearable, but I'd rather keep it to myself. "I asked Vance and he was pretty clearly that he doesn't want to help…"

"Then I guess he's changed his mind." Harper winks at me. "I'm sorry Romeo has had to replace me so far. But I just don't have enough time to be by your side this semester. I've failed so many exams. My schedule is busier than New York at Christmas and I have to take tutoring in everything…"

"Oh, I didn't know that." I was so distracted by my own studies last semester that I never asked about her grades.

"It's bad." For a moment, I see the exhaustion in her expression, the tiredness that develops in someone who works too much and sleeps too little. "I don't think I'll make it through sophomore year."

"You shouldn't let my problems distract you."

"That's why Vance is here now. If we both take care of you, things will get better. And like I said, he's *not* Romeo. Tell him if he wants money, I'll pay it. You talk to him alone, I think that's better. He doesn't really like me. I'll see you in philosophy, yeah?"

I sigh. The last thing I want is a paid bodyguard, but do I have a choice?

When I open the door, I see Vance is indeed waiting for me. Déjà vu. First Jaxon, then Romeo, now Vance. They all

172

seem to love my dorm room and like to make themselves comfortable there while they wait for me.

"What do you want?" I ask.

He approaches me in silence. "I told you I wouldn't help you, but I have something you can use to get revenge."

"Revenge on who?" I'm not quite as confident in his presence. Even though the Kings and their behavior towards me have strengthened me in some respects, Vance is a different caliber.

"All of them." Vance holds his smartphone out to me. The voice memo app is open. He presses play and Reece's voice fills the room.

"You know, Dole. You can't have any real fun as a man with most of the sluts on this campus. They're all whores. They want our names, our money, our influence, or at least our looks. No woman who gets mommy and daddy to fund her studies at Kingston hasn't been drilled beforehand to snag the richest, most powerful, most influential guy on campus. They want to be the next First Lady. Harper wants Sylvian's position. But you, you just want us, don't you?"

"Where did you get that?" I ask, distraught. How can Vance have a recording of the conversation Reece had with me on Halloween night? No one was with us. No one!

"The Kings record everything they say and pass it on among themselves."

"Excuse me?" I gasp. "And they put it online? They put everything online?"

"No. Not their private conversations. They're connected to each other like a live broadcast. They do it to be able to control each other. They claim to be friends, but they also distrust each other as if they were enemies. I hacked them a while ago. At least I know one of the passwords to their security protocols. Whenever it changes to the one I have, I can listen in and record what's being said. It doesn't happen often, but I was able to make this recording. You just have to send the recording around. The students aren't going to be thrilled when they hear Crescent talk like that."

I look at Vance doubtfully. "Why don't you do it? Why do you want me to do it?"

He stumbles. "Why should I do it?"

Ah, of course. Why would he grow a backbone?

"You're the one who has to show she has guts," he explains calmly with a shrug of his shoulders. "You have hurt them, so they'll respect you. If I do it, you won't win anything."

I bite my lower lip so as not to say anything nasty back, because he seems too cowardly to use the recordings himself, and take out my own smartphone. "Can you send me the messages?"

"Yes. I also have this." He switches on another recording.

"The first night of the Thanksgiving vacation. That must have been after sex. They're talking about you."

I shiver as I hear Reece's voice again.

"We could lie down next to her."

"This is still my bedroom." Sylvian. "Fuck off to your own." Silence.

"What's going on, Jax?" asks Reece. "Are you thinking about putting a ring on her?"

Silence again.

"She liked it, didn't she?" asks Jaxon.

174

A shiver runs through my entire body. I've never heard Jaxon's voice so gentle before. So... loving.

"We could all stay here and lock us in with her on Thanksgiving... have fun... that's what vacations are for, right?"
"Did Jax really just suggest that?" Reece.
"Do you understand now," Sylvian growls close to the microphone, "why I wanted to protect her? From everything?"
"Yes."

That's all Jaxon says, but this 'yes' alone sounds real. So... true. Like the moment he told me I was beautiful.

"I'm not the one who wants to stick with this stupid game come hell or high water." Reece. "What's stopping us from just ending it? We don't care about all the idiots out there. All the money hungry bitches and the ridiculous assholes who go running to their parents for help. Why are we candidates for the circle if we don't use it? We are the kings of this university. So we can also decide what happens to Mable."
Silence.

I hold my breath. Another reference to the 'circle'. If the Kings are talking about it among themselves, it must have great significance. "Do you know more about the circle?"
Vance does not answer.

"Jaxon," Reece implores him urgently, "those people out there are the real playthings, aren't they? The real pawns. They're useful to us. Sooner or later. And we just let them

think they have something in common with us. Why don't we finally show them what's really going on? That we don't give a fuck about them? That we despise these worms? Why do we have to kick our sweet little knight from the board? What's the real reason?"

I'm looking at Vance with big eyes. This clip has huge potential. It... It could actually disempower the Kings.

"Because this isn't about a game, Crescent," Jaxon say sharply. "I brought your lives to this level. Without me, you're nothing. If you want to drop me now..."
    "No."
    "Good. Because ultimately, I am the one who says what happens with the scholarship students."
    "Jaxon is right," adds Sylvian. "The sooner she disappears, the better."

Vance switches off the sound recording. "That reveals a lot, doesn't it?"
    Yes, it reveals too much. The Kings' true feelings. Did I perhaps mean something to them after all...? "What do you know about the circle?" I ask, trying to distract myself from the actual content of the recording.
    Vance looks at me silently for a moment. Under his gaze, framed by his dark lashes, I feel smaller by the second. He manages to make me want to cringe and feel judged for not knowing much about the Kings. "The circle is the reason. The reason this is all happening in the first place."
    "Really?" I ask nervously. "The Kings are playing with our scholarships... because of a secret organization? Who's behind it?"

Vance snorts. "No one I want to know more about. You want the recordings?"

I nod and give him my phone number. He sends the files, waits for me to save them and deletes the sent files from our message history.

"Can you also give me that password to their security protocol?"

"Do you know anything about IT?"

I shake my head. "Can't you show me?"

"You have to be able to write and read code. If I get something new that you can use, I'll give it to you."

"Okay." I'm not going to rely on that, but it sounds pretty good.

"You've collected a few email addresses with the challenges. I think that's enough to make it go viral."

I look up at him and put away my cell phone. "Yeah. Maybe."

"What does 'maybe' mean?"

"I'll save it for later. That's fantastic leverage, thank you."

His eyes widen. "You're not sending it now?"

"No."

"Damn." He cranes his neck, trying to get rid of the tension that seems to be affecting him. "I put a gun in your hand and you won't use it?"

"I'll think about it."

"That's bullshit," he growls, coming closer. "Send it out. Do it now."

"No, you do it! Are you just trying to use me? Are you too cowardly? Thanks for your help, but I'll decide for myself when the best time is!" His right temple twitches and I unconsciously back away from him. Damn. Who is this guy? And what does he really want from me?

"Trust me," he demands. It sounds more like a threat.

"I don't trust anyone anymore."

His eyes narrow and his shoulders tense. "That's basically the right attitude. But you've as good as lost anyway. What harm can it do you?"

"I'm not going to do it." This isn't about me, is it? He just wants to use me to get back at the Kings for whatever. He didn't want to help me at all. I'm just another pawn to be moved across the board. "I won't do it without thinking it through, and I certainly won't do it if you try to force me."

He looks like he wants to throw a whole novel of arguments at me, but he just exhales in frustration. Like a bull about to charge. And then he really does. "I'm not forcing anyone's happiness on them," he growls, then he steps past me and stomps out of my room in big strides.

As he slams the door behind him, he leaves behind an oppressive silence in my room.

And Jaxon's, Sylvian's, Reece's voices that whisper to me, forbiddenly, that they... feel very differently on the inside than they show to the outside world.

JAXON

When there's a girl in front of me, I feel a lot. Namely a lot of emptiness. It's always the same. The same big eyes, the same seductive smile. I'm just a credit card to them, and the prospect of bearing the name Tyrell makes them all drop to their knees immediately.

Suck me hard.

Those are the three words I would use to describe myself.

Because I'm not interested in these whores.

So what good would it do to tell them what I really care about?

18

MABLE

In the days that follow, I can't help but notice that Reece, Sylvian and Jaxon cross my path in the corridors or in the park more often than usual. Is it because our schedules have changed this semester? But shouldn't they all be working on their Bachelor's theses and instead of attending class?

Whenever I notice them, I keep my head down and steer past them, and miraculously they let me pass. Thank God they don't stop me or confront me in front of everyone. Romeo is just a shadow most of the time instead of an actively present companion.

Because this new development makes me a little overconfident, I go to him at the end of February. I ask him to let me work at Crowns again. Having to buy a new cell phone because I couldn't read anything on the broken screen has torn a deep hole in my savings, and on top of that, my mom and sister are still dependent on financial support. Working at Crowns while Romeo is around seems like a good option. For a few glorious evenings, it even feels *normal*. Like nothing worse has ever happened on campus than the chicken feather prank.

Crowns is run by the Alpha Rex fraternity students, but there are a few other employees besides myself. Romeo is my favorite person to work with. We don't talk to each other, we work. And there are moments when we can signal orders to each other just by looking across the room. We are a good team.

I shouldn't even like him, but I can't really hate him either. And now that the unfriendly, gray weeks of February have passed, I'm starting to look forward to the evenings at Crowns even more with each day of spring.

Of course, I would never admit it openly. Especially not to Romeo himself.

When he greets me on the Wednesday before spring break with a "I gave you the day off", I'm disappointed.

"Oh."

"We're playing poker today," he informs me curtly, taking off the apron he sometimes wears when tapping drinks. "Rebecca will be taking your shift."

"I had confused it with tomorrow."

"No problem." He washes his hands, dries them and I stand in front of him, looking a bit stupid. "I didn't think it was a good idea for you to serve us," he adds.

It's definitely not. Because there's this tingling in my stomach when I think about what happened the first time I served the Kings. And the nausea when I think about what happened the *last* time. "I'll be back here tomorrow then." With those words, I turn away because I get the feeling Romeo could have read every thought on my face.

"Do you *want* to stay here, Weaver?"

Blood rushes to my head. No, if I turn around now, he'll see I'm not indifferent about his question. But I should be. I'm not going to wait tables when the Kings are playing poker.

Not after what happened last time. Not ever.

"You could… join the table."

I close my eyes, not sure if I've misheard. I hope none of the guests are watching me, though they are anyway. I'm like an unpopular tv actrice everyone loves to hate. No one likes my show, but everyone is talking about me. "Why would you suggest something like that?" I ask Romeo and turn to him. "Why would I play?"

Romeo starts to speak, but someone from the side beats him to it.

"Never."

I turn to the voice. Reece. His blue eyes narrowed, his lips curled in rejection. "You're not going to invite her, Portcharles. I'd prefer an evening without the subject of 'Dole' coming up and making me sick."

All of a sudden, Crowns has gone quiet.

Romeo gives Reece a warning look, but I'm not going to let him show me up any longer. "Reece is right," I reply nonchalantly, although his manner towards me doesn't exactly leave me cold. "I would *never* sit at your table. Ciao."

With these words, I walk to the door, but something in the room has changed. The eyes are no longer just on me, watching me as they usually do when I wait tables here. There's laughter and insults and then someone kicks a chair into my path.

I stumble over it and Romeo is immediately at my side to push it away.

It could have been a friendly gesture, but it's so much more. He's protecting me. From what, though, I'm not sure. Tension builds throughout the bar. Everyone seems to be waiting for something to happen.

"Take her home," Romeo hisses at Reece, who raises a

brow in disapproval. "Go on."

"I'll go alone, it's fine," I mumble and storm out.

Fuck, what was that?

It seemed like Reece's attitude towards me has made me fair game. The slightest hint that he wouldn't mind if I suffered and people turn on me? Is that possible? Is Romeo not just there to protect me from attacks from Clarisse's side – but from the whole campus?

Deep in thought, I only notice the Tesla when it stops right next to me.

"Do you really want to walk?" Reece smiles at me and everything seems forgotten. The electric car's engine is silent, the passenger door window is open. This man has nothing in common with the idiot who just mocked me. His clear blue eyes and white sweater, along with his ivory-white skin and blond hair, make him look like a prince.

"Yes, I do," I say stubbornly.

He drives up beside me. "I'm sorry about what just happened. Come on, Mable. Get in."

I shake my head. "No."

"Every girl at this university wants to sit in this car and you turn up your nose at the opportunity?"

"Obviously the *girls* at this university are only after your money and don't mind your obnoxious character. So no, I don't want to be like them."

Reece stops the car. "You're right, that's probably it ." He opens the driver's door and walks towards me.

I pull a face. "Okay, fine," I shout. "Before you run after me all the way to the dorm, I'll get in with you! But if we end up in some fucking woods, I'll kill you, you understand?"

Reece frowns, but the smile on his manly features doesn't disappear. "Okay. No woods. Got it." He's like a changed

183

man. Like a completely different guy. What the hell is this? Is he a schizophrenic?

I roll my eyes and get in his car. As soon as I feel the expensive leatherette underneath me, I hate Reece even more. Why does he have to drive a Tesla of all things? Why does he have to look so good? Why can't I just live my life away from these lunatics?

Lunatics who play with scholarship students as if they were pieces on a chessboard.

Lunatics who can kiss like gods.

Lunatics who my body craves like nothing else.

When Reece gets behind the wheel and smiles at me again, something is definitely different. He may have looked good at Crowns just now, but there was no magic. No positive spark that comes over to me like it does now and makes me tense. He really does have two sides to him.

"Listen," he begins in a serious voice, making my stomach vibrate. "I know I can be an ass, and I don't expect you to look past that. But I'm sorry for everything that was done to you. Especially that I stood by last semester instead of helping you."

"Of course," I say with a sneer. "So sorry you didn't do anything at your party back in August when Romeo drugged me and Jaxon kidnapped me. Your compassion knows no bounds."

"It's not that simple." An apologetic expression comes into his eyes. "When Jaxon drugged you, all I could do was watch."

"That's why you said you wanted to *watch* back then?"

"I wanted it to sound like I was enjoying watching you suffer. But in fact, I just wanted to be there and make sure he didn't do anything bad to you."

"He drugged me and kidnapped me! Great job, Reece!"

"I know." His voice becomes brittle and he runs his hand over his mouth. "Mable, it was me who got Harper to come looking for you. I didn't realize Jaxon would take you so far away, and I thought she'd find you pretty quickly."

"I don't believe you, if that's what you're hoping. What was that all about? Your nasty comment about me? I know exactly how you feel about me. Why is Romeo so desperate for you to take me home?"

"You need to be protected. If people see me taking you home, they'll know to leave you alone. Because the queens belong to the Kings, as silly as it is. You've seen how easily everyone can be turned against you just because… I made a stupid comment."

I would love to tell him that I don't *want to* be protected, but it would be a lie. I want to live a normal life at Kingston. And if it takes Reece, Romeo and whoever else surrounds me from time to time, I'm not going to turn down that offer of help. "Do us both a favor, take me home and just leave me alone," I mumble and turn away.

Reece sighs and switches on the radio. A slow version of 'I Feel Good' fills the air around us. He alternates between looking at the road and looking at me. As the road network around Kingston is made up of many one way streets, he has to take a detour to get me to my dorm. "I'm doing all this so no one on campus gets suspicious. It's better for you if the other girls don't think I'm interested in you. Clarisse is already fuming with rage because Jaxon hasn't touched her in weeks. And I don't want any more girls to get jealous of you. So I thought I'd make some stupid comment. One that makes them think I don't think much of you. But I didn't expect them to come straight back at you for it. I know it's sick and you can judge me for it. But I want to tell you one thing: I'm sorry that it got this far in the first place. And even if it seems otherwise on the outside, I'm here for you."

"Thank you," I say coolly, stubbornly looking straight ahead. I hope he doesn't think I trust him now. And why doesn't Jaxon touch Clarisse anymore? Is that a lie? Is Reece lying to wrap me in his web? Or is some of what he's saying really true?

"What you said to me in your room the other day..." he begins as he pulls up to the street in front of my dorm.

I bite my lip. Do we have to talk about it?

"Tell me what I can do to make you forgive me."

My hands get sweaty and I force myself not to let on as I look into his face. But I'm lost as soon as I do. Reece Crescent isn't just anyone. He's not Jaxon and he's not Sylvian and has not – yet – broken my heart. He is so incredibly attractive and captivating in his own right that I can't fight his attraction. Everything about him is flawless, seductive, sexy, and I can't help but think back to how it felt with him. In his room and later in the frat house. How he came in my mouth... in me.

"Okay," I manage. It's the opposite of what I wanted to say.

"Okay...?" he repeats, stretching. His eyes flash with interest. "So, what can I do?"

"Clarisse has deleted my files from my cloud. And Support can't give me the data back." Unfortunately, I sound terribly nervous. Why can't I just be immune to the effect the Kings have on me? "I've asked my professors to send me the material again, but some said I should ask my fellow students. Which I can't do because no one will help me. If you want to make amends, then... I would need your help with this."

"Clarisse deleted your files?" he asks skeptically. "When?"

"After... our first philosophy lecture." When I kissed you.

186

You, Sylvian and Jaxon. I know I've turned beet red.

Reece's eyes widen. "Vance told us something happened. But not that your data has been deleted."

"Well, he's just a bad stalker." Although I try to laugh, Reece remains serious. What kind of stupid conversation is this? Why am I even talking to him? Like he's going to help me! Him! Me!

"Why don't you ask Harper for help?" he asks thoughtfully.

"What can she do? Go to my professors and explain to them that I'm being bullied? That's a great idea. No, I'm asking you because you… because all you have to do is smile at the professors and they'd do anything for you. They'd give you all the exam answers."

Reece laughs and shakes his head in amusement. "I see. They probably will, at least when it comes to older exams. Give me your laptop and I'll try to recover the data. *And* I'll get you the material."

I take a shuddering breath. "You would really do that?"

"It's no trouble for me." He smiles warmly, and it would be so wonderful if I could just trust him. His gaze goes to the parking lot behind which my dormitory building is located. "Do you want me to… come in?"

My mouth opens helplessly. Reece. It's Reece Crescent. A god. A god who didn't help me when I was down. And who would have to do penance forever for me to *even consider* forgiving him to some extent.

"I could look at your laptop right now."

"No!" I gasp, a little too panicked, and move back to the passenger door. "No, that's a stupid idea. Everything about you is a terribly stupid idea."

Reece's smile stretches into a grin and he leans over to me. His hand plays with the folds of my shirt, and though he doesn't even touch my skin, the spot flares up just from the idea of him caressing me. "I'm just going to look at your laptop," he promises me, and I know he's lying, "then I'll leave."

I bark out a laugh and almost choke on it. "Sounds really nice, but unfortunately I don't believe a word you say because you hang out with psychos and are one yourself. Forget I said okay. Nothing is okay. Okay is if I get out now and we never speak to each other again."

Reece frowns thoughtfully and begins to touch my upper arm in gentle circles that drive me insane. His eyes hold me in place as if they were captivating me, and his lips are sensually parted. His blond hair falls seductively in his face, his lean, muscular body glistens in the lantern light and everything about him screams 'too good to be true'.

He comes even closer, leaning on the dashboard with one hand and on the back of my seat with the other. Reece wedges me in, and it would make sense to open the door and get out very quickly. A ravishing scent of fresh linen and peppermint stuns my senses. I can't resist. I simply can't.

And the devil on my left shoulder says: "If you come in with me, I won't wear a blindfold."

Reece pauses in front of my face. His breath tickles my skin. Only a few centimeters separate our lips. "So you want to watch me again?" he asks harshly.

My entire body is gripped by an electric current. The idea of Reece making himself comfortable in my dorm room. Stripping off his pants, lying down on the bed and touching himself like he did at the party in his glass mansion… And me just sitting there, watching him, him coming, while he looks into my eyes…

"We could… both watch each other, what do you think?" he asks.

My mouth goes dry. Dry as dust. "May…" I can't finish the word.

"Maybe?" he finishes for me with a smile.

Oh God, no. You can't let this happen. You can't! "How long will you stay if you come in?" I ask anyway.

"How long do you have? An hour? I might have to take your laptop with me if I need additional equipment."

One hour. That sounds good. One hour is just sixty minutes. I can control myself for just sixty minutes. He'll give me his show, I'll enjoy it and then I'll kick him out. Sounds like a good plan, right? An absolutely *safe* plan.

Wordlessly, I reach behind me and slip out of the car.

Reece is confused. "Was that a yes?"

"Do you need a handwritten invitation?"

He also gets out and throws the door shut behind him. "Sometimes I'm not sure what you really want."

"Hm," I just mumble and walk towards my dorm. I know I'm inviting a devil to my place. *He's watched me hit rock bottom. The way Jaxon showed me up. He fucked Rachel. He's played in the Kings' macabre chess game every year. He might still be playing now.*

No, not just might be.

He most certainly is.

As hot as it is, do I really think I could play with fire without burning myself?

My naivety and physical weakness seem to know no bounds. So I should never have been accepted by Kingston. Obviously, I'm just stupid. And my hormones have taken over most of my brain.

"Tea?" I ask as we pass our communal kitchen.

"Don't hold it against me, but I don't drink anything you can buy in the supermarket."

"I see." We stop outside my bedroom door. I try not to think about the fact that Reece knows our kitchen particularly well since he had sex with Rachel in it. And I also try not to feel any satisfaction because he wants me now and not her.

He doesn't want me. He wants me too. *That's a very big difference.*

I turn the key in my door. Maybe it's just my imagination, but I think I feel Reece's hand on the back of my neck as we step into the darkness. Trying to avoid the bright overhead light bathing my flaming red face in harsh light, I head for my bedside lamp and bump my foot on the way there. "Ouch!"

Reece switches on the light and I stare down at my chair in the middle of the room.

At least I think there's a chair hidden under the black velvet cloth. "What the…"

Reece sighs.

"What's this?" I reach for the letter lying on a pink cardboard box that fills the entire seat of the velvet-covered chair.

"An invitation from Jaxon."

I remember last semester when the Kings invited all the scholarship girls to their frat party to officially kick off the arena. Are they really going to do that again this semester? "To what?" I ask Reece, turning to face him.

He leans bored against the wall, his hands in the pockets of his sporty chinos. A bored god who has descended from Olympus to seek distraction among the people. "Who knows? A date? A party?"

I roll my eyes and open the envelope. Inside is a black card with delicate silver lettering.

Amabelle,

Be my date on Friday.

Jaxon

"On Friday?" I ask incredulously. "Which Friday does he mean?"

"The last Friday before spring break."

"How do you know that?"

"Because the Friday before spring break is the same party every year."

"How should I know that?"

"Anyone on campus could tell you that."

"And *where* is this party exactly?"

"Again: anyone could tell you that."

I exhale in frustration. "Jaxon's not really thinking clearly anymore, is he? If he invites me and thinks I'm coming?"

"Or else he feels the same way I do." Reece sounds disapproving, like he has something against Jaxon asking me out on a date. Which I would *never* go on anyway. "Spring break parties are one of the most important of the year. Anyone who shows up there together is making a statement."

I stare at him and the card almost falls out of my hand. "A statement?" I squeak. "To who?"

"To everyone. Sylvian and Harper were there together last year. And until they break up, no one even *dares* to make a pass at either of them."

"And Jaxon…?" I ask, stunned.

"Obviously wants you to accompany him."

I laugh coldly. "He could have saved himself the trouble."

Reece looks at me blankly. "I'd think about it if I were

you. If Jaxon really takes you there, no one will even dare *look at* you."

The glow in my head is starting to feel like I'm burning up inside. "Why would he do that? Does he want to show me off to everyone? Does he really think I'd be stupid enough to let him do this voluntarily?"

"God, Mable." Reece groans and runs both hands over his face. A moment ago he seemed content, now he just seems tired. Tired and bored. "What else does he have to do to make you realize what he wants from you? If he wanted to humiliate you in front of everyone, why would he cancel his actual date – which he surely would normally have – at such a big party? Just for... you? Sorry, but even Jaxon isn't childish enough to waste his time on a fake date."

"But –"

"I would have asked you too," he interrupts me. "But I'm not so conceited that I think you'd be ready for it."

"You would want..." My voice is just a breath. "That we go there officially... together...?"

He shrugs casually. "Yes."

"Why?" I look at him and don't understand the world anymore. What is this all about? And why do I think it's all real? And if it isn't real: why would they do this? There are a thousand better ways of humiliating me, hurting me and ultimately driving me off campus than by inviting me on... *a date.*

As Reece takes a step towards me, he grabs my top again, just touching the fabric, twirling it between his fingers, lost in thought. "I want you, Mable, and I'm not the only one."

My breath catches and I look up at him. His words sound so genuine. And far too good to be true.

"It would be best if you just threw me out now."

I take a shuddering breath. "Because otherwise you're going to watch me get hurt and abused again?"

"We're not the ones you should be afraid of. It's the other students. The other sororities. Clarisse and her friends... Even pawns can beat a king, Mable."

"Then why should I throw you out?"

Reece looks at me in agony, and the sorrow that shines in his eyes makes me suddenly soften. An impulse goes through his body and he steps even closer. He reaches into my hair with desire, pulling my head in front of his and smelling me as if my scent beguiles him. His voice sounds rough as he puts his mouth to my ear: "It would be wiser if you stayed away from us. But if you can't, take me. I promise you that I will no longer stand idly by and watch how they treat you. Go to the party at the beach house with me. Let's officially be together."

Butterflies begin to dance in my chest and I try to drive them away with all my might. "How could I be with you after everything?" I ask, whispering.

"You can't. I know you still need time. But if you at least pretend, you'll end the game. If a King chooses a queen, then she's a winner. For everyone."

I inhale quivering. It can't be that easy. None of this is real. They just want to hurt me even more. How could I trust them?

When Reece slowly pulls my face to his lips, I let him. He kisses me. As gently and sensitively as a prince kisses his fairytale princess. His tongue slides between my lips and he opens his mouth wide. His scent of freshness and mint overwhelms me and I let myself go completely. I let myself fall into his grip, into his arms.

His words turn to mist and I can't remember any of them.

Reece makes a demanding noise, pushing me back. It feels absolutely natural that I sink back onto the bed, land on my mattress and he comes over me.

His lips nibble on me, caress me and he is everywhere. Everywhere on my body, in my thoughts, in the air I breathe.

He opens his mouth wider, engulfs my chin and his hand begins to run over my upper body. He grips my waist, holds it tight and pushes his body between my legs. I flinch nervously as his stomach touches my crotch. Another longing sound escapes him and he begins to bite down on my neck, kissing me in such an electrifying way that I feel dizzy.

"I want it," I gasp.

When he lifts his head and looks at me, a storm rages in his eyes. A storm that passes over to me and scares me because it seems deadly.

"Me too," he says quietly, so agonized that I feel bad for him. "But if you want more to happen, I'll have to blindfold you."

"You're… not making an exception?"

He shakes his head and it's as if this fact tortures him a hundred times more than it tortures me. I'm lying in bed with a hot guy and I'm supposed to give up all my control so that he can sleep with me.

"Why?" I whisper. "What was different at the frat house?"

"*Everything* was different."

I swallow hard as I think back on it. "What happens when I'm blindfolded? Or… what doesn't happen?"

"It's my rule," he replies seriously. "Maybe I'll break it if you choose me at some point."

"But…"

Reece sinks onto the mattress next to me, his head resting on his elbow as he begins to stroke himself. "We can have fun like this if you're not ready yet," he explains gently, running his fingers over his chest.

I find the courage to reach out to him as well. The storm in his eyes fades, leaving behind a satisfied expression as I push his sweater a little higher and let my fingers dance over his muscular skin.

Just touching him creates another rush in my body. Reece gently unzips my jeans, undoes his belt a moment later and pushes my right hand towards my crotch.

His gaze rests on my face as he embraces the bulging length of his dick. "Touch yourself," he whispers.

Nervously, I do as he says and wince as I touch my pulsating clit.

"More!" he demands, rubbing his shaft firmly.

I slide my fingers deeper, stare at him and lose myself at the sight of him. My gaze alternates between his fist and his huge cock, then back to his angelic face.

"How could I have gone so long without having you in front of me like this?" he asks roughly and kisses me again. His tongue is restless and turns me on with its ferocity. I caress myself more intensely, succumbing to the idea that this is just foreplay. I imagine Reece holding his cock as he lies on top of me and guides it between my legs. That he pushes it into me, deep inside, fills me up and starts to fuck me in full thrusts.

I moan because it seems so tangible, almost as if it were true.

In my mind's eye, he is above me, we are naked and I belong to him.

Him and not *just* him.

I close my eyes. Close my eyes because it makes it easier for me to give up control completely. It's no use judging myself.

I succumb to this guy. He fucking looks like a Greek god.

What should I do?

His lips glide over my chin and he pulls my hand out of my jeans. Reece's body comes closer, as if in my imagination, and yet there are still too many clothes between us.

I sigh his name with feeling as he lets me know that it won't be just a hand job and lean my head back. I claw my way into my blanket and give myself to him. I imagine what we look like. How we look from the outside, lying on this bed, making a mismatched couple. A waitress who has to scrounge clothes from others and a millionaire whose sweater probably costs more than I earn in a month.

As his lips slide lower, something else entirely blends into the picture. There are ice-blue eyes watching me, with a mixture of desire and arrogance, and I look back into them. Being desired by several Kings fuels my inner fantasy world.

I open my eyes to pull Reece's mouth back in front of mine and cry out in panic.

He moves away from me and drives around in the direction I'm looking.

I blink rapidly, but it doesn't make the apparition at the door disappear.

There he stands – the product of my imagination – with his arms crossed in front of his chest.

"Still so easy after everything, Dole?" Jaxon scoffs, twisting one corner of his mouth.

"Fuck," Reece groans, hastily fastening his belt as I do my jeans. "What is it, Jaxon? You want in on this or why are you sneaking in like a peeper?"

"Thanks for the offer. But I thought you didn't want to share anymore? And didn't you swear some kind of oath? I seem to remember something…"

"It was just a kiss," replies Reece, bored. "As you can see, we both still have our clothes on."

"Of course." Jaxon smiles narrowly. "And it would have stayed that way if I hadn't interrupted you."

"What do you want?" Reece asks again.

"Making sure my gift has arrived."

"It has," Reece replies tonelessly.

"So?" Jaxon asks me with interest. "Are you going to be my date?"

"Uh, no?" I answer, flabbergasted. "Of course not."

The corners of his mouth twist into a condescending smirk. "You'd rather go with Crescent?"

"No!"

"Ah, you haven't decided yet."

"I'm not going to go at all!"

"You don't want to go with either of us?" he asks, but it's clear from his voice that he'll force me if necessary if I don't come willingly. "Are you hoping Sylvian will break up by the weekend?"

"No!" I hiss.

Jaxon raises a brow. "Let's go, Crescent. You've turned our lady's head enough."

Reece seems to resign himself and then turns to me. "Do you want me to take your laptop?"

There is no important data on it anyway, so I simply hand it to Reece.

"Good night, Mable," he whispers. "Text me if you change your mind." With these words, he follows Jaxon out.

He leaves behind my lips burning with desire.

With a black invitation card.

And a pink box.

Things could be worse for me, really.

How long will the butterflies be allowed to dance inside me this time before the Kings catch each one and tear them apart in the cruelest way?

JAXON

Hm, you think we want to share you. That we just want to have *fun*. That we have no problem with you fucking each of us in turn.

You are spot on.

But what kind of game would it be if we just told you?

When we tell you that you'll never get one of us, never us apart?

We are always together. We know everything about each other.

You are smart enough to figure it out.

It won't be easy to convince you otherwise, but we're running out of time.

The rules of the game are clear.

You will choose.

One of us.

And it will always be the wrong choice.

19

MABLE

Jaxon's present is still there when I wake up the next morning. So it wasn't a dream. Reece's words weren't a dream and neither was Jaxon's request for a date.

I can't help but think the Kings *not* hating me and wanting to expel me is almost as challenging as the end of last semester.

I'd love to bury myself and not resurface until my last midterm exams are written, but I can't hide.

"You could be my date," Harper chirps as we wait for philosophy class to start. I just told her about the Kings and their invitations. "The party at the beach house is really nice, you know? And I deserve a party because I've been studying every free minute for midterms."

"Don't you already have a date?" We've stopped mentioning Sylvian's name. As I hardly ever see them together, I can almost convince myself that they're no longer together.

"No. I've already been there once with… him. This time I'm not going to embarrass myself. But showing up at the beach house without a date is frowned upon." She winks at me. "Lesbian couples are allowed, though."

"And gays?" I ask with interest as we arrange our writing utensils.

Goldman arranges the exams on his lectern and waits until the examination assistants finish roll call.

"No one at Kingston is gay," Harper murmurs to me. "Well, I don't know. I think there are some who wouldn't be open to it. A lot of the families who send their children to Kingston are damn conservative. When my father got hold of a photo of me kissing a woman, he almost cried. Getting heirs for their massive dynasties is the most important thing for these people."

"I'm sorry about your dad."

"Oh, well. I don't really care that he's conservative, what's worse is that I have to study law because of him." She sticks a finger down her throat and pretends to gag.

I watch as Jaxon, Reece and Romeo enter the room. They show their student ID to an examination assistant, then walk towards their usual seats in the front row – and pass them by. Chatting casually, they come up the steps and take their seats in the row behind us, of all places. They sit far apart, as is the rule.

My cheeks glow and I lower my gaze shyly. I haven't talked Jaxon or Reece yet.

"Don't panic," Harper whispers to me. "None of them are right behind you."

Relief floods through me. But I can't think about anything else for the entire exam except what they're up to. As was to be expected from Goldman, the test is completely crazy and consists of only one question: *How do you define 'nothing'?*

When I finally get so nervous that I start biting my nails, Harper gives me a dirty look. I stop and wait tensely for the exams to be collected.

"Please, it's such a bad habit," Harper whispers, scooting closer to me and looking at my fingernails.

"Sorry," I mumble.

"You don't have to apologize to *me*."

"Can you maybe talk to Jaxon and Reece?" I glance furtively in their direction. They're just handing in their sheets and don't pay any attention to me, but the whole exam I had the feeling they were watching me.

"What?" Harper asks me incredulously. "Since when are you so shy?"

Her wavy hair falls gently over her shoulders, and I notice again how pretty she is. So much prettier and more perfect than me. A good indication that what the Kings are asking me for can't possibly be real. A date? An *official* date?

"They don't believe me," I whisper. "Tell them what I've already told them. Maybe then they'll get it. That I will definitely *never* go on a date with them. That we're going together. You and me. That's a great idea."

At first she seems surprised, but then she smiles warmly at me. "Okay," she whispers and gives me a fist bump. "Bossgirl vibes, all right?"

We laugh quietly and then discuss the exam task at length until Goldman dismisses us.

***

Thanks to Harper, I manage to escape the Kings before they accost me. I can still see Reece looking discontentedly in my direction as Harper stands in their way, allowing me to disappear into the crowd. Since it's not a good idea to be on campus without Romeo, I head straight to my dorm.

Harper and I text each other in between, looking forward to our 'date' and thinking about what outfits would suit us. The fact that she doesn't want to go with Sylvian shows me that she's not taking the engagement quite as seriously as she did in January. If she officially breaks up with him now, we could almost be friends, right? Provided she doesn't hate me for cheating on her...

When I get out of the shower in the early evening, I know immediately that something is wrong. My towel is no longer there.

Neither are my clothes.

Fuck. A prank from the other scholarship students? I really didn't miss it... Since I don't know what to expect in the residence hall, I pull down the shower curtain without further ado. It's transparent in some places, but it should hide the essentials. I go to the door, prepared to be photographed or subjected to another prank, and see another shadow.

Then a muffled sound. My eyes close of their own accord. Pain jolts through my head. I fall to my kneels, half fainting. Cold tiles on my bare skin.

Someone grabs me.

"Come on, help me!" Rachel's voice. It sounds damn far away, considering she must be right next to me. My senses fade and I realize I'm being dragged down the hall. Past my room. The shower curtain drags behind me.

A door is opened.

Rachel's room?

Whatever was knocked against my head has taken me out, so I can't fight the hands pulling me along.

Dim light, several men, dark shadows in the room. My arms are yanked roughly onto my back. I blink.

Two, three, four times.

Then I can see more clearly.

"Here she is. Go on, have at it!"

One of the guys laughs. "She's pretty skinny. I imagined her tits would be bigger."

I tear my eyes open, trying to focus my vision. There's this hellish pain at the back of my head and my hands are being held down behind my back by Rachel…

"Wake up, trailer park girl," she hisses in my ear and shakes my head.

That doesn't necessarily help me to see more clearly, but at least it awakens my defenses.

"Come on!" Rachel groans. "We'll put her on the bed!"

More hands grabbing me. The shapes become clearer. Three guys. Rachel, Brittany. A dorm room, two beds. I'm pushed onto one of them and someone rips the curtain off me.

"Shit, what are you guys doing?" Although I feel like I'm shouting, I just mumble. My head is pounding so hard. Whatever I was hit with, it must have been something really big and heavy.

"It's okay, sweetie." Rachel squats over me, a crooked smile on her red-painted lips and a greedy look in her eyes. "You're going to score points now. Because then you'll play along and the arena will go on. And then *we'll* win."

"You're crazy!" I gasp in panic and try to escape. She presses down my elbows with both knees.

"You have a choice, Mable. Give them a blow job – or they fuck you."

My eyes and mouth widen. She can't be serious.

When she jumps off me and leaves me lying there as if I were cattle on the slaughterhouse floor, I realize that the *guys* in particular are serious.

They surround me. Three big, muscular guys. Dressed in expensive clothes, varsity jackets around their shoulders.

"Come on. I have more to do." Rachel.

"Hey, don't stress," the one guy who has already grabbed his belt tells them. "You can wait outside."

One of them comes up to me, grabs my hair and unabashedly holds his cock in front of my face. "You heard her, Dole," he says with a laugh. "Suck or get fucked. What do you choose?"

I press my lips tightly together, shake my head and wriggle out of his grip.

"Shit, don't you know how to do this?" Rachel shouts. She grabs my damp hair from behind and pulls my head up. "There, you see that dick, Mable? You're going to suck it until he comes."

The situation is too serious for me to have time to insult her. She pushes my head with all her might towards the hip of the half-naked guy standing in front of me.

The men laugh.

"Go on, suck it!" hisses Rachel. "You have to earn your points by doing favors! And if you don't volunteer, they'll use the hole that can't bite!"

"You can't really want them to rape me," I say powerlessly and I try to roll off the bed. The others hold me tight and then my mouth is forced open. A glans on my lips, even though I don't want it.

The reflex to bite comes automatically. But how I could exert so much force that the guy starts screaming is beyond me. My spirits return, the adrenaline rushes through my veins and I shake Rachel off.

"What are you doing?" I shout at her. Naked, upset, head throbbing, unable to cope with the situation. "Are you trying to *force* me to play along?"

"If you don't do it voluntarily? Yes!" she screams.

"Fight later," says the third guy. He sounds fucking drunk. When he gets half on top of me, his weight pushes me down, but I only have to move a little under him, and he can't even find my hip to lock it in place.

"God, you guys are really bad at this." Rachel squats over me. She pulls my mouth open with all her might. "There!"

Three men in front of me. All exposed below the abdomen. Their faces are shadowed, there is hardly any light in the room.

Another cock is shoved down my throat and this time I can't defend myself.

But what's much worse is that one of them is fumbling with my crotch. I can feel his finger trying to push it inside me. All my struggling, moaning and screaming is useless as Rachel and the other guy brutally hold me down on the bed.

Can Vance hear me?

Or another of the scholarship girls?

It can't be that nobody hears this noise!

A rumble at the door.

"Damn it," Rachel hisses, letting go of me in a panic and lying down flat next to me. "Go on!" she hisses at the guy on top of me. "Go on!"

She grabs his hand, pulls it onto her breasts and screams in pain just as the door is broken down. She wants to pretend she's being raped too. *What a crazy woman.*

Glaring light, five men.

They fill the room and, without meaning to, I'm damn glad to see every single one of them.

Vance is at the front, but Jaxon pushes him aside the next moment. Sylvian, Reece and Romeo follow. Everyone stares at me.

Jaxon is the only one who remains standing when the

other four storm towards the three guys at the same time and pull them off me. There's a hint of a fight, but the three drunks don't stand a chance against the four Kings. They're on the ground faster than I can count to five.

It's the first time I've looked Jaxon straight in the eye since he interrupted Reece and me. But it feels like an eternity since we last faced each other. And in that one moment, as the others wrestle the guys down, none of the terrible things ever seem to have happened.

There is only this hope. I want him to save me.

Save me from this hell that my life has become or has always been, and I want to forgive him. Even if I will never be able to.

As the other Kings and Vance slowly stand up again and I finally realize that five pairs of eyes are staring at my naked body, I sink into myself. My eyes are closed. This is not really happening. This is college. It can't be this bad. I can't be at the mercy of those cruel bastards.

"Belle…" Jaxon's voice, very close. A hand on my sweaty forehead.

"It was awful!" Rachel gasps behind me. "Thank goodness you came!"

"One more word and you'll be the next one down." Sylvian.

"But… Reece!" says Rachel accusingly, scrambling off the bed. "Why are you letting him talk to me like that?"

"Because you're a little cunt who doesn't deserve it any other way," Reece replies dismissively. "I only fucked you because it was the obvious thing to do. I hope you didn't think I saw you as anything else than a whore?"

My eyes flicker and I look for Reece in the room. I recognize the voice, but it's not him at all. He wouldn't talk like that. He wouldn't call me Dole, and he wouldn't call Rachel a whore. "Zayn," I manage to get out, and his eyes dart from Rachel to me, then I slump back down.

Too powerless to think about what I may have just realized.

"I want to sleep," I mumble.

"She's hurt," Jaxon says alarmed, grabbing the back of my head. "She was probably knocked out."

"Did you do this?" Sylvian immediately asks sharply. Rachel screams out. "Talk!" he hisses.

"You!" grumbles Vance. He must mean Brittany. "What hit Mable on her head?"

"A glass bottle," she says in a shaky voice.

"How long have you been in here?" asks Jaxon.

"Not really for long," she replies anxiously.

"Was one of the guys..." Reece. "... in her?"

Brittany seems to give a wordless answer and I breathe a sigh of relief. "No. Only in my mouth."

"Bad enough." Jaxon.

I feel his fingers dancing across my forehead and try to open my eyes again. His head is directly in front of me, his cheek resting on his elbow so that he can look at me at the same angle as I look at him.

"Don't worry," he whispers. "You're safe now."

"Am I?" I ask back even more uncertainly. Someone has spread a blanket over me. "Why should I believe you of all people?"

Jaxon turns the corners of his mouth into a genuine smile. "That's a good question. But you actually have a good sense of when I'm being honest and when I'm not."

"Do I?" I whisper, enjoying the gentle dance of his fingers on my cheek far too much. "I actually think you're a rotten, cowardly asshole through and through, and I believed you when you said your every word was a lie."

He laughs. Everything about him is pure warmth. "I've missed you, Belle."

A shiver rushes through my entire upper body. His words are those of a psycho, because none of them match what he said to me *last* semester.

"Jax," Reece asks behind him. "What do we do now?"

Jaxon lets go of me and slowly straightens up. His gaze glides over the men on the ground, the two women standing anxiously between the Kings, and then over Vance.

"We're not wasting any more time." His commanding tone is sharp. "Vance, you get the two doles to the frat house. Get the Asian girl with them. Romeo: help him."

Vance doesn't look like he wants to do anything. "I'm staying with Mable."

The Kings laugh derisively.

"You might want that," Jaxon replies calmly. "But who do you think you are? Someone she shouldn't be afraid of?"

"I don't care what I think of myself. *You* are the danger."

For a few seconds, no one in the room moves. Vance looks at me, caring, and the Kings look at him, stunned.

"Shit," Reece finally groans. "Don't even dream about it, Buchanan."

"We'd castrate you before you touched her," Sylvian growls.

"She is ours." Three words out of Jaxon's mouth.

Vance's face mirrors a little of how I feel. Run over. Fainted. On the ground.

"I don't belong to anyone," I hiss and slowly straighten up. Sylvian and Jaxon are with me immediately and push me back into bed.

"Stay down," mumbles Sylvian. "We have to check if you have a concussion or if anything else is wrong."

209

"I don't belong to anyone, Sylvian!" I throw at him.

"Whether you're ours or not," Jaxon explains softly. "Buchanan will pay for thinking for one minute that he could stand in front of you. *Against us.*"

Vance's face turns dark as night. "You damned fuckers. I've watched long enough. The fact that Rachel set this shit up is because of *your* sick game. Not mine. You're going to have to kill me to get me to leave Mable's side tonight."

"Well, that would be a hassle," Jaxon replies in his usual cynical tone. "But what was it again? Your poor mom? Doesn't she have cancer and *really* needs our money?"

"You bastards!" I shout and I would have jumped up if Sylvian wasn't with me, still pushing me down on the bed.

There is a pain in Vance's eyes that I instantly feel deep inside me. He's being blackmailed. With his mother's life, who probably has no health insurance or any other help.

"Trust us," Reece says to me. "Vance taking blackmail to help his family is the only good thing about him."

"Then he's already got more good points than you!" I shout.

Vance smirks, but Jaxon points to the door.

"No time to question your loyalty, Buchanan. Go, damnit."

Vance admits defeat as he grabs Rachel and drags her to the door. "I'll stay close," he promises me, before leaving the room with Romeo, who is holding Brittany captive.

He stays close to me, which is not a particularly reassuring promise when he leaves me alone with the Kings anyway.

"Put this on," Sylvian murmurs, taking off his jacket and putting it around my shoulders.

"Wait." Jaxon kneels down in front of me, pulls out his cell phone and shines the flashlight into my pupils. "She seems to be able to stand up."

He watches me anxiously and I want to scream. What's wrong with them? And am I really *happy* to see them? Shouldn't they actually be pleased about what has just happened?

I angrily shake off Sylvian's hands and jacket as I stand up. Two hands on my upper arms pull me to my feet and guide me down the hall to my own room.

"Okay, thanks," I mumble. "Now get out of here."

They do nothing of the sort. Reece goes to my closet, looking for something in it.

"The box with the dress, where is it?" he asks me. I don't answer, so he just pulls out something else and puts the clothes on the bed next to me. Sylvian closes the blinds and turns on the light, and Jaxon stands there without taking his eyes off me.

"Get out!" I shout louder now.

"We're not going anywhere without you," Jaxon replies calmly. "Get dressed."

"I'm definitely not coming with you! Whatever you're planning to do, it –"

Sylvian steps forward. "Put some clothes on already," he growls darkly.

I flinch away from him. He has so much power over me that I obey him, even if I hate him all the more for it. "Can you at least turn around?"

Jaxon and Sylvian do, but Reece continues to stare at me. "Crescent," Jaxon hisses.

"What? We've all seen her naked anyway." He rolls his eyes and turns around too.

What the hell is happening here? Reluctantly, I slip into the panties, bra, shirt and skirt Reece gave me. On the floor under my bed is the box with the dress Jaxon gave me for our date. It just appeared one day, though I refuse to wear it. I'm not surprised that he has access to my room. He seems to own the whole university anyway.

While I'm still getting dressed, Jaxon looks curiously around my room.

"Leave my things alone," I mutter angrily.

He was just about to take down one of the photos from the photo wall that Harper had given me. "Nice present."

"Yes!" I bark. "*She* had the balls to apologize to me! Unlike you guys."

"Do we have to talk about Harper?" asks Reece, annoyed.

"No, if it's up to me, no one needs to talk at all." I straighten up. "What do you want?" By now I feel mostly recovered from the blow to the head, although a dull throbbing at the back of my head remains.

The Kings take their sweet time checking me out.

Jaxon.

Sylvian.

Reece.

If I was able to do that with the buzzing in my head, I would certainly feel uncomfortable.

"Nice," says Reece. "Who actually allowed her to wear those skirts?"

"Definitely not me." Sylvian growls something unintelligible, and Jaxon turns back to my jewelry box that I bought on eBay last semester. It still only contains one pair of earrings.

"We have to go to the party," he says casually. "Where's the dress I gave you? And why don't you even have any jewelry, Belle?"

"Leave my things alone! And I'm definitely not going to the party with you!"

Jaxon wheels around to face me, his ice-blue eyes fixed

hungrily on me. "Behave yourself," he barks. "Do you want that to happen again with Rachel? Then keep it up. Talk to me like I'm nobody and treat us like we have no power over what's happening. Or practice patience, give answers when we demand them, and be happy that we' re not interested in you getting raped right now. Or some pathetic nobody touching your pussy at all."

My breath quivers. "I'm going to the party with Harper."

"She's not coming." Sylvian has now bent under the bed and found the box with the dress. "Is that it?"

"Yeah, have her put it on there. Vance will make a scene if we don't arrive in time," Jaxon says impatiently. "Crescent, take her hand. You will follow us to the limo quietly, unob-trusively, and completely compliantly, Belle."

I clench my jaw, let Reece clasp my hand, and follow him out reluctantly. It's cold as fuck, but Jaxon's car is parked right on the street, and I'm glad to see it without having to think about how he abandoned me in the woods with it.

The men wait until I get in, then they follow me.

Sylvian, Reece, Jaxon.

It has never ended well when I've been in a room with them, as Goldman's first lecture demonstrated. Not that night at the frat house, not at the poker night, not after the 'show' in front of everyone in the lecture hall. These men are poison to me. Trouble and crumbling self-control.

As soon as the car drives off, something changes. Jaxon leans his head back, suddenly looking tired. I remember exactly how he last sat like this in front of me in the back seat. It seems like years ago. So much has happened since that moment and everything between us has changed.

Reece sits next to me, his arm outstretched to the right, his expression deadly serious. Sylvian is as dark as ever, and seeing him in front of me reminds me again of what happened between us over winter break. And for what I have to condemn myself.

"You have to make a choice, Belle," Jaxon begins. But his voice no longer sounds smooth like it usually does, it's now attacked. As if he's struggling to get the words over his lips. "That's the game now."

"A fake game," Reece interjects. I look at him and wonder whether he has changed again. The undertone of his voice is a lot friendlier. "Officially, it will look like a game. But you'll know it's not. The game will protect you."

"From whom?" I ask doubtfully. "You've been my only problem so far."

"From me."

Everyone looks at Sylvian, who has said these words.

When I think about how hard and demanding our last sex was, I feel hot and cold at the same time. Harper didn't find out, and it hurts *me* most of all that they're still together.

"Yes, well, from him too," Reece interjects. "We've got Sylvian under control to some extent."

"It's important that you listen very carefully now," Jaxon says insistently before I can say anything back. Their brief exchange of words confuses me. Jaxon is sitting alone in the back seat, just like the first time we met in this car; legs apart, hands clasped together, he looks at me piercingly. I haven't seen him up close since January, so I can't help but notice everything about him. The black shoes. The loose chinos. The azure blue shirt, with an elegant, close-fitting coat over it. Black leather gloves that he holds in his hands. An expensive watch that flashes in the light of the LEDs. Many rings on his hands, including the Kings' signet ring. The dark blond hair that falls into his forehead, long enough to feel dreamy under my fingers, short enough to be fashionable.

"Just tell me when you're done checking me out. Then I'll start talking." A sly grin forms on his masculine, handsome features and Reece and Sylvian laugh.

I squeeze my eyes shut for a few seconds, trying not to let the shame arise inside me. These men have driven me over the edge. They don't even deserve me to look at them.

"I'm listening," I say coolly and open my eyes again.

Jaxon's grin is lewd, and my mind instantly imagines what it would be like if he pressed my head into Sylvian's lap again. Fuck.

"When we all want the same thing, we usually make a bet."

"Like the one about the first time with me?" I ask mockingly.

"Exactly," says Reece.

I don't look in his direction, but the fact that he's sitting next to me and being the nice version of himself again makes Jaxon's words seem all the more forceful.

"If there's one thing you've learned so far," Jaxon explains, "it's probably that we're not exactly… harmless when it comes to getting something. Unfortunately, you've caught our attention. Starting with the fact that Sylvian warned you – and you didn't leave. If he'd made the same announcement to Rachel as he did to you, we'd probably have got rid of her by now."

The mention of her name makes me feel even colder. "So?"

"What he's trying to say, Mable…" Reece waits until I look at him. "When we pulled something like that with a girl like we did with you, we were aware of all the consequences. And we didn't care about them at all. But none of them were ever warned. Or knew who we were. We tried to convince ourselves that it was because of your naivety that you got involved with us anyway…"

"But that's not it, is it?" asks Jaxon smugly.

I look back and forth between them. "Where the hell are you taking me?"

"Just listen to them!" growls Sylvian.

"But I don't want to know what you have to tell me!" I snap at him. He sits opposite Jaxon and looks completely out of place with his leather jacket, the tattoos on his hands and his flashy gangster look. "I'm not interested! In none of it!"

"You want us," Reece murmurs and reaches for my hand, which I immediately snatch from his grasp. He leans toward me, his eyes infiltrating my gaze. "You knew who we were, what we do, and what our... sexual preferences are, and you didn't run away from it."

"You gave yourself away to us," adds Jaxon.

"And you trusted us to never go further than your will allows us," Sylvian concludes.

"You're just as rotten as we are," Reece whispers in my ear and I helplessly pull away from him.

"Don't push her," warns Jaxon. "Not after what just happened."

My heart beats wildly in my chest. "And what do you want from me now?"

Silence fills the car and suddenly everything is different. I can answer the question myself. It is too obvious what they desire. Too palpable in the electrified air. I wish I could feel the aversion that I should be feeling right now. The hatred that should fill my chest.

I wish I could laugh at them, insult them, hurt them with words, but I do none of that. Not a word leaves my lips as I realize that the Kings haven't spared me because they're planning a much harder blow or Romeo has turned on them. They don't want to get rid of me at all. Not yet, anyway.

"If it were up to us," whispers Reece, "we'd stop playing immediately. But the people out there are greedy. They want a game, a show, a lie they can hold onto. We can't stop the game, and just sitting it out gives a Rachel the wrong idea as well. That's why you have to make your choice."

"Forget about the fucking game for a fucking moment," Jaxon growls and my gaze flickers in his direction. "Or Rachel. Who is this little bitch anyway? We'll destroy her tonight, but that won't erase Amabelle's memories. Nothing will."

"What just happened," Reece chokes out, "is nothing compared to what you did to her, Jaxon. So stop being a fucking moralizer."

Jaxon's expression remains inscrutable. "I'll stop if you stop, Crescent. I don't remember you helping Amabelle last semester? And what do you think will happen when she finds out you've been lying to her at every meeting?"

"What are you going to do now? A dick measuring contest?" asks Sylvian cynically.

"Yes," Jaxon says seriously and leans forward. With his arms propped up on his knees, he fixes me insistently. "In a way, that's what we're going to do. Make up your mind, Belle. Reece or me. Or Sylvian. Which would please me personally the most, because his engagement is the purest farce."

"You want me to decide who I'm going to the party with?"

"Decide which King gets you. Not just for the party."

They can't be serious. "You'll never get a second chance," I whisper.

"Absolutely understandable," says Reece casually. "None of us really expect that except Jaxon. But we have to maneuver you through college somehow by making you a winner. Option one: the arena stays as it is and you play along. But none of us will let anyone get too close to you for favors."

"You really want to make me the winner?" I ask helplessly.

He doesn't respond to me. "Option two: one of us will officially end the game tonight. We've decided on option two."

"It's very simple," explains Sylvian. "You just have to choose one."

My mouth is terribly dry. "Choose one…? For what? To kill him first?"

They all grin at the same time.

"Not quite what we had in mind…" says Reece. "But it comes close."

Jaxon raises a brow in a sneer. "Kiss her, Reece."

"What?" I gasp as he has already grabbed my chin, turned it towards him and lowered his lips to mine. In those first few seconds of his touch, time seems to stand still. Emotions fight for supremacy inside me, and the only thing still moving is my pounding heart. Reece's tongue touches mine and I automatically open my mouth a little wider. Let him in, let *myself* into *him*, touch his cheek, savor for that tiny moment of peace how familiar he is to me.

And then it all washes over me. Tears well up in my eyes.

Rachel pushing me down on a bed, opening my mouth. Rachel lying on the kitchen table, being fucked by Reece. Rachel laughing maliciously at me while playing poker. Rachel standing by Reece's side in the lecture hall as Jaxon shows me off to everyone.

Her nastiness digs a long fingernail into my heart, just as Harper's kindness does. They both got a guy I fell in love with. Much worse, though, is that I fell in love at all. With several guys at the same time. How the hell does that even work? And why does it have to happen to me of all people?

Maybe that's one reason why I didn't expect it to hurt so

much. I thought my heart was unassailable because I liked them all equally. I could never have favored any of them, especially not that night at the frat house. If Reece had been missing, I wouldn't have trusted it. If Sylvian hadn't been there, I wouldn't have wanted it. And without Jaxon…it wouldn't have been so damn hot.

Reece takes a step back and strokes my damp cheek. His eyes are filled with compassion and concern, but it's different from Romeo's. Romeo feels sorry for me. Reece feels it. At least, I think he does. How am I supposed to trust myself?

The realization that I will never again be able to be sure that the men's intentions are sincere takes away the last remnants of my self-control. I start crying, tears streaming from my eyes like waterfalls, a huge knot slowly loosens in my throat and Reece pulls me close.

He pulls me tightly against his chest and I let him.

Let his arms wrap around me, hold me even tighter.

Everything is there at the same time. Protection, warmth and comfort. Closeness, connection, trust. His gentle hands run over my back, enclosing me, and I cry all over his sweater for an eternity, even though it makes absolutely no sense to lie in the arms of my tormentor.

"We're here," Jaxon says quietly, waking me from my lethargy.

I wipe my tear-stained face and try to see where we stopped. "Not the woods again, is it?" I ask them, already too broken to be scared. Nothing can shock me anymore.

"No, forget the fucking woods, Mable," Sylvian growls. "That was just because Jaxon wanted to draw me out so I could fuck you."

Icy rain cools any warm feeling I just felt against Reece's chest. "What do you mean?" I ask, my voice quivering. It hurts so much to think back on it. I should never have let it happen. I should never have let him take me, even though I felt something. It was wrong and it tore my heart apart.

"I made a bet that I would manage to stay away from you," Sylvian explains tonelessly. "And lost in the very first week. If I had won, Jaxon would have left you alone forever. That's why you weren't allowed to tell anyone about it. Because if the others had found out that I'd already lost, it would have been even worse."

I swallow. "You made a bet…? For my future? And you just fucked me, even though you knew my *life* was at stake?"

Sylvian's face becomes endlessly shadowy. "You lay underneath me and talked some shit about being attractive. You licked my finger like it was my dick. You didn't run, you didn't scream, even though I was acting like a psycho –"

"I did run!" I shout at him.

"But not far enough!" he growls.

Jaxon and Reece follow our conversation with interest.

"Can you two please argue later?" asks Jaxon.

"No!" I hiss. "Do you know what you're doing to me? Not only was my first time a fucking bet, which I was counting on, but *my first time cost me my fucking degree!* I wonder what it would be like if you were punished so harshly for sleeping with someone? What are you? Ultra conservative Catholics who don't want women to have *fun* too?"

"It was your first time?" asks Jaxon, puzzled. His eyes dart to Sylvian. "In the woods? With Silvano? Never. No virgin would go along with that."

I snort. "Oh, fuck you." With renewed vigor, I slide out of the limo, open the door and get out. Jaxon follows me, and for a moment I'm too absorbed in taking in my surroundings to think about escaping.

We are on the middle of a jetty on the open sea. Behind us lies the beach, a gloomy forest, in front of us nothing but a stormy sea illuminated by moonlight. There's a multi-story villa on columns before us, made entirely of wood. It's gorgeous. Floor-to-ceiling glass windows look out in all directions, and balconies, terraces and interlocking floors make create nooks, making the huge house incredibly cozy. Inside, people are standing around partying everywhere. There can't possibly be valet parking, so the students were brought here somehow.

After my eyes have had their fill, I think back to the reason why I'm here. The limo driver gets out, one of the Kings' golden masks on his face, and Jaxon, Reece and Sylvian suddenly have one in their hands too.

"No," I gasp and I back away. The last time I saw these masks, I was presented like a slaughtered deer to a jeering crowd. I have sworn revenge. I vowed to become a problem for them. A real opponent. Instead, I am still nothing more than a victim.

Their victim.

"No, I'm not going in there with you," I groan, backing away over the footbridge.

Sylvian is already wearing his mask, but Jaxon rolls his eyes. "Is she going to run now?" he asks.

"Probably," replies Sylvian.

Reece pushes the mask up again. "Mable, please, what would you want to escape from now?"

"More importantly: where to?" asks Jaxon, annoyed.

I look at them one by one, three arrogant assholes who don't even question whether I'll ever get involved with them again, but simply take it for granted that I'll forgive them so quickly. Then I turn around and run.

221

I can hide in the forest. It seems dense and dark, and they certainly won't be camping on the beach to thwart my escape. But where else can I go? By Monday morning at the latest, when I'm back at Kingston, they'll be able to get me again. They will always get me if they want to.

I hear footsteps behind me, but mine are much louder. The stretch of beach is short, I rush across it and reach the forest.

"Please, Belle, what are you doing?" Jaxon calls after me.

I storm into the forest, run until I find a suitable spot and slump against a tree trunk. I watch anxiously as the Kings approach the wood.

"Look, you must realize that something has changed just because we're running after you," Jaxon shouts into the forest. "What do you think we are? Morons who need a victim so they can rape them? Wrong. You just escaped from those people. So what stupid reason could there be for three of us to run after you, other than that we care about you?"

I lean my head back, trying to hold back the tears. None of this can really be happening. It can never be true. I didn't fall, hit the ground hard, just to get up again as if nothing had ever happened.

Jaxon, Sylvian and Reece are my tormentors. They humiliated me in front of everyone, bullied me, threatened me, tried to drive me away and I'm still suffering from the attacks of their followers.

And now Jaxon claims they *care* about me?

I ball my hands into fists and hold them in front of my chest, trying to protect my heart, to preserve it, to close it. Branches crack around me and I don't feel strong enough to face them defiantly. But neither do I feel strong enough to flee. The hope that one of Jaxon's words might be true pins me to the forest floor, against the tree trunk, and makes me hold out.

"Do you want to get up?" Jaxon finds me first and looks at me with a mixture of disinterest and impatience.

"No," I whisper and I remain seated.

He takes a deep breath and does something I would never have thought him capable of. He sits down on the forest floor in front of me and leans against a trunk opposite. He watches me in silence. The light from his cell phone flashlight is just enough to illuminate his smooth face. But I can't read it. I probably never could.

"Listen, Belle, I'm not the type to have regrets. What we do is much more important, isn't it? And I seem to remember that I made it clear to you what would happen when you returned. And *none* of that has happened yet."

"Because Romeo turned against you," I whisper.

He laughs, showing his white teeth in the dim light. "Romeo," he says seriously, "would *never* turn on me. You were supposed to think that, yes. Everyone on campus was supposed to think that. But everything he did, he did for me. For us. Because we wanted it that way."

That doesn't really surprise me, even though it sounds pretty far-fetched. "Whatever you say," I mumble. "I'm glad that some synapse in your head has finally been sending the right signals since Christmas."

"Stop talking to me like I'm nobody," he demands again. His voice is raised and cold. "Do you want things to stay the way they are? That Romeo is there when the others attack you? That the game ends when you choose one? Then practice some fucking respect and be aware of who you're talking to."

I cross my arms in front of my chest. "How am I supposed to respect you? You're an asshole who mistreated me because he can't deal with his feelings."

His eyes flash. "My *feelings*, eh? I'll teach you respect, don't worry. Right now you're just on a break because we didn't get there fast enough to stop Rachel."

Well, that inspires confidence.

"Here you are." Reece stumbles out from behind a leafless bush in surprise. "What's going on now? Are you going camping?"

Sylvian also finds us. He says nothing.

Jaxon keeps looking at me and I pull my legs to my chest to protect myself from him. It's freezing cold. The leaves, the ground, the tree trunk, but I'm not cold. Everything inside me is glowing.

"Why can't you just leave me alone?" I ask.

Jaxon laughs and shakes his head. "That's not how the game works."

I'm not going to tell him again that the game is stupid. "I'm not going to choose between you just to end it!"

"You will."

"No!"

Jaxon rolls his eyes and Sylvian steps forward. "Get up, you'll get hypothermia."

"No!"

"Fuck," he growls and he pulls me up.

Jaxon also stands up with a flourish and he brings his face close to mine. His lips open sensually, he comes closer to me than I would ever allow if I wasn't in Sylvian's firm grip. "When we want to get rid of something, we're cruel," he whispers right in front of my lips. "But when we desire something, we get it. You don't stand a chance, angel. Just give in, it will be easier for you. Every woman at Kingston would be all over what we have planned for you. So be a good girl and stop running away. *You won't get away from us.*"

I shake Sylvian off. "I hate you guys. I hope you never forget that."

"As long as you fuck us like you fucked Sylvian the other day, hate is perfectly fine with me." Jaxon licks his lips, and I feel hot and cold in equal measure.

JAXON

Y ou think you could get away from me?
How cute.
I'm pulling all the strings. Everyone who touches you is controlled by me.

If you choose, then you choose the one I want you to have.

Everything, fucking everything, even every glance in your direction, is controlled by me.

I just sometimes pretend otherwise.

But that's just part of a perfect poker face.

20

MABLE

The Kings take me to an empty room in the beautiful villa on the water. 'Beach house' is an understatement. The masked driver follows us, carrying the large box that Jaxon put in my room a few days ago and places it on the table. Jaxon lifts the lid and pulls out the fine fabric. "Put this on."

I take the dress and let the fabric slip through my fingers. The blue fabric has red and gold embellishments. The waist is accentuated, the neckline low-cut. I know the dresses the Kings have for their ladies. I wore one myself. It was beautiful, princess-like, and it was just a sham like everything else. "I've always wanted to wear dresses like that," I whisper, convinced that no one cares what I say.

I run my fingers over the embroidered beads. *How much did it cost? And how much good could have been done with the money?*

"I've always dreamed of being a princess. To wear dresses like this. At the latest when I've reached a high position in business and am invited on a date or to a glamorous party…"

The silence in the room pierces me and I turn around, unsettled. All three Kings look at me as if my words mean something to them. As if they care about me. Next to them stands the masked driver, dressed in the same fine, tailored tuxedo as the others.

"I could buy you thousands of these dresses," Jaxon replies tonelessly.

"All of us," says Reece.

"But that won't do her any good," growls Sylvian. "Let's give her time to change."

They seem to agree with Sylvian's words, but none of them move. The idea of them leaving me behind suddenly becomes just as agonizing as the idea of them staying and continuing to look at me.

Once I'm alone, what Rachel has just done will come crashing down on me. Knock me down. I will fall and not be able to get up. Distraction is good for me. Not having to think about it, to push the memories away.

"We're such bastards," Reece mumbles suddenly, throwing the mask he's been holding to the ground and stepping towards me. His thumbs wipe over my tears, which I didn't know were there until just now, and his lips find my cheek. He kisses my temple. So innocent and harmless that my chest shakes with despair. He has touched Rachel. He fucked her. Nothing can ever make up for what he's done. "Mable…" he murmurs.

I look up at him, into the soft blue of his eyes, and then, following an impulse, I look in the direction of the driver. In a matter of seconds, I make a comparison.

The same stature.

The same suit.

Every detail is the same.

Zayn.

Reece and Zayn.

"Reece," I mumble back and everything becomes clear to me. If Reece has a twin… Then his twin is the nasty one. Then his twin slept with Rachel. But does that make anything better? It would mean that Reece – and his brother – are the biggest liars of all time. Who did I kiss in the lecture hall? Who was in bed with me?

The thought seems so cruel that I suppress it again before it can settle in my head.

"Why did you sleep with *her* of all people? With Rachel?" I ask, hoping he can explain it to me other than that he's a twin. What would be worse? That he let me believe that he wasn't? Or that he really had slept with Rachel? "I can never forgive you for that. Never," I breathe, not even sure what I mean anymore. Reece. He's the one I've trusted the most so far. He was my anchor when the others made me feel like they wanted to see me dead. And he of all people is supposed to have been dishonest in the most brutal way?

There are five Kings. Romeo is on the outside, but all four of the others were there.

How could Vance's hints mean anything other than that two of the Kings look like the same person? That's why there are five Kings, but just four faces I've seen around campus…

It seems too logical for it not to be true.

And Zayn is in the room with us. I'd just have to go over there and rip the mask off his face. Can that be true? Can anything about this horrible theory be true?

Jaxon steps next to Reece and pushes him aside. "It's not important, Belle." His words bring me back to the real issue with difficulty. "The question is, who haven't we fucked? You'll never be first for men like us. But maybe the last."

I inhale a hiss of air. As if he means those words! My gaze flits over them all. Which one of them is my biggest tormen-

229

tor? Which one of them has allowed all this to happen to me? Jaxon, who made me apologize to Hilbredge for trying to rape me? Or Sylvian, who shagged Harper so loudly that I woke up every single night from it? Reece? Who did nothing and had his way with Rachel?

Shit.

I am so done with these assholes.

Take what you need, Sylvian's words echo in my ear. *Take what you need.* That's funny! How is that supposed to work if I need more than sex in a changing room with a guy who's taken?

"We're going outside," Jaxon says harshly, puts on his mask and turns around.

I see Reece and Sylvian reluctantly want to follow him, and then I put all my eggs in one basket. A bad, worthless, unsafe basket, but maybe the Kings aren't the only ones who like to gamble anymore. "I don't think I can do this alone."

All the Kings turn around at the same time.

We stare at each other appraisingly.

Their masked faces and mine, which they can read like an open book. At least that's what they think.

Three kings desire me.

One is probably the biggest liar in the universe.

The other is engaged to my only friend, of all people.

And the last one is the most perverted asshole of all time.

But they desire me, and I would be stupid if I didn't learn to take advantage of that. They used me, so why wouldn't I use them?

"What can't you do on your own?" Sylvian asks harshly. A wild jungle in his green eyes. "Changing your clothes?"

I hold up the dress and nod.

Nothing happens for a breath, then they stir. They get into

position like predators, waiting with their black and gold masks on their faces.

"And how… should we help?" asks Jaxon slowly.

All the energy between us condenses. Electrified air. Breath held.

"Do I… really have to explain that to you?"

Jaxon hesitates, but then he steps towards me first. But Sylvian stretches out an arm to stop him. "No," he murmurs. "We're not going to take advantage of her condition."

Jaxon whips his head around. The black and gold mask suits him best of all. "Of course."

"What kind of condition?" I ask coolly.

"Something terrible happened to you today, Mable," Reece explains tonelessly. The restraint in his voice crumbles. "We wouldn't be gentlemen if we took advantage of you being beside yourself."

I roll my eyes. "You're not gentlemen anyway!"

"That's true," admits Sylvian. "We're the opposite of that. Still, after today, you should think three times about who you –"

"Oh, shut the fuck up, Sylvian." Jaxon pushes forward, rips off the mask and reaches both hands out for my head. I back away, bump into the table, take two steps backwards. He looks at me with a flash of anger. "What?" he growls. "What else are you going to do to torture us?"

I swallow hard. To… *torture* them? "Could what you did to me ever be repaid?" I ask them, whispering.

"No," says Reece.

"Yes, it could be!" Jaxon glares at me. "We've already given you everything back. You can study. You're under our protection. Romeo breathes by your side day in, day out. That's all you'll get."

"Good," I reply bitterly. "Then *you* won't get any more either." I take off my shirt defiantly and throw it on the table. I play with the lions, holding the meat right in front of their greedy fangs. Longingly accepting the resulting coldness that seizes my heart. Cold and blackness are what I need to get over the pain. *Am I becoming just like them? Insane and calculating?* "You don't really expect to ever get me back, do you?" I enjoy watching their faces slip away as I unclasp my bra and drop it to the floor.

The Kings' expressions each change in their own way.

Jaxon looks surprised.

Reece agonized.

Sylvian even darker than before.

"It must be a terrible thing for guys like you to want something and not get it, right? Or maybe no one wants you anymore because you're so obnoxious? You have to resort to impoverished girls like me?" I open the zipper of my skirt with an ironic smile and slowly slide it down.

Desire is in their eyes, longing. It's impossible that's all because of me. If they cared about *me*, they would never have done all these things to me before, would they? Vance must be right: men want what they can't have. No matter what the object of their desire is, it's all about the principle.

Right now, their desire for my body seems to be my only weapon. A weapon I can barely fire without the recoil throwing me to the ground. Because if I give myself to them to challenge them... I will lose again.

Again and again.

Can I play with them? Can I give back some of the agony? Or will I always succumb to them?

I don't know.

But I've never been the most cautious person in the world

when it comes to the Kings anyway.

"Too bad, isn't it?" I ask challengingly and drop my skirt. "We could have had so much fun together… So many hours of good, hot sex…"

The party is raging all around us, but it's quiet in here.

"Stop that," Reece demands harshly.

"What?" I ask lasciviously and grab my panties.

"Don't be like them, Belle." The blue in Jaxon's eyes deepens. "You don't have to pretend in front of us that you're some unfeeling bitch who thinks she can control us with her physical charms. Everyone at this fucking party is like that."

I look at him, and the thin mask I've been trying to hide myself behind breaks. The mask that should protect me. *Must* protect. "But what else am I supposed to do?" I ask them, trembling. "What do I have to do so that I don't fall again?"

"And us?" asks Sylvian, moving imperceptibly closer. "Have you ever wondered how far we've fallen? What we've had to endure to do what we do?"

"We've all had our experiences with this world, Mable," Reece elaborates. "It's not often that someone *doesn't* deserve it when we're cruel. Most of the scholarship students are Rachels. And if they're not Rachels, they're Brittanys, watching."

"Harper didn't warn you about us for nothing," says Jaxon with a wry but sad smile. "But it's too late now. We are here. And if you don't want to choose…"

"Then what?"

Jaxon gives Sylvian and Reece a meaningful look. They are now standing close together again, approaching me like panthers in the night.

And I step forward.

It seems to be the only thing I can do right now. Holding out my hands to Sylvian and Reece respectively, I pull them

233

towards me by the shirt and lean up to Jaxon.

I kiss him, hot and brief, then turn to Reece, who instantly lowers his lips to mine. He slides his tongue to mine and breathes in with feeling, then I break away from him and am grabbed by the chin from Sylvian. He pulls me in front of him, his mouth wide open, and devours my lips while the others approach me, kissing and touching me tenderly.

A frenzy takes hold of me and I float into a paradise of tongues, kisses and hands that surround me from all sides. I kiss Jaxon again and am touched by six hands at the same time. Again I kiss Sylvian, who becomes more dominant with every second.

Then Reece.

They surround me from all sides, stroking my hair, touching my shoulders, my neck, my back with their lips, and I know in this moment of heavenly closeness to them that it is worth it. No matter what happens, this experience is worth it.

The tingle is worth it.

The butterflies are worth it, bursting out of me and carrying all my infatuation away, across the room and beyond.

Jaxon finally grabs my hair roughly and kisses me for a particularly long time, while Reece pulls my panties down. I've already forgotten that the fourth masked person is in the room, and I realize that the thought that it could be Zayn doesn't bother me.

He stands in the shadows, watching us stiffly.

And then I've already forgotten it again, because the three men help me onto the table without letting go of me. They are so close and intimate and tender that I melt completely between them.

Reece sinks into a crouch in front of me, kisses my stomach, my inner thighs, but Jaxon grabs his shoulder. He looks up and they come to an understanding.

"You want me to make amends, don't you?" Jaxon asks me profoundly, then sinks between my legs and runs his tongue through my slit.

I hold my breath, can't believe he's doing this, and I'm engulfed by my lust in the next moment. Sylvian kisses me urgently and passionately, while Jaxon licks me and Reece caresses and kneads my breasts with his tongue.

Jaxon's stimulation between my legs makes me quiver inside. It's so hot and dark and so much like my forbidden dreams that I can't help but sink back.

I'm lying on the table. Legs spread wide, Jaxon's tongue deep inside me, I bring Sylvian and Reece towards me one after the other. Unlike me, they are still fully clothed. I hastily undo the buttons of their shirts. They laugh and take them off after my pitiful attempts.

My breath catches in my throat as they present their muscular bare chests to me, but it's nothing compared to the feeling Jaxon creates between my legs.

I reach for them with both hands, touching Sylvian and Reece's flawless skin as they bend over me, kissing and devouring me, and then I come. It's wonderful, intimate and deep.

My body feels hot and the orgasm sweeps through me. For a moment, I feel nothing but pure pleasure.

A smile on my lips. After all the heartache, it feels like I've been lifted to heaven. Jaxon straightens up. There they are. Looking at me like there's only me. The one true queen.

Even if they're not serious, I have to savor this feeling. In this one moment, it is true. In this one moment, it is real. They are here and they want me. And I want them even more.

As Jaxon steps around the table, he runs a hand over my heated naked body. "So beautiful," he murmurs.

Reece laughs at him, then he goes between my legs too. He kisses me right where Jaxon's lips were before and sends a thrill through my body.

Breathlessly, I look at Jaxon and Sylvian as Reece shoves his tongue deep inside me and starts fucking me with it.

"Poor, delicate little bird," Jaxon quips, running a long finger over my cheek. "If only she realized what it means to be desired by us."

"She should choose Reece." My gaze darts to Sylvian. His expression is serious. "He knows what he's doing."

Jaxon laughs harshly. Seeing them both above me while Reece licks me is too much for my brain. They're a blur. A figment of my imagination. Like they're not even real. "She'll kill Reece when she finds out what he's done. At least with the two of us, it's just our egos getting in the way."

"What…what do you mean?" I stammer, trying to prop myself up, but Jaxon playfully puts a hand on my bare chest, and Reece licks me even more greedily at that very moment, causing me to jerk and convulse on the table in front of them.

"For you, it's your ego," Sylvian replies. "For me, it's something worse."

"We need someone who will treat her well and not destroy her," muses Jaxon. "But unfortunately, Romeo just doesn't seem to like conscious women."

Sylvian growls something unintelligible, but Jaxon grins even wider. "Just kidding. We'd never expose you to Romeo, Belle baby." Jaxon runs his thumb over my lips and looks at me lovingly.

My breathing becomes more frantic as Reece begins to lick me vigorously.

"Oh, by the way, did I tell you that she likes spanking?" Sylvian asks with interest. "You shouldn't miss out on that."

"You're such assholes," I gasp, then they both grab my hand, and I hold them tightly as I come a second time. Under Reece's mouth, who licks me passionately and purposefully to orgasm. I tense up in Jaxon and Sylvian's hands and lift up off the table. This climax is much more intense than the one before. I have to hold onto them. They do nothing but stand above me, smiling at me and watching me. Only when I sink back onto the table, breathless and my whole body trembling, do they bend down to me.

Jaxon breathes a kiss on my lips before kissing my chest, and Sylvian slips his tongue between my teeth dominantly before he takes over my neck.

"Choose."

I open my eyes. Reece is standing at the end of the table, between my legs, looking down at me. "I can't," I groan. Choose one of them? Decide who I want? Impossible.

Reece quirks an eyebrow. "We can't all fuck you at the same time."

My chest trembles violently. *I see. Of course. It's about sex.*

"She just doesn't want to choose," Jaxon says smugly as he looks into my eyes and I still can't come up with a name. "Cute. How about she gets us all?" Jaxon extends his arm in Reece's direction. Reece reaches into his jeans pocket.

From there, he pulls out the velvet cloth with which he has already blindfolded me once. He drops it into Jaxon's hand and he spreads it out in front of my head. "You won't know who's starting. And it'll be all the better."

I imagine what it will be like to see nothing and feel everything, but I know I'm not ready for that. Give up control completely? No. I shouldn't let that happen. Not today.

Take what you need.

When I realize how vulnerable I am because Sylvian is with me and yet so far away, I have to fight back my tears. When I breathe his name, his hand tightens in mine, but he understands.

"You could push the girls off a cliff and they'd still want you." Jaxon's voice carries contempt, but I don't think that contempt is for me, it's for Sylvian. "How do you do it?"

Sylvian is silent. He leans forward, gives me a kiss on the temple and steps around me. As he undoes his belt and pulls my legs towards him, our eyes meet.

And there is everything and nothing at all. Love and so much betrayal.

He looks at me, spreads my legs, pulls my ass towards him, but we won't have sex. We will punish each other. Like every time we get close. He pushes himself into me and I am once again caught up in that current that always connects us. Under normal circumstances it'd be called love, but between us it's a sickness.

The green of his eyes infiltrates me intensely, and we look at each other as he begins to fill me. Deeper and deeper, harder and harder. The others are present, but they are meaningless now.

Sylvian's hands are on my thighs, his dick slides in me relentlessly and it's hot. So fucking hot to watch him fuck me with a rock-hard face.

Rock-hard and yet full of feeling.

"Shit, how does he do that?" Jaxon asks from far away and I look up at him. His gaze is much warmer than Sylvian's.

"You should have seen you both at the frat house," Reece murmurs. "It couldn't get deeper."

"Do you hear that, Belle?" asks Jaxon, chuckling. "Reece

claims we have a *connection*. What's it like when Sylvian fucks you? Do you like it?"

I nod. Sylvian's thrusts slow down for a moment.

"You know we're not going to end this until everyone has been inside you, right?"

I inhale hissing air and shake my head.

"Reece and I have been waiting a hell of a long time to feel you again. Have you had any others this semester, Crescent?"

"No," Reece simply replies.

"Well. I have rejected Clarisse and her plastic friends too, little Belle. Do you see what a gentleman I am that I've been giving up sex for weeks just for you? Because I've been waiting for this moment?"

"I don't believe a word you say," I mutter.

Jaxon and Reece snicker at each other.

"You will feel what it's like to get all our semen in you." They unbuckle their belts at the same time and I automatically grab their long, bulging dicks. Last semester I would probably have been ashamed to indulge my depraved desires so readily, but now I know that there's no point in holding back.

I run my hand down the voluminous length of both of them at the same time, and grab their balls. And yes, they are… full to bursting. I lick my lips nervously as Reece approaches my mouth and I take in his tip.

As soon as he has pushed himself deep inside my mouth, Sylvian becomes rougher again. He puts one hand on my stomach to hold me in place and fucks me hard.

Jaxon and Reece help themselves to my mouth one after the other and I love the feel of their wet dicks between my lips. Of course, Sylvian is thrusting far too hard for me to concentrate on Jaxon and Reece, but it feels good to me. It is hot and horny and heavenly.

I suck on one of them, giving the other a handjob in the meantime and feel Sylvian approaching an orgasm inside me. I deliberately hold back so that I can fully enjoy him coming inside me.

He pulls me towards him, pumps himself into me, closes his eyes and opens them again shortly afterwards. When we look at each other now, all the hardness is gone. Instead, a thousand other emotions flit across his face. Longing, love, fear, compassion, self-hatred, pain.

"Sit here, Crescent." Jaxon pulls Reece a chair over, then takes my arm and helps me up. "Sit on him, Belle," he murmurs against my ear, "but so I can look at you."

A shiver trickles down my spine as I obey. I sit on Reece's lap with my back to him, who pulls me against him and slides into me. Gradually, he enters me and we both moan. It feels incredible. Especially knowing that Sylvian was inside me just moments before. I feel so desired and cherished, and I'm endlessly wet.

Jaxon approaches me, runs his hand around my chin and waits until Reece is all the way inside me. Then he presses a thumb between my lips, which I lick greedily, followed shortly afterwards by his dick.

My moans are drowned in my mouth, which he fills deeply. I forget myself in the sensual feeling of being filled by Reece with gentle thrusts and caressing Jaxon at the same time. It's so hot and forbidden and exciting that I end up just closing my eyes and letting it happen. Jaxon inside me and then Sylvian. They both devote themselves to my mouth while Reece fucks me in my pussy.

I rise between them, feel one of their hands on my clit and am driven to orgasm by them.

I greedily grab Jaxon's and Sylvian's dicks, bring them to my lips and run my tongue over their tips at the same time, just before I come.

Reece lets go at the same moment I do and the storm of my third climax sweeps through me to the tips of my toes. He moans beneath me, holding me tightly by the hips as he comes inside me, and I savor the feeling of his throbbing hardness inside me.

As soon as I've caught my breath, Jaxon kisses me and pulls me up. The warmth in his gaze feeds my inner fire, and Sylvian grips my hair tightly, pulling me into his lips. Reece straightens behind me, and as he steps in front of me and kisses me, he spins me around to face the window at the same time. He pins me against it, his hand on my chin, and kisses me, demanding and greedy.

"Move aside." Jaxon pushes Reece's arm aside and takes his place in front of me. For a moment, I look up at him breathlessly because I know it's the last thing I ever wanted to do. To stand naked and demanding in front of him.

Despite everything.

But it's as if I'm particularly drawn to the danger he could pose to me and his penchant for the hideous. Jaxon Tyrell is insanely beguiling.

He smiles as he seems to divine my thoughts, reaching out a hand for my damp strand. "Why do I love it so much when we do this?"

I'm utterly intoxicated. His words can hurt me deeply yet also catapult me into the happiest spheres.

"You're so fucking hot, Belle. I don't think you have any idea *how* hot you really are."

"You... not a total turn-off when it comes to sex either."

Jaxon and the others laugh, and then he leans forward.

He kisses me softly, gently, like our kiss started in the lecture hall, and pulls me tightly into his arms. "I'm not just about sex, Belle," he whispers in front of my lips, trailing his mouth along my cheek, towards my ear. "I could do without, if that's what you want."

My eyes widen.

His smile is as dark as the night. Distraught, I look at Sylvian and Reece and then I realize.

"Ah, you want me to beg for it." I can't explain how I know that. But it suits him. It suits him like everything else, and the fact that he's challenging me like this – trying to get me to *beg* him to sleep with me after everything that's happened. That's Jaxon Tyrell.

There is no better way to describe him.

His lips go to my ear again. "I want to hear you beg, Belle. I won't do anything until you do."

I find it harder than ever to say the words. Giving in to my lust is one thing. Switching off my thoughts is easy. But *consciously* making a decision *for* him? Even if it's just this one brief moment?

"You know I'll never go that far," I whisper back.

His gaze darkens abruptly.

"I will never ask you for anything again. Rather, *you* should beg me to forgive you. Beg me to be so gracious to even *consider* forgiving you."

Jaxon's eyes narrow and the other Kings approach, as if to protect me from him in an emergency. "We'll see which one of us gives in first," he murmurs, then whirls me around.

I gasp as he pulls my ass towards him, spreads my legs and sinks into me with one thrust.

"Fuck, Belle, you don't know how much I needed that," he moans. He is wild and rough. To cushion his thrusts, I hold onto the window frame, seeing my reflection and wondering if anyone out on the open sea could be watching us. If so, they'd be in for one hell of a show.

Jaxon fucks me quickly and persistently. One hand on my hip, the other on the window frame to give us support. When Sylvian steps next to me and gently strokes my back and breasts, I burst.

I let all the lust that I've suppressed over the last few weeks run free and moan loudly and uninhibitedly with every hard thrust Jaxon gives me. He comes inside me and I couldn't be happier.

It's forbidden and hot and *very* forbidden and simply...

Beautiful.

As soon as he lets go of me and takes off the condom, he kisses me sensually. All of them do. Reece brings the dress, they help me into it, touching me tenderly, making me feel cared for.

As I stand there wrapped in the evening gown, my cheeks glow and I wish I could just stay with them forever.

"So?" asks Jaxon, turning to Sylvian. "Can you finally break up with your fake fiancée now?"

Sylvian steps back, takes out a lighter. The snap of the mechanism, the glowing spot of his cigarette and smoke in front of his face after he has taken the first puff. "No."

"And why not?" asks Reece. "Why hurt Harper and Mable?"

Sylvian laughs dryly, and I suddenly realize that it gives him *everything*. He loves that we suffer. Harper and I equally.

I open my mouth to draw him out, but Sylvian shakes his head warningly. "If Jaxon is going to force you to make a decision right now, you couldn't bring yourself to do it. And you shouldn't either. The same goes for me. Harper is hot so I fuck her. Why should I pass that up?"

My heart grows cold and my lips tremble, but the fact that Reece looks the way I feel gives me some strength.

"He's such a jerk, Belle," Jaxon sighs, straightening his suit. "I'm sorry we brought him in at all. He deserves you the least of all of us."

"I wanted it that way," I mumble and I look down.

The dynamic between the Kings intensifies. Whatever Sylvian has done with his words, there is more tension in the room. The limo driver – Zayn? – has disappeared. It's just the four of us. Three kings and their queen. Who won't be able to stand on the chessboard unscathed for much longer.

I open my mouth, but before I can say anything, the door bangs open.

Vance bursts in, taking a barrage of party music with him. "It's all done –" He falters when he sees us. "What the hell are you doing here?" Alarming panic enters his warm eyes as he looks me over from head to toe.

"Nothing," Sylvian growls and lets smoke escape from his mouth. "Get out of here."

Vance closes the door behind him. "Did you bastards make her cry?"

I quickly stroke my cheeks. Do I look that upset?

"Get out of here, Vance," Reece hisses. "We'll be right there."

Vance doesn't look like he wants to leave. His eyes fall on the clothes on the floor and he seems to be putting one and one together. "You miserable fuckers fucked her after tonight of all nights?"

"God," Jaxon groans. "Can you please let him bleed, Silvano. I'm so sick of this guy that I'd welcome the thought of him being tied to a bed in hospital for a few days."

Vance bares his teeth. There they are. Three kings, a pawn,

a fallen queen and no prospect of checkmate.

Or maybe there is?

Do I have any control over any decision the Kings make?

Is it still a game?

Or are they really serious about their remorse?

"You're not really blackmailing Vance with money he needs for his mother, are you?" I ask them. If they're going to pretend to be reformed, I might as well put them to the test.

Vance's face hardens instantly, but the Kings won't let me know what they think in response to my words.

"So?" asks Jaxon. "We wouldn't have to give him any money and could force him to work for us in other ways. So you can call us real Samaritans." He smiles wryly, and I see the corner of Reece's mouth twitch as well.

When Reece notices my look, he immediately becomes serious, as if he didn't want me to recognize his cruel streak.

"You're not Samaritans," I hiss. "You're blackmailing him."

Jaxon rolls his eyes, Sylvian's expression is hidden behind the smoke of his cigarette, but Reece speaks up.

"A Rachel is a Rachel, Mable," he repeats his words from before. "A pawn is a pawn. We don't have to do much for them to be who they are. Vance can't hide behind the fact that he needs the money for his family. He'd find other ways if he wanted to. We take advantage of the situation, yes, but we're not *forching* anyone."

"And what has Vance done?" I ask demandingly. "What could he do that's anywhere near as bad as your atrocities?"

Vance's eyes widen, but he remains silent.

"For example, he made sure that a girl called Eleanore got addicted to pills and ended up on the streets," explains Jaxon smugly.

Vance growls.

"She was a queen and Vance wore her down to the max without us."

"I trusted Zayn!" Vance snaps. "You can't blame me."

"We're not," says Sylvian dismissively. "But Mable asked what you *did*, Vance. And I still have the video of you dunking Eleanore's head in the toilet like it's a toilet brush on my phone. Do you want me to show them to her?"

I cross my arms in front of my chest to protect myself from the disappointment. Of course, I could have guessed that Vance is no innocent angel. But hearing that he doesn't even shy away from such low bullying makes me understand why the Kings are warning me about him.

When he notices how I close myself off from him, he shakes his head. "They're just fooling you, Mable. Maybe they have this one video of me, but no one recorded what *they* did."

"We don't just have this *one* video," Reece remarks tonelessly.

"What are you guys up to tonight anyway?" Vance asks the Kings and stands up to his full height. His muscles are impressive and his entire body fills the room with an overwhelming presence. "Are you going to humiliate her again? And Mable, do you really think they *won't*?"

"Don't you dare," Jaxon replies coolly. "Don't you dare even think you're someone who's going to protect her. We had to blow a lot of money up your ass this semester to get you to leave her alone, remember? Don't act like something you're not, Buchanan." Jaxon spits on the ground in front of him. "Now get out of here."

"You didn't give me the money to leave Mable alone," growls Vance. "I wouldn't have done anything to hurt her anyway."

"Oh yeah? Then why did we give it to you?"

Vance grinds his jaw. He doesn't seem to be able to say anything back, which is an indication that the Kings are right.

"Fuck," Sylvian groans, stepping out from behind me. "Do we really have to do this, Buchanan? What are you and what are we? Exactly. We're the ones who've chosen in our lives not to do other people's shit, and you're the exact opposite of that. But if it weren't for little fuckers like you whose loyalty can easily be bought, Mable wouldn't have woken up tied to a chair in the lecture hall last semester. Did you tell her that it was you and your childish pawns who cut up her clothes? Wasn't it you who kept breaking into her room to make her day a living hell? Where would we be without assholes like you? You can't talk your way out of it. Not even with your fucking family. If they knew what you do for the money you send them regularly, they wouldn't take a single dollar of it. You're not weak. You're not a loser. You are an asshole. That's why you work for us. You're just too good at your job for what you say you don't want to do."

Vance's eyes stare fixedly at Sylvian, but then his gaze shifts to me. Remorse and infinite guilt are etched on his face, and I realize that every single one of Sylvian's words is true. "It was… wrong…" he says hoarsely. "You don't have to forgive me, but at least I can help you now."

"Shut up," warns Reece. "No one wants to listen to you whine."

Do the Kings realize how ridiculous they are making themselves look with their behavior? Yes, I've just had heavenly sex with them. Yes, I like it when they ensnare me. But there's so much about them that I hate. And them stubbornly claiming that Vance is worse than them is one of them.

"You know what? I want to hear it." I bravely step forward.

"What if I just choose him?" I stop just short of him and look up at him. His dark charisma envelops me and I have to ask myself whether I'm venturing a little *too* far into the lions' den.

Sylvian laughs bitterly at my back. "I thought you weren't a whore? Then you're not going to start anything with Vance just to spite us."

I clench my teeth, trying to suppress the anger I feel. Again and again. Again and again, Sylvian hurts me in brutal ways when we've gotten close before. "Maybe I do it because I just want to?"

Vance checks the reactions of the kings, who don't make a sound before he takes the hand I hold out to him. "What do you have in mind?" he asks gloomily.

"Just a little revenge. Are you in?"

His expression slips when I put his hand on my waist and the other on my back. I imagine how this guy, who always radiates warmth, would really protect me from the Kings. It would be heavenly to trust him, to *be able* to trust him. To let go and be the little girl who nestles perfectly in his arms.

But then I think about how he, of all people, dunked the head of a scholarship student in the toilet. How he bullied and tormented her. How he drove her into a pill addiction. All of that becomes so real and yet it fades into the background.

It's not about him now.

Or me.

I just want to prove that I don't belong to *anyone*. Not Vance, not the Kings, not anyone. And if I get involved with the Kings, why not with one of the pawns? They're all the same anyway.

My gaze lingers on Vance's lips. I wonder what it would

be like to kiss him. There's more than my desire to prove to everyone in the room that I'm standing up for myself. A spark between Vance and me that tells me he's someone I can trust the most out of anyone. But can I trust myself?

As he slowly leans down towards me, Jaxon lets out a hissing breath.

"Don't you dare, Vance."

"Let her go immediately," Reece demands harshly.

Anger rushes through me. *Who do they think they are?* I hold his hand on my waist and turn in his arm. "Oh, he isn't allowed to touch me," I sneer. "But I can touch him, can't I? You don't have much leverage against me. Or are you going to threaten me with my sister's life? It won't take much longer, I bet."

Reece turns white as I take Vance's hands, push them towards my breasts and grimace in delight. I open my lips sensually, stretch up towards him and look at him sideways. Although he is only an object for my revenge, I am still hurt by the distaste with which he looks at me.

I freeze in his gaze. He doesn't let go of me, holds me all the tighter, but he is also infinitely angry.

"Are you doing all this just for them?" he asks with suppressed rage. "You'd offer yourself to a guy like me to get one over on *them*? Why, Mable?" he snaps at me. "I gave you that stupid footage and you'd get involved with them again?"

"That has absolutely nothing to do with it!" I gasp, wanting to tear myself away from him, but he holds me tightly, trapped in front of him, and I know why he's doing it. It's not because he wants to assault me. He wants to hear an answer. He wants to know why I fall for them over and over again.

Why I am so weak.

Why I become just like them instead of staying true to

myself and showing them in other ways that they are not worth my attention at all.

"You're becoming like them," he mumbles. "Yet *they* are the ones who should become like *you*."

"Enough!" Jaxon snaps.

Sylvian yanks me out of Vance's arms and Reece is with me, pushing the straps of my dress back into place.

The Kings don't ask what recordings Vance is talking about, and perhaps I should be wonder why. But they seem to be preoccupied with other thoughts.

"Enough, Mable," Reece says in such a bitter way that I feel bad for what I was about to do. "You don't have to overdo it and fuck every bastard on this campus."

Jaxon also stands in front of me, his arms crossed. The Kings have been watching the spectacle, presumably to see how far I would go and how far Vance would allow it. But now they're present again, posing as my owners. "If I catch you even *looking* at her again, thinking of more than your duty to us, Buchanan," Jaxon growls, "I will destroy you."

"Have you fallen in love with Mable, Buchanan?" Reece asks mockingly. "Is that why you stutter around her? Give her these rueful looks? Trust me, she'd marry one of us before she even shortlists you."

"That's not true!" I hiss, and Vance's eyes widen as if I've already forgiven him with those words. "You're all equally bad! Just because Vance did things for money doesn't make him worse than you! You have much more reprehensible reasons that aren't as obvious. It's probably about money too, so much more money, power and influence. You're all bastards, no matter how nice Sylvian's speeches are. I would never marry or even choose one of you. Never!"

Reece runs his hand over his mouth at my words, Jaxon

looks at me seriously and Vance smiles.

"Bring her on stage, Sylvian." Jaxon adjusts his mask. "And you." He fixes me. Dark and black and gold and menacing.

"What?" I challenge.

"You will choose one. Whether you like it or not." With that, he pulls the door open and rushes outside.

Vance grins at me as he follows Jaxon out. "We should do this again, Mable. You got balls."

"Unlike you," I mutter.

Sylvian laughs behind me, which I can't understand. None of the Kings or pawns have anywhere near the strength I have. They would probably howl and run home to mommy if they had to go through what I had to go through.

But I am stronger.

I will not give up.

And the way it looks right now, I just don't have to make a choice to win.

21

REECE

Vance takes Mable to a podium where the other scholarship students are already waiting. Maybe their dresses look as good on them as Mable's does on her, but I don't even look. My problem is that I haven't seen anyone else for months. Ever since she was in my room and gave herself to us. No. No, since she asked me for sex at the party.

It's agonizing. She has no idea how agonizing it is to want the same things as Jaxon and Sylvian. And it's even more agonizing not to want the same thing as Zayn.

As if he's heard my thought, he steps next to me. The mask hides his entire face. Wherever he's been, he smells like sex.

"Rachel?" I ask bitterly.

"I had to do it," he confesses to me. "It's so easy to manipulate her. She'll do anything, really anything I ask, and she's nowhere near as trite as a real hooker. I don't understand why you're missing out on this."

Without having to say anything back, he knows everything I think about it. *Jaxon, Sylvian, Zayn. They're all in my way. The only thing missing is that Romeo also wants something from Amabelle... Or Vance. Fucking Vance Buchanan. I'm going to have to kill him if this keeps up. She seems to have absolutely no idea what is even remotely good for her.*

Zayn sighs as he starts to look in the same direction as me. At Mable, who is now illuminated. Jaxon stands up in front of the four other ladies and the music is turned off. The conversations fall silent and everyone turns to the front.

"She's boring as hell, Reece," Zayn tries to me convince me. "A really boring, stupid virgin who thinks she can stand up to us. Can you please stop putting her on a pedestal she doesn't deserve?"

"No."

"But why? What do you want to do? Mourn her forever?"

"I still have no reason to mourn."

"Jax will never let her be happy with you."

Now I do look at him. "Jaxon is *nothing* without us," I hiss. "And we're supposed to listen to him of all people? Grow up, Zayn. It was clear we'd go our own ways sooner or later. Our college days are coming to an end."

Panic enters his irises at my words.

"Stop fucking Rachel," I demand harshly. "If you don't want Rachel to suffer after what happened, you're no longer a King."

"Maybe I don't want to be one?" he asks defiantly.

I feel nothing but contempt for him. "Go on then." Without waiting for his reaction, I turn away and make my way across the room. Every eye in the room follows me. I'm Reece Crescent. I'm not just anyone. I'm one of the ones they look up to. And I can do anything I want.

Above all, getting justice.

When Jaxon begins his speech, I stand next to him.

Rachel looks up at me. She expects me to save her. She sees in me a man that I am not. My smile is tender.

Tender. Because everything that follows will be hard.

Poor little Rachel. You will serve to show Mable what we *really* do with sluts like you.

JAXON

You're just as fucked up as I am.

That's what sets you apart from others.

Your morals crumble when examined under a magnifying glass. You didn't fall for us for no reason. You knew what you were getting yourself into. Your heart screams for more, your head says "fuck me", you want all of us and everyone just as much. We're not so different, Belle. There's bad blood simmering inside you. Maybe you'll never be cruel, but you're far from innocent either. You want us.

That alone proves that you long for the darkness.

All you have to do now is admit it.

Just say it: "Yes, Jaxon. Anything you want."

And it will happen.

22

MABLE

Jaxon paces in front of us. It's just like the last time. The same spectators, the same longing for a spectacle, the crackle of tension in the air. The black and gold mask that hides Jaxon's features.

The first time he stood in front of me like that at the party in the Alpha Rex house, I didn't know who he really was. Although my instincts told me to stay away, I already suspected that I would never be strong enough to do so. That he would make me fall for him over and over again.

Unlike the last time in the lecture hall, I am not sitting alone in front of him, but next to the others. The eyes of the masked crowd glide over me, giving me the feeling that I have become the center of their interest.

Collect fans.

That's it.

Do they even want me to leave? Do they want it to end?

Lien is sitting on the other side of the wooden stand. I haven't seen her in so long that I wasn't even aware that she was still studying at Kingston.

"Hi," says Jaxon, casually widening his arms. "Nice of you to honor us with your presence again."

Laughter from the audience. They know that we have no choice but to be here.

"Normally there would only be three of you left here today, but one of you had to defy the rules, didn't you?"

I raise an eyebrow, and it's not just boos that follow. It almost seems as if some people want to cheer me on. I'm still here. I'm still not broken. And I'm going to win. Not my place as a scholarship student. But in general.

"We're going to change the rules."

Silence fills the packed hall.

"This time, *we're* not choosing. *You* will." Jaxon's lips twist into a patronizing expression beneath his mask. "You will choose one of us. Each of you. And depending on who you choose, your future at Kingston will be decided. If you choose the right one, you will be his queen and win the game. If you choose the one who wants nothing more from you than sex, you'll go through to the next round unscathed. And if you choose the wrong one…"

A murmur goes through the room.

"I can only advise you not to do it."

The door to the hallway is opened again. Jaxon turns to his left as three men are ushered in. Although the inside of the wooden villa is beautiful, I can't enjoy the ambience for a second.

I recognize the three men immediately, even though they are wearing masks. They have just tried to rape me.

Pushed me onto a bed.

Pulled their dicks out.

Humiliated me.

A feeling of unconsciousness spreads through me, fear and panic intensify.

Sylvian leads the three men onto the stage.

They are far too close to me. Far too close for them to ever get close to me again.

Jaxon turns around and smiles mischievously. Combined with his mask, it's dark and almost disturbing.

"Ah, how wonderful of you to join us," he calls out.

The crowd falls silent. Everyone is waiting for the big bang.

"May I introduce you all?" he asks, turning to the audience. "Tonight's heroes."

It's like someone is twisting my guts. He's being ironic, isn't he? No. No, he isn't. You fell for it again! You've been tricked again!

No, no, no!

"We all know that one of the four ladies didn't want to play this year," says Jaxon smugly. "And no matter what we did, she still came back."

It seems as if an underlying anger is spreading through the crowd. I, on the other hand, feel nothing but coldness and powerlessness. I couldn't even stand up. Although there are no chains to bind me in place, I remain seated, my insides hollowed out by the realization that Jaxon has betrayed me again.

"We warned her, didn't we?" he asks with relish. "We warned her what would happen if she didn't leave. And did she listen?"

A clear "no" sounds from the audience.

"But it wasn't just our three heroes who showed her what it means to stay at Kingston without permission. There was also a heroine."

When Reece steps next to Rachel, she smiles broadly. She seems to think she has won. She probably has and everything up to this point was just for show.

All Jaxon's posturing.

Reece's loving nature.

Sylvian.

I want to jump up and just disappear, but the weight of my failure presses me down. Reece. Reece of all people! It's all been another farce? All another lie?

Jaxon notices me sitting stock-still and his eyes flicker. Then he just carries on. Continues with his praise of my rapists. "Rachel showed tonight what she's willing to do to stay at Kingston. She showed commitment. Courage."

I can't believe he's saying all these things.

"And she will get what she deserves in return. She will be the first to choose."

My stomach feels like a fist is closing around all my guts. I feel so sick that I want to scream, but I don't want to expose myself. Of course I should never have trusted them. Of course we had meaningless sex. But I... Fuck, I really thought it would be different this time.

Fuck, fuck, fuck!

"But let's get to our three heroes first. Have a seat."

The pawns push in chairs and my three rapists sit down. I can't see their faces because of the masks, but they look satisfied. There is no sense of guilt in their movements. No remorse at all. They look self-confident and seem certain they have done the right thing.

When the door opens again and three scantily clad women enter the room, I can't believe what's going to happen next.

"We reward those among us who show particularly great commitment, don't we?"

The crowd applauds, and Jaxon beams at the women, steps aside and motions each of them to sit on the lap of one of the guys. They are masked, but beyond that their bodies are clearly visible. Huge breasts, big asses and athletic figures.

They seductively lower themselves on the guys' laps, and the crowd cheers and roars as the women begin to tie the men to the chairs with their arms and legs.

There's something almost innocent about it. A college strip show that everyone enjoys. If it wasn't about them being rewarded for what they did to me.

I desperately search for Sylvian's gaze. Reece's.

Are they really okay with what's happening?

But they pretend I'm not even there, looking at the strippers just as enthusiastically as everyone else. I quickly look towards the door. I won't be able to escape if the crowd tries to stop me. I'm too far away from the saving door for that. How could I have been so stupid?

So naive?

Why didn't I just stay in the forest?

Why did I follow them voluntarily?

Tears sting my eyes as the cheers for my rapists continue to erupt and knock me down. There I remain, unable to move. Trapped and humiliated.

A movement at my back, a hand digging into my shoulder and a voice that is now more than familiar to me.

"Look closely," whispers Romeo.

I move my head around. Why should I even look at what's happening? He never wanted to help me, did he? He just wanted me to be tortured even more. He did what Jaxon asked. Made me trust him, and by extension, all the other Kings.

Romeo shakes his head in warning, then nods at the spectacle in front of us.

On stage, the masked women tear open the three guys' pants in sync to thunderous applause and rousing cheers.

I only realize that something can't be right when Romeo

picks up his cell phone next to me. He films the scene and some people do the same. Not the audience, but the masked 'pawns' on stage.

As soon as more than ten phones are pointed at the three guys, the women turn around. They rub their butts against the dicks of the assholes at the same time, stretching all the way and wiggling their hips. As the women lower themselves to the ground in front of them, the crowd gets louder and louder. They demand the three guys get a blow job in front of everyone. And it actually happens. The women lift their masks only slightly, take the men's dicks in their mouths and when they are deep inside them, they pull off their masks and throw them away.

Suddenly there is a cruel silence.

"No!" my rapists yell in unison, trying to get the 'women' away from them, but because they are tied to their chairs, they have no choice and have to let it happen.

Although everything about the three women looked sexy and hot, it wasn't three female beauties hiding under the masks. Quite the opposite. They are three men.

They suck the dicks of my tormentors for a few more seconds before turning around and presenting themselves to the crowd. The approval is muted. No one expected this turn of events.

But the cheers grow louder as the three cross-dressers make faces, sit back on the guys' exposed laps and move around on them. Apart from the fact that I was also shocked at first, the cross-dressers are impressive. Their bodies are well- groomed, they look like they came from a beauty salon and their faces are gorgeous.

And they seem to have a lot of fun shocking the students around us.

I don't know what to make of them being used to carry out the Kings' revenge, even if I am relieved at first. So relieved *not* to have been wrong this time that I just sit there and take a deep breath.

The laughter gets louder and louder so that my three tormentors start shouting and swearing.

Then suddenly everything happens very quickly.

The three men are each held down by two masked pawns. The strippers step back to make room for three more pawns.

Then three metal rods flash.

Screams.

Panic.

A helpless roar.

And the stench of burnt skin fills the air.

The roaring and laughter has stopped. Everyone stares in bewilderment at the three rapists who have been branded below their stomachs. Although the letters are mirror-inverted, I can see what is written on the metal bars.

Rapist.

"We have no room for rapists at Kingston." Jaxon's voice rings hard over the speakers, filling the room with a resonance that reaches everyone, drowning out even the howls of the men.

The pawns let go of my three tormentors.

"Get out of here," orders Jaxon. "Before we brand your forehead as well."

The masked pawns cut the men's ties. They scramble up fearfully, back away from Jaxon and disappear outside through the patio door. Everyone backs away from them as they flee, as if no one wants to touch them with a six foot pole.

"Well, let's get to our heroine tonight."

Rachel is held down in her chair, struggling. She gives me an angry look. I'm probably just as stunned as she is. I would never have expected this. *Never.*

"Rachel thought," Jaxon explains cheerfully, "that she could continue the game by forcing another scholarship student to do favors. She was wrong. We don't want scum like you at Kingston. Especially not ugly rapists. We've already taken care to make you deeply regret your little scheme."

"I didn't do anything!" Rachel yells at him, but someone immediately covers her mouth with his hand. She struggles against the hands holding her to the chair.

"But as I promised you, I'll give you the choice. You can decide. Which one of us do you think will save you?"

Rachel opens her mouth helplessly, looks at Reece, gives him a demanding look, but Jaxon shakes his head.

"You promised to help me!" Rachel hisses at Reece. "You just did! You fucking fucked me and you promised!"

Reece's face is hidden under the mask. He doesn't move, and it's hard to tell what he thinks about her words. Rachel's statement only confirms my assumption that Reece *must* have a twin. One who likes to fuck Rachel despite everything. Is Reece really willing to lie for him?

"No," Reece replies tonelessly. "I'm not going to help you. My words to you never had any meaning."

"That's not true!" Rachel scolds. "You're lying! You're a fucking bastard and you're lying!"

I'm experiencing déjà vu, only this time it's Rachel who's being paraded around by the Kings. I still don't know if I really like it. Even if she deserves it. She deserves every little bit of suffering.

"Reece is the wrong choice, Rachel," Jaxon tells her smugly. "But we all knew in advance that you would choose him.

Tonight, your family's accounts were emptied and the loans were maxed out to the last cent. The money went through your card and we've just withdrawn it thanks to some contacts at the relevant banks." Jaxon holds a paper bag in front of her face and lets her look inside. From where I'm sitting, I can see banknotes wrapped up in it. "And unfortunately, your family will think you stole from them. Which fits your character really well."

He holds the bag in front of Rachel's face and lights it.

She gasps as the paper bag catches fire. Jaxon throws it into a metal bowl that a pawn hands him, and I stare at all the bills that are simply destroyed.

"But that's just the beginning. Just the icing on the cake. Because we're going to make sure everyone in the entire United States knows what you've done. Your career will end before it ever begins. Not a single reputable law firm, not a single company will want you anymore. And neither will your parents. Do you want to send a scholarship student back to where she came from?" he asks the audience. "Here you go!"

The pawns pull Rachel up. She is dragged away, cursing and struggling. I watch as Romeo follows the group outside to the balustrade, pushes his way between the pawns, grabs Rachel's hair with one fist and cuts it off. Then he nods and the pawns simply throw Rachel over the balustrade into the sea.

My heart falters.

"That leaves three ladies."

My gaze flits back to Jaxon.

An awed silence fills the room.

Jaxon Tyrell stands in front of us as if the crowd is giving him energy. Quite different from how I would feel. I'd be nervous and flustered if I had to speak in front of so many people, but he…? *Am I starting to admire him again?*

"Amabelle Weaver." A snarl on his face, a clear look in my direction. "Which King do you choose?"

23

JAXON

It's just like last time. Three remaining victims sit in front of us, looking at me as if I were the ruler of the party, waiting for my lips to move and for me to continue the round.

Three women in the spotlight.

Three ladies wrapped in expensive dresses.

Three celebrated downfalls.

But I only have eyes for her.

I know that's a real fucking problem. Since when do I care if one of our ladies cries? Gets raped? Something happens to her?

You warmed my fucking cold heart, Belle. It doesn't feel good. Not good at all. And I hate you a little bit more for that.

The expensive dress Amabelle is wearing doesn't make her any more or less pretty than her cheap clothes from the supermarket. Fuck, how can I think that? How can I not care which designer dressed her?

How can I only care about her fucking skin under the fabric?

Although I should be concentrating on putting on the show for the ravenous crowd at my back, all I can think about is how we're fucking her. To keep my dick from getting hard from the memory, I run through all the reasons why I *must* not care about this woman.

Clarisse can help me advance. I have to marry her. Not just for the Kingston line. There's a lot of money involved. Without marrying Clarisse, I'll always be dependent on my father.

Good, but of course that wouldn't stand in the way of an affair with Amabelle.

Reece could marry her. He fancies her anyway and I can trust him to treat her well. If it wasn't for Zayn, and Zayn will always mean more to Reece than anyone else.

Sylvian…

Romeo for appearances?

Shit, am I thinking about the future again? I was just thinking about sex!

There you see in which fucking direction you're leading my thoughts, Belle.

"Amabelle Weaver." I widen my lips, but my smile is empty. If she knew how much I don't give a damn about this shit and that I'm only doing it to protect her, she'd choose me in a heartbeat with no further inhibitions. Unfortunately, she doesn't know. She can't see through me. She doesn't understand what it means that she is still sitting in front of us, even though we would normally have destroyed her long ago. "Which King do you choose?"

She looks at me and I can see from the expression on her face that she desires me. Me and the others.

"You understand the rules of the game, don't you?" I ask her, impatiently waiting for her to say Reece's or my name. "One of us will save you. Another will let you keep playing. And the last one means… your death. It's a wicked game.

267

Utterly reprehensible, the worst of its kind."

I know the entire crowd is wondering if we would really kill one of the scholarship students. We would. Only no one is allowed to know.

"You only have this one choice, Belle. Choose the right one or let the campus become your personal hell again."

"That really is a tempting offer," she replies ironically and the crowd behind us laughs. *Are they laughing with you or at you? It seems many of them no longer see you as the victim. No, for them you're the one lady that everything revolves around.* "But I'd rather choose hell than you."

Silence spreads through the room.

Sylvian and Reece approach me. They approach as if they crave Amabelle's precious blood, her cute little heart. She is completely in our hands, with no prospect of escape unless we let her go.

"You choose hell?" Sylvian asks. *I love hearing his voice carry all that darkness to you.* Would he be the wrong choice? Who knows? "I don't think you have any idea what awaits you there."

"If you don't decide, someone else will do it for you," Reece explains coolly. "Don't waste the opportunity to end it. Now."

"No," she replies nervously, "no matter who I choose, it will be the wrong one."

I smile, the crowd murmurs and Sylvian steps forward.

"You don't seem to have understood." Sylvian growls. "This is not a *request*. It's not an *invitation*. It's an *ultimatum*. You only have one choice. Make it." He is angry. But that's exactly what he wants. He doesn't want her to choose anyone. He wants her to stay away. Disappear, protect herself from us and all the shit he comes up with when he's not annoyed that Amabelle just won't listen to him.

"Are you still not afraid of what might happen?" asks Reece impassively. As if he didn't care about what was happening. As if he has long been sure that Amabelle would take him if her pride didn't get in the way.

"There's only one thing I'm afraid of," she whispers.

"Oh yeah?" I ask, stepping closer. My breath touches her skin and I enjoy the connection that has always existed between us. There's more between us. More attraction than I know what to do with. And more desire than I can fend off.

Not just because Sylvian wants to protect her from me, not just because Reece pines for her.

It's about me. Only about me.

No matter who you choose, I'm going to have a lot of fun with you, Belle.

"And what is this thing that you're afraid of?" I murmur, my voice quivering. "If it's not us?"

"That you're taking away the most important thing in my life. My studies. I want to stay at Kingston. But not at any price. You want something from me that I'm not prepared to give."

"You just have to give a name. That's all. Sylvian's, Reece's or mine," I summarize smugly. "And you won't even do that to save your fucking studies?"

She swallows hard.

What the hell is stopping you from just calling a fucking name? Making a choice? You don't really want us all equally, do you? How is that supposed to work?

"Maybe you haven't noticed," she whispers, "but you're not exactly guys a woman would willingly choose."

Again, the room erupts in restrained laughter and I laugh too.

"Are you really going to force me?" she asks anxiously.

269

All the masked students behind me follow our conversation with interest. It's not quite the show they're used to. But they don't expect us to let Amabelle win either. They think we're going to destroy her, one way or another. If it's not us that drives them away, it'll be the pawns and bitches at my back.

"Of course not, *Belle*," I whisper back. "No one will *force* you. If you don't choose, be prepared for us to *destroy* you this time. But so much more. Until there is nothing, nothing left of what you once were. Do you really think you know what it means to defy our rules forever? What it means for your *life*?"

"So I have to choose? Come what may?"

"Or you can leave," I clarify. *Belle, that really would be better for you. Go and stop exposing yourself to the masses demanding your downfall. The Kingston students who are jealous of your grades. The scholarship holders who want to defend their place. The women who see you as competition. Or the circle. None of them want you to stay.* "If you leave Kingston, it will save you from what will happen otherwise."

She raises her chin. And I know she won't give up. She will never fall, our beautiful queen. At least not if it' s not me who gives her the final kick. "Never," she whispers and I am grateful for her words.

I don't want our game to end any more than she does. I don't want her to leave.

I want her to stay.

And maybe it's *my* downfall that I'm fueling.

JAXON

Do you really think you could choose the right one?
Sylvian acts as if he could exist without me, but that's a lie.

Romeo will kill you rather than ever develop an interest in you.

Reece always shares.

And Zayn doesn't know how to leave girls whole.

There's only one you can choose if you really have monogamy in mind.

But it's not me.

24

MABLE

Jaxon grins. "Then choose. Now."

It could be so easy. I would just have to say a name. Reece. It's Reece. He's the one I trust the most. If it wasn't for Zayn. And because Zayn might be his twin brother, Reece is the one I can trust the least.

Sylvian. Do I need to think about it? Yes. Because if I pick him, he might part ways with Harper. Maybe the game will even force him to. But do I really want to be with him? No. He'll keep hurting me.

And Jaxon?

Who is he and who am I?

It would be easy to mention his name. I wouldn't mean it, but he would have his satisfaction and I could finally get off this vile stage. But what if I'm wrong? What if he's the one who means my death? What if he's just waiting for me to let him catch me so he can clip my wings?

Is Clarisse in the audience? Does she enjoy seeing that I will always make the wrong choice?

I open my mouth. All the Kings look at me through their masks. I have to say a name. Any of theirs. Maybe I'll just count off? *One, two, three, and the game is over...*

A massive shaking of the floor and a huge thunderclap suddenly interrupt my stream of thought. Jaxon looks around at everyone in the room, then the first floorboard cracks.

As abruptly as I stopped making my choice, panic breaks out in the room as a large part of the building suddenly sinks.

The crowd screams, the woodwork groans. Everyone runs for the doors, away from the hole that is forming more and more. It is as if the room as a whole is sinking, as if it is breaking in two.

Just a second later, almost all the Kings are with me and I am swept away. Off the stage, away from the floor, in the opposite direction of the screaming crowd, towards the balcony.

Another violent explosion underground and the house sinks deeper. It creaks. Beams break directly above our heads. Chaos ensues around us, desperate shouting, the first casualties.

"What the hell is that?" I hear Reece shout as Sylvian pulls me out in the opposite direction to the flow of people. We take a door deeper into the house as the ground beneath our feet crumbles away more and more, and then suddenly there's Vance.

He grabs me, heaves me over the broken floorboards.

"Over here!" he calls, beckoning the Kings to a window, which he runs to with me. I feel like I'm in a 2D computer game, as if I'm trying to run away from a gigantic enemy at my back. One look back and I see the catastrophic scale of the explosions. Half of the house has already toppled into the sea. The Titanic in house form. Students everywhere are struggling to stay afloat or sliding down into the sea.

When I reach the window, four hands grab me, pull off my shoes and push me through. Before I can brace myself,

I fall into the dark night, a silent scream of horror on my lips, and I hit the water hard.

I'm diving under.

Panic, shortness of breath, cold. Icy, icy cold. I struggle, fight my way up and am swept away again. Someone grabs my arm, I can't see anything in the darkness with all the sea water in my eyes. I can't do much more than pedal. The body pulls me past the lights of the house. My ears are filled with the sound of the waves and the screams in the night.

For a moment I think I'm going to die, but then there are four hands pulling me along.

"We're almost there." Reece is by my side.

Reece and… Reece.

I blink, my eyes are burning. I can't see clearly in the night. We swim towards a boat shimmering in the darkness ahead of us and four hands help me up. Then a woman stands over me. Her face is ghostly, haggard, but her gaze glows, even though I don't know how the hell I notice that in this situation.

She pulls me up. I fall over the railing into the interior of the small motorboat and catch my breath. Then I notice a fight behind me. Something is happening, but I'm too busy spitting up salt water to deal with it.

"We got her," someone says. "Let's go."

The boat's engine is started and the icy cold wind sweeps around my ears. As I straighten up and sink against the railing, I freeze.

Rachel.

She sits in front of me, wrapped in a blanket, and looks at me coldly.

"What the f–" I gasp and look at the others. I don't know any of them. There's just the girl with the haggard face.

"Hi," she says to me. It seems like she's happy about everything that's happened. "You're welcome."

"You're welcome?" I ask in alarm. "Where's Reece? He was just with me!"

"We didn't want him to come on the boat," explains one of the guys at the helm. He is wearing a thick winter coat.

"I'm Eleanore," the woman in front of me purrs and she hands me a blanket. "We didn't expect you to be at the party tonight, but Rachel told us about it. That's why we stayed around to save you, despite the blast."

"To save me?"

She smiles warmly. "Yes. It would have been really bad if you had been killed in the action." She laughs wildly. It's too dark to make out more of her than the deep, black hollows of her eyes and the haggard face. "We are the resistance, Mable. Together we will destroy the Kings."

I stare at her. My gaze flits to Rachel. Has she been part of this the whole time? "Destroy?"

"Yes," Eleanore replies happily. "Blowing up the house will only be the beginning. Every single one of them will get pay for what they did to us. Every single King."

"And where is Reece?"

She narrows her eyes. It seems to really bother her that I'm worried. "I hope he drowned after he got our lifebuoy against his head. Then we'll be rid of the first one." She smiles again. "You're on our side, aren't you?" she asks, and her words leave no room to disagree. "Because if you're not, Mable… Then it's going to end just as badly for you as for the Kings, who make you believe they would ever feel anything more for you than loathing."

I clench my teeth. What can I say? I'm on a small boat with a person who has admitted to carrying out a huge attack.

A lunatic. One who hates the Kings and the elite as much as I should.

But does that mean they deserve to die?

Does Jaxon deserve it?

Sylvian?

Reece?

And am I in a position to decide that? Or have I long since fallen into their darkness, that I would… choose them? Even though they brought all the suffering upon us scholarship holders? Am I well on the way to… forgiving them?

No.

No, I can't do that.

I look at the stranger called Eleanore with a tentatively convincing smile on my lips. She's the one Jaxon was talking about today. She's been through the same hell I have. She needs me as an ally. "Thank you," I mumble.

Her eyes flicker with approval, then she lowers her voice conspiratorially. "Let's destroy them together, Mable. Ready for the next round?"

Bonus material

CONVERSATIONS DURING PART 1
THE FOLLOWING CONVERSATIONS TOOK
PLACE WHILE I WAS WRITING PART 1

Shortly after the erotic scene at Crescent's party

Me: Hey, Reece.

Reece: Yup?

Me: You're such a dumb idiot, you know that?

Reece (mocking laugh, leaning back against the wall with his arms crossed): Oh yeah?

Me: You got clear instructions. Tease her, tease all of us. Show everyone how hot you are.

Reece, unimpressed: I turned you on. And your readers too. And that Mable of yours is…

Me: Yeah?

Reece: She's a little devil.

Me: Huh?

Reece: You don't see it?

Reece: She's impossible to handle. One guy doesn't stand a chance with her on his own. You really came up with a fun little bitch this time. Every man's nightmare.

Me: More like every man's wet dream.

Reece (shrugs): I'm gonna go screw someone else. Later.

Me: No! No, no, no, no! Come back, asshole! Reece! (I throw my keyboard and mouse at his head. And my mousepad. And I start screaming!)

***

After the limo scene with Jaxon

Me: Oh, I love you, Jaxon. You're so bad. A real bad boy, with your heart buried so deep you don't show a single emotion. I love you! You do exactly what I tell you. And then some.

Jaxon: I don't do what you tell me, sweetheart. You write all this for me. Because I want you to. Don't think you can boss me around.

Me: No, no, of course not (hiding shyly behind my iPad and doing everything Jaxon tells me to).

Jaxon: Good girl.

***

Right at the beginning, when there wasn't much sex in part one…

Me: Why do you even sleep with them?

Mable: I don't. But why would I say no if they're into it? Have you seen what they look like?

Me: Yeah, they're hot. But don't you seem a bit naive starting something with them?

Mable (thinks for half a second): No, why? The Kings are the naive ones if they think I'm hanging around them because I'm in love.

Me: So you have thought this through.

Mable: Let's just say I'm taking advantage of the opportunity. I don't get why women can't sleep with whoever they want. Guys do it all the time and no one cares.

Me: Hm, yeah…

Mable: What?

Me: I'm not getting much done today. I'm nervous about the cover.

Mable: Oh, now you've got me nervous too.

Me: Want to be nervous together?

Mable: You could start writing about… Halloween. I get the feeling it's going to be a pretty dark night.

Me: Depends on whether Jaxon's in a good mood. Should I ask him?

Mable (raises an eyebrow): If you let Jaxon decide everything, I'm out. That guy's seriously messed up.

Me (panicked): Shh! Are you insane? If he hears you, Halloween won't just be dark – it'll be bloody.

Mable: Are you saying that you actually listen to him while writing? To that… that…

Me (quickly shutting my mouth): Things have gone pretty well for you so far, right? If we both stay calm, sweet, and nice, maybe he'll show some mercy…

Mable (stares at me, shakes her head in disbelief, and walks away…)

***

Me: Okay, so what do you guys actually like about Mable?

Jaxon: Aside from her fuckable mouth, you mean?

Me (rolling my eyes): Yeah, Jax. Aside from her mouth.

Jaxon (ironically): And I'm guessing aside from her tits and that gorgeous ass too?

Me: Yeees.

Jaxon: Nothing. That's enough.

Sylvian (facepalms): He just doesn't want to admit she's the perfect combination of a challenge and easy to get. Touch her once and her heartbeat speeds up. She's sensitive, observant, quick to catch on, and she stands up for herself. She won't let anyone push her around and she never would've started anything with you, Jax, if we hadn't been there.

Jaxon (snorts): You're just a poor, pathetic, lovesick boy, Sy. Mable's just like all the others.

Reece: No, she's not.

Jaxon: Oh, just because she wants to fuck you? What makes her so different? The fact she's always walking around with that stupid ponytail?

Reece: That she wants all of us.

Jaxon (smug): Who wouldn't?

Sylvian: You know what he means, Tyrell. Nobody wants all of us at o n c e.

Jaxon (mocking): Wow, so she's a slut. Congrats.

They all roll their eyes.

Me (jumping in): Can we give the readers something more than just Mable's hot body? What makes Mable Mable?

They all just stare at me blankly.

Me: Okay, never mind… This is going to be the most meaningless caption ever.

Jaxon: Not my fault you describe her mouth like that. Make her ugly. Then I'll show you what else she's got to offer.

Me: I'll make *you* ugly.

Jaxon (grabs my red pen and glares at me): Don't you dare.

***

During a date with Reece — which later got turned into the frat house scene where Reece and Mable talk about virginity

Me: Reece?

Reece (mockingly polite): Yes, ma'am?

Me: You got clear instructions, right?

Reece (curious): Give Mable an indescribably good date?

Me: No, it can't be indescribable because I have to describe it. Okay, why are you finally alone together?

Reece: So we can talk without anyone bothering us?

Me: No! No! No! No! You're supposed to –

Reece: Fuck?

Me: Yes!

Reece: Not gonna happen.

Me: No!

Reece: Have you seen her? I don't think she even knows what sex is.

Me: Bullshit!

Reece: She's way too inexperienced. Why does she have to be a virgin?

Me: She's not!

Reece: Oh, now you tell me.

Me: Yeah! So you'll ruin the date!

Reece (smug): Your readers will see it differently. I'm so damn attractive. Definitely points for #TeamReece.

Me: There is no Team Reece. You're not even a team.

Reece (offended): Hello? Then what am I? Some side character for decoration?

Me: Yes!

Reece (gives me a doubtful look, then gets up from the table): Well, fuck Mable yourself then.

Me (muttering): I hate you...

***

When I wanted to extend the poker scene and Jaxon and Sylvian suddenly started talking about their fathers.

Me: Hey, what are you guys doing?

Jaxon: Talking. It's fun. Leave us alone.

Me: This is a sex scene.

Jaxon: Yeah, so? We can pick it up again anytime.

Me: But this is a sex scene!

Sylvian: This is important.

Jaxon: More important than our lovely princess's orgasm.

Zayn: Well, she's not crowned yet, right?

Me: Stop with the nonsense and get back to the hot stuff.

Jaxon and Sylvian look at me like I'm speaking another language.

Me: Hellooo?

Zayn: Let the two have their deep moment, Jane. They're going through it and need to exchange silent looks that no one else understands.

I slump back in my chair with a sigh, flipping through a newspaper while I wait to continue writing. Always these guys, using their mouths to *talk*.

✳✳✳

When I was figuring out Mable's last blow before she'd give up.

Me: Okay, we still need to decide what Mable's final punch will be before she throws in the towel. Anyone got a creative idea?

Reece: Ugh, do we have to? Can't we just have sex instead?

Jaxon (smacks him on the back of the head): No, idiot.

Mable (sitting far away, not even looking at them): You have to hit the Kings where it hurts.

Me: In the balls?

Mable (snickering): Yeah. But I can't get close enough to hurt them physically.

Me: It has to be something that gets you fans. Something super cool. But all I've got are feminist ideas. Nothing against feminism, but in erotic romance, that's not exactly *sexy*. A middle ground would be perfect. Jaxon? Any thoughts?

Jaxon (raising an eyebrow): Amabelle as a feminist? What's not sexy about that?

Me: So you wouldn't mind if she walked around in manspreading jeans to make a statement?

Jaxon (cold laugh): The moment I "spread" my masculinity, it's without jeans, and then she'll…

Me: Okay, never mind.

Jaxon: … want to suck me off. So she might as well pretend to be the kind of woman who'd never start anything with guys like us.

Mable (yelling across the room): Feminism's got nothing to do with prudishness! As a feminist, I can fuck brainless guys like you just as well. You sleep with Clarisse, right? Equal rights for everyone.

283

Me (still stuck without a good idea): Clarisse… Clarisse, could you somehow mess with her, Mable?

Mable: Does she even have enough brain cells to realize I'm messing with her?

Jaxon snorts.

Sylvian (reluctant): Jane, there's nothing she can do. We've played this game before.

Me: Could she hurt you with a viral video?

Sylvian: No.

Me: By making fun of you?

Jaxon: No.

Me: By saying only one of you is a real man?

Reece (rolling his eyes): No.

Me: Then tell me what I should do!

Jaxon: Nothing. Just don't let her screw up even more.

There's a knock on the door.

Me: Yeah?

A huge, muscular guy steps in, shoulders as wide as the doorway. Everyone stares.

Vance: Hey.

Mable (nervous): H-hi.

Jaxon (rolling his eyes): Jane, you're not seriously putting this pawn on the board, are you?

Vance (walks in, ignoring Jaxon, looking annoyingly hot): If needed, I've got an idea.

Mable and I are basically drooling, and I automatically start writing because I have no choice…

Me: Hi, Vance, come join us and tell me how good you can fu– eh, help Mable.

Vance (with a crooked grin): No objections to the first one.

All the Kings look at me.

Reece (whispering): Vance is worse than us, huh Jane?

He's done things I wouldn't even think of.

Jaxon (smug): Right, that's my job.

Sylvian (coldly): Vance is the epitome of a dirty bastard who'll do anything for money.

Vance (sitting down casually): That was me. Until now. Time to help Mable so I can screw you guys over.

Suddenly, they all jump up with clenched fists, Sylvian pulls out a knife. Looks like they all want to kill each other.

Me (holding my red pen over the manuscript): Sit. Down. Now! Or I'll make all your dicks two inches shorter!

Luckily, they listened… phew.

***

When I had to plan the ending of part one…

Me: Hey, guys.

Three Kings sit down in front of me.

Me: What do you actually want from Mable?

They stare at me in disbelief.

Reece: You don't know?

Me: You want to destroy her, right?

Reece: I wouldn't put it like that.

I look at Jaxon.

Jaxon (smiling): Nothing. I don't want anything from her.

Sylvian (snorts): I don't want to destroy her. I just don't want any of us to do it.

Me: So you want to protect her.

Sylvian: How can I protect her from me?

Jaxon (suddenly paying attention): It's not about her. We're just using her to reach our goals.

Me: And "using her" means destroying her?

Sylvian (jaw clenched): No, Jaxon wants to hurt her. He wants to hurt everyone. But his usual game doesn't work on her.

Me (sorting papers): Okay, okay, maybe that's something for part two. But what's the focus now?

The Kings look at each other one by one.

Reece: I think we just like her. That's all.

Me (frowning): You're not exactly nice to her.

Reece: Because we like her. She needs to keep her distance.

Me: But she doesn't.

Reece: Well, you're the only one who can change that.

Me (laughing): You think I control Mable?

Reece (shrugs): Yeah, who else?

Me (shaking my head): Fine, so you like her. But how do I wrap this up? Do the readers need to think you like her too?

Sylvian (expression darkening): We tie her to a chair. Let her believe for a while that –

Reece: Man, you're not gonna shoot her, are you?

Sylvian (even darker): Haven't had a reason not to yet.

Jaxon (listening calmly): So a chair, and then?

Sylvian doesn't answer.

I look at Jaxon again. He's the king – he should know what's next.

Jaxon: I'm gonna fuck her.

Me (holding my breath): Just like that?

Jaxon (matter-of-factly): Just like that.

Me: You… all of you…?

Jaxon raises his eyebrows.

Me: I mean… if you want… me to write that, then…

Reece: God, does this woman write erotic romance or is she a nun?

When I wondered if I should end part one right after the frat house sex scene.

The Kings laugh, and I throw an imaginary crumpled note at their heads.

Me: Fine, so if you're having sex –

Jaxon: Yeah?

Me: What's the cliffhanger?

Silence.

Me: Hey, think with me here! You can't just think about sex and forget the cliffhanger!

Jaxon: How about, for a change, we don't have a cliffhanger at all?

Me: That's not possible!

Sylvian: Maybe you'll come up with something later.

Me: Jaxon could tell you guys something... something you really didn't see coming.

Jaxon: Like what? That she's a slut and I'm only using her? Wow, shocker. Been saying that for three hundred pages.

Me: It has to be mean, but not *too* mean. Otherwise she won't want you in part two.

Jaxon just laughs.

Sylvian: Just keep writing. You'll change the ending later anyway.

Me: You know me too well...

Sylvian (winks): Because I mess with your mind all the time.

Me: Fine, who's first?

Reece: Is it gonna be 18+?

Me: I need to know beforehand, otherwise you'll start arguing in the middle of the scene and we'll end up with pages of pointless chatter and no action. So, cooperate, please.

Jaxon: Why are you even asking?

Me: I don't want you thinking you have certain privileges here.

Jaxon: I don't just think it…

Me: You're not doing it out of the goodness of your heart.

Jaxon (cold laugh): And the others are?

Me: Sylvian… maybe a little?

Sylvian says nothing.

Me: Okay, so not you either. Reece? You like her!

Reece: I don't want to.

Me: What?!

Reece: Not really my thing.

I look at him, confused.

Reece: What? We might actually end up bonding. You know, first time and all that… nope.

Me: You're afraid of… bonding?

Reece: And?

Me: What's wrong with you guys? I thought you'd fight over this. At least you, Sylvian!

Sylvian (sighs): I don't think we should decide this. Seems more like Mable's call.

Mable: Uh.

Me: Can you just make the call already?

Mable (blushing furiously): Okay, so Reece was…

Me: Yeah?

Mable: He was always nice to me.

Me: Okay, got it. Too nice. So which one of these bastards do you want? Sylvian or Jaxon?

Mable (turning red, avoiding eye contact with any of the Kings): I just can't… you know… because…

Me: I don't get it. You want *him*? After everything he's done to you? Why are you always like this?

Mable: Like... addicted to darkness?

Me: No, so predictable! Surprise the readers for once.

Mable (guilty): Sorry. I think it's because nice guys are always so boring.

Me: You said it...

***

While writing the last thirty percent of the book...

Me: My dear Kings...

Jaxon (ironically sweet smile): Yes, Jane?

Me: I love you so much. I adore you.

Reece: Didn't see that coming.

Me: You're so cruel and nasty, it's almost unbeatable. And there's probably no one else who would dare to write down just how awful you are. Except me.

Jaxon (unbothered): Not like our colleagues C, Ly, and so on, you mean?

Me: They never hurt my girls.

Sylvian (crooked smile): I seem to recall Crack Amber with those drugs...

Me: That was justified! More or less! She wanted to rat him out, that's why he did it. But you guys... you don't even need a reason to be awful. And I love that. Makes me love you even more now.

The Kings exchange glances.

Jaxon (leaning back casually): So you're saying you love us because we're... such bastards?

Me (with a look of pure adoration): Yes!

289

Jaxon: While we're breaking her mind until there's nothing left?

Me: Yes, yes, yes!

Jaxon: While we show no mercy? Break her down to nothing?

Me: Yessss!

Reece: Stop it, she's about to come.

Me (trying to compose myself): I don't think anyone's ever been this evil before. And you know what's so great about that?

Sylvian: What?

Me: Mable's going to get her revenge. It'll be bittersweet. By the end, you'll each have cried at least once, and I will lovingly describe every single tear…

The Kings stare at me, puzzled.

Jaxon: She's talking shit, right?

Reece: I don't think so…

Sylvian (cold laugh): I don't even know what tears are. How do they work?

Me (with an even more smitten look): I'll show you. Oh, Sylvian, you're gonna have it so rough. And Jaxon, I'll drag you down so far you'll cry your eyes out. And Reece, you'll suffer in silence. You'll question your entire existence. You'll all be begging me to kill you, because it hurts too much.

The Kings look horrified.

Jaxon: Okay, hand over that stupid book, she's lost her mind.

Reece: Last night was too much for her, eh?

Sylvian says nothing. He's the only one who knows I'm right.

Me (satisfied): Get ready for hell, my little kings. I can't wait.

When Jaxon still wanted to keep Mable out of the game, but she had already taken the wheel.

Me: Come on, Jaxon. Got a killer last line for me? How am I supposed to wrap this up if you won't let her play anymore? What's she supposed to do now? You have to give her a chance. Hello! Get over here.

Jaxon (annoyed): She crossed a line. She knew what would happen.

Me: No, yeah, okay, but you've gotta react differently. Give her a chance!

Jaxon: Jesus, what kind of chance?

Me: Don't yell at me.

Jaxon (runs a tense hand through his hair): Your plot sucks. Come up with something else.

Me: No.

Jaxon: I'm not giving her a chance. She blew it. You should've saved those revenge plans for when they made more sense.

Me: I've already told you I'm not in control of Mable.

Jaxon (furious): Then get in control!

Me: Again, if you don't let her play anymore, it's all been for nothing. All you have to do is give a mean little grin and say, "Okay, last chance." Don't mean it too seriously and we're fine.

Jaxon (rolls his eyes): That goes against my principles.

Me: I'm sorry.

Jaxon (jaw tight): Fine, I take back what I said. But she better be convincing. I'm not being played. If she wants something from me, she has to give something in return.

Me: Got it. (Starts typing furiously, deleting Jaxon's last line with satisfaction.)

***

Last thirty percent.

Me: God, I'm editing the last part and… why are you always such filthy bastards? I hate you! A little more with every sentence! You're so mean! Such incredibly mean assholes!

Mable: Yeah, tell them, Jane!

Jaxon (unimpressed): Sorry, but which one of us is actually coming up with all these twisted ideas? I seem to recall it wasn't me…

Me: Yes, it was! You said I should do whatever you tell me.

Jaxon (cynical): And that's how you want to talk your way out of it? Jane, no one's really forced to do anything. You *want* this. You *want* to put Mable through this. Which makes you the only guilty one here.

Me: No!

***

When I wondered when the pre-order should start…

Jaxon: Sit down.

The Kings take their seats.

Jaxon: Put your phone away, Zayn.

Zayn rolls his eyes but puts his phone down.

Jaxon: I've got something important to discuss.

Reece: I should hope so, otherwise you dragged us here for nothing.

Jaxon (lets the silence drag on before speaking in an ominous tone): We have to decide when Jane will upload the e-book so readers can pre-order it.

Silence.

Zayn: Do we have to do this now? (reaches for his phone again)

Jaxon shoots Zayn a look so deadly he puts it away again.

Sylvian: How are we supposed to know the perfect timing?

Jaxon: We're the Kings, the best at Kingston. If we don't know, who does?

Reece (pretending to take it seriously): Okay, what are the options?

Jaxon: Tomorrow. Or next week.

Sylvian, Zayn, and Reece exchange looks and then burst out laughing.

Jaxon: Damn it! (slams the table so hard everyone flinches) Don't you get it? If the "visibility" comes too soon, it could hurt the book. And if it doesn't release on May 28, that could be just as bad! And if Amazon screws up part one, this won't be an epic series – it'll be a very short detour to Kingston. Fewer wild parties, less sex, fewer filthy things we can do with Mable. Are you taking this seriously?

The Kings all look like they've got stomach aches.

Reece: Wait, are you saying our entire lives depend on this? On fucking Jeff Bezos?

Jaxon (dead serious): Yes.

Sylvian (growls, pulls a gun from under the table): We shouldn't leave this to chance.

Zayn (eyes wide): I think we should use all means possible, but –

Jaxon (firm): No. Even then, we can't beat that algorithm. So, what's the best timing, assholes?

***

Jaxon: Hey, what's wrong, princess? (strokes my neck)

Me (laying my forearms on the manuscript, crying): It's so good!

Jaxon: Huh?

Me: My *Catching Beauty* series! Way better than anything else I've written!

Jaxon (looking up, the Kings moving closer because he keeps massaging my neck, and damn, he's good at that, the bastard): Did she really say that?

Me (whimpering): Yes! *Catching Beauty* is unbeatable! Have you read it? It's packed with such brilliant dialogue I'm jealous of the author the whole time. Whereas you guys...

Jaxon (threatening): Yeah, what?

I wail even louder.

Crack walks in, sees the scene, whistles, and signals for Wres and Ly to join him. When he's almost at Jaxon, Jaxon steps in front of me, possessive.

Jaxon: Her breakdown is nothing. She's gonna write my story now. You're old news. Leave.

Crack (laughs, unbothered because Jaxon's colder inside than he is): Okay, kid. Grow up first, then try stopping me.

Ly (joins him): Us.

Zayn (steps forward with all the Kings): Who, you guys?

Crack (evil laugh): Wow, five rich boys still living with their mommy. Quite a challenge, right, Wres? Ly?

Wres laughs darkly.

Vance (emerging from the shadows, crossing his arms): It's my story too, motherfuckers. Back off.

Crack, Ly, and Wres laugh harder, and soon they're all facing off. The Kings barely have weapons, but they're heirs to America's elite and will one day rule the world. Crack, Ly, and Wres are as deadly as guns, but not exactly diplomatic. The Kings will win. Because they don't fight; they make others do it for them.

Me (looking up through tears): It's no use if you kill each other!

Their murderous stares instantly soften.

Ly: What's wrong, little Jane?

Me: *Catching Beauty* was so much better! (more wailing)

Sylvian and Jaxon roll their eyes.

Sylvian: And you're just figuring that out now? Ages later?

Me: That's what's so awful! I got such a bad review for part two back then that I thought it was all worthless, but now I realize I should've never doubted myself! (loud sobbing)

The Kings, Vance, Crack, Ly, and Wres all look annoyed.

Me: No! With the Kings, I *should* doubt! And rightly so! It'll never be as good as *Catching Beauty*!

Wres steps up and smacks me on the back of the head.

Me: Ow! What the hell?

Wres: You needed someone to knock some sense back in there.

Vance: I'll do the same next time she threatens with that red pen.

Crack: You let her scare you with that pen?

Jaxon (shrugs): Wanna risk a smaller dick?

Crack (laughing): Ah, now I get it. If you let Jane hold you back like that, you'll never amount to anything. You have to take over. Only you should decide what happens.

Reece: Is that helpful advice or do you just want to see her shrink us?

Ly (stepping forward): Trust him. Think Smoke would've been impressed? Remember what Smoke did? Compared to him, Crack's an angel.

Crack: Well…

Jaxon (folds arms): We don't need your help. Who even are you? Three losers with illegal side gigs who convince themselves they're saving women by making them work for you or forcing them into prostitution? Maybe you're well-written and funny, but compared to us, you're nothing.

Ly: Wow, you're a cocky little shit.

Sylvian: Your appeal's nothing but violence, cruelty, and anal with virgins. So impressive. Now go. And don't forget your walker – it's still outside.

The Kings grin, Crack and Ly laugh.

Me (sniffling): Make jokes all you want, you're not even close.

Reece (eye roll): You wrote a whole intro to a bully romance/college romance/reverse harem. If you can't imagine what can happen in that…

Me (tearful): I should stick to dark romance with a kidnapping. I'm good at that.

The Kings look like they want to kill me, so Crack, Ly, and Wres step in front of me.

Ly: Leave her alone.

Jaxon: You don't get a say in this. You're out.

Ly: I've known her ten books long. Three of those were mine. You have to be patient with her. Don't let her control everything. Be the filthy bastards you can be. Let the whole book drip with tension, use all your weapons, and sometimes, be nice. You can't hold back anymore, or Jane will doubt herself so much it'll ruin everything.

Jaxon (grinding his teeth): Fine. Now get the hell out.

After finishing part one.

Me: Hello, everyone.

The Kings are partying, it's vacation. Loud, thumping music.

Me: Hello, everyone!

Reece chokes on his drink, spinning around.

Sylvian, about to light a cigarette, glances up.

Jaxon (pushes a girl off his lap): What?

Me: Party's over.

They stare at me like I just killed the mood. Even Romeo (who I'm slowly starting to like) frowns.

Me: We have to start writing part two.

The Kings keep staring. Zayn's the first to laugh. Then they all do. Sylvian turns the music back up, Jaxon gets a blowjob.

Me: I'm serious!

They ignore me. Great.

I look around helplessly. Vance is in a corner, almost like he's somewhere else.

Me (running to him): Help me!

Vance (studies me): With what?

Me: The Kings need to start part two!

Vance: Seriously, Jane, you haven't even finished part one.

Me: Almost! I deserve a reward! Plus, I've got ideas for part two that will top everything! It's going to be my best book ever!

Vance (deflecting, in true Smoke fashion): You say that every time you think of something good. Then you write three sentences and start looking for other work. Let them have their fun and come back when you've really finished part one.

Me (furious, holding up my red pen): Just like before, I can decide how big your dick is!

Vance (looks like he wants to snap my neck): You're such an annoying bitch. (He pulls out a gun I didn't even know he had and fires into the air.) Party's over!

Immediately, all five Kings group together, glaring like a pack of snarling dogs.

Jaxon: Says who? And why would some insignificant little mercenary dare to speak to me?

Reece: Insignificant, yeah.

Romeo rolls up his sleeves, flashing brass knuckles I didn't know he had.

Sylvian (finally lights his cigarette, nodding at the door): At that range, you'll only hurt yourself with the recoil, Buchanan. Get lost.

Me (clearing my throat): If you don't start part two right now, Vance will be the next one to sleep with Mable.

Jaxon (expression darkens): You wouldn't.

Me (triumphant): Wanna stop me? Get to work on part two!

Four hours later...

Vance: Well? What did I say?

Me: Yeah, yeah.

Vance: Didn't I tell you to finish part one first?

Me: Yes.

Vance: And what happened with that?

Me: Nothing.

Vance: Exactly. Because you wouldn't cut anything, you couldn't fix the plot holes.

Me: Not true.

Vance: And you didn't make that scene a thousand percent hotter. Way better than before.

Me: What do you care? You're not even in it!

Vance: Oh, I love being right. And besides –

Me (glancing at my red pen): No.

Vance: Two inches bigger.

Me: That'd make it a horse dick!

Vance (smirks): Do it.

Me: No! I'm not writing that you've got the biggest. Never!

Vance: But deep down, you know it.

Me (a bit guilty, since I've honestly never thought about size before – though in a reverse harem, it does kinda matter): Goodnight, Vance.

Vance: Goodnight, Jane. Sweet dreams… (filthy grin)

Me: Oh, for fuck's sake!

***

Part one releases

Me: I'm so nervous I can't even write a dialogue for you guys.

Jaxon: That's nothing new.

Me (switching to turbo mode): Yes it is! I'm great at dialogues. Like when Mable shut Reece down – that was pure magic.

Jaxon (pitying look): Yeah, Reece. He's happy with crumbs.

Sylvian (interested): Are you two fighting?

Romeo (always nearby, like Jaxon's shadow): Jaxon's got the red pen – keeps things exciting.

Reece (joining in): Who's gonna win?

Jaxon (eye roll): Me, obviously, you idiots.

Sylvian (cold laugh): Dream on.

Me (sternly): See? I can't even write a decent dialogue like this.

Reece (reaches for my laptop to shut it): How about you take the rest of the day off? No Instagram, no panic. Go cuddle your daughter or something. We can manage a few evenings without your writing.

Me: But this is when all the genius scenes come! I just don't know whose POV. Reece? Jaxon? Sylvian? Mable?

Reece: Decide tomorrow.

Me: But –

Jaxon: Today, the dialogues can go to hell. Everything can go to hell. Three and a half hours to go; enjoy it after months of hard work.

Me: But –

Sylvian: God… Sorry, Jane, but this is the only solution. (He stands in front of me, pulls out duct tape, and tapes my fingers together.)

Me: Endless swearing emojis.

Bonusmaterial

INTERVIEW
VERY BAD KINGS

Do you guys have a leader?
Jaxon: Always the one with the biggest ego. So me.

Should we be afraid of you?
Jaxon: No, no. Ignore the warnings, it's more fun.
Sylvian: Yeah, definitely.

Will it be a happy ending?
Jaxon: First we have to define "happy"…
Reece: That our fans are happy.
Sylvian: And that no one dies, I guess.
Jaxon: Will that happen?
Reece: Tough call.
Sylvian: Maybe, if you listen to me.
Reece: Why you? They should listen to me.
Jaxon: Me.
Zayn: Me.
Sylvian rolls his eyes

Do you share women?
Jaxon: Only if they deserve it.

What was your first thought when you saw Mable?
Sylvian: Too weak for me.
Jaxon: Hot, but virgin type.
Reece: Unremarkable, but interesting.

Why is it okay if she sleeps with one of you, but not others?
Jaxon: Have you ever shared a beer with friends? You don't want a stranger's mouth on it. Same with girls.

Do you give the same "performance" with each girl?
Zayn: Yeah.
Sylvian: Yup.
Reece: Hm.
Jaxon: Absolutely.
Romeo: Yeah.

What are your best qualities?
Zayn: You don't mean my dick, right?
Sylvian: No one's asking you.
Jaxon: No one really knows us, so "best" feels like cutting our balls off.

Any weaknesses?
Jaxon: Even if we did, there are always four others to cover them. Together, we're unbeatable, baby.

Who is the most underestimated?
They all look at the guy in the back, Romeo.
Sylvian: If you mean just the three of us…

Jaxon: Then Crescent. Acts sweet and harmless with that baby face, but what he's capable of… I'm not telling yet.

Why do you target Mable?
Jaxon: Because we like her. Dangerous thing for a girl like that…

Who's the meanest?
Jaxon: Sylvian breaks your heart. Crescent breaks your mind. I break your soul. Until there's nothing left. So yeah, definitely me. Want a taste?

What is a trait you hate in others?
Zayn: I don't get the question.
Jaxon: Are there any traits we *don't* hate?
Reece: Can't think of just one. There's plenty to hate.
Sylvian: This question's a fail.

Who's the favorite among you?
Jaxon: You mean between us? I think we all find Sylvian adorable.
Reece: Definitely. The broken hero thing.
Zayn: Agreed. Always plays innocent, never admits how twisted he is. That sweet, crazy little guy.
Sylvian: …

Bonusmaterial

CONVERSATION DURING PART 2
THE FOLLOWING CONVERSATIONS TOOK PLACE WHILE I WAS WRITING PART 2

When the beginning of volume 2 was a bit more tearful...

Me: Phew, she cries a lot.

Jaxon: We're just assholes.

Me: Yes, but that really gets to me. I kind of like the fact that she wears her heart on her sleeve. But I like you guys less.

Reece: Excuse me?

Me: Yes, I think I only like Romeo and Vance now. She doesn't cry over them.

Jaxon: Oh, we can easily arrange for her to cry over them...

Sylvian: Do you remember what I said at Thanksgiving?

Me: That was a lot.

Sylvian: She has to burn to ashes before the phoenix can rise. She's still burning.

Me: But it hurts! Burning really hurts! And anyway: Why does it have to burn? What's wrong with you? When are you finally going to suffer?

Sylvian: Really now?

Reece: We're already suffering, Jane.

Vance: She means your tears. She wants to see your little fucking tears.

Jaxon (rolling his eyes): The only one who's about to cry here is you. Have we invited you or do you go around, bursting in everywhere since lately?

Vance (shrugs): I'm there when you need me. And Jane practically always needs me to protect Mable from idiots like you.

Me (drying my tears): It's fine now. Do you actually want to have sex in the next scene or not?

Vance (groans): As if those sex-crazed vultures would ever say no…

***

After a few readers compared Davies and Alec (from the Dark Prince series) to the Kings…

Davies (sharpening knife): Did you hear that, boss, they're actually comparing us to those campus kings. They're comparing me to… (he can't even pronounce it)

Alec: Are these opinions important enough for me to listen to you?

Davies: Absolutely not. Just in case you want a little laugh.

Alec (sighs and puts his incredibly important work aside. Then he looks at the sketches of Kingston, the character sheets, the readers' opinions and Jaxon's profile): Comparing me to this Tyrell would be like comparing my career to *Game of Thrones*. An absolute disgrace.

Davies: I'm fine with being compared to Wres. Smoke;

absolutely respectable guy. But what kind of psycho jerk is Sylvian supposed to be? He's not a sadist anymore. I don't even know what he is. An elitist little bastard from an elitist unimportant mafia family in America. His lineage alone says it all.

Alec (slowly paling in the face): Comparing me to Tyrell is the worst insult. Who is this Mable? Do we have to save her?

Florence: I think you're crazy. You're mine.

Davies and Alec ignore Florence's objection and bend lower over my notes.

Alec: You broke her, Davies. That must be what's going on. With your sadistic streak, you made sure Jane went completely crazy.

Davies: Me? Come to think of it, this Tyrell is just a less fierce 'I'm the only asshole at the top' version of yourself. If he was a royal, he'd have done it just like you. Here, see? The notes clearly show it.

Alec (hissing): Jaxon Tyrell only thinks about himself. I never thought about myself. And then I met Florence.

Davies (relaxed): Any way you look at it, Tyrell is just at a different rung on the ladder. Let's say he were to become president…

Alec (growling): Don't give Jane the wrong idea…

Davies: He would probably be a pretty good stroke of luck for the States.

Alec: The states have elected Bush twice in a row. For them, anyone without a pot shot is a windfall.

Davies laughs heartily.

Alec (grins): Look, they're even comparing you to Romeo. The only thing missing is that they compare you to your stinking cat.

Davies: Romeo is cool. Something different.

Alec (rolling his eyes): He jerks off next to unconscious women. Totally different.

Caleb: You know what I'm wondering, brother.

Davies: Who are these two?

Alec: The guys who shut down a mafia ring in New York. Your book is called Bastards.

London: Yes, dear twin?

Caleb: If they knew us, they would know that our profiles are pretty similar to Jaxon's and Sylvian's.

London: Wait a minute. But they're not brothers.

Caleb: Possibly the only difference.

London: Possibly.

Davies and Alec have been listening and are back to their work.

Davies grinds his knife.

Suddenly Nike appears: Well? What are you up to?

Davies: Nothing for a know-it-all little bird like you to worry about.

Nike: Oh yeah? (He makes himself comfortable on the royal sofa and throws a grape into his mouth). I wanted to drop by since you're discussing important stuff.

Alec: Not anymore.

Nike (ignoring him): Do you know I'm Mable's age? Maybe even a year older?

Davies (laughing derisively): So, she's got plenty of choice and she'll never want you.

Nike: I'm not into trailer park girls anyway. But I have been thinking...

Alec (suddenly looks up critically): What?

Nike: Are you paying for your brother-in-law to study at Kingston, Alec? I am, after all, the queen's brother. More famous than Rosalie and the missing Ella, so to speak. I could build up contacts in the meantime.

Alec (dismissively): Contacts where?

Nike (his eyes shine): The circle.

Alec and Davies look at each other.

Alec: The Kingston circle…

Davies: Never been a bad idea.

Alec (again disparagingly): Never. The circle is behind a lot of assassinations lately. You're going to do nothing of the sort and study at Cambridge.

Nike (grins): Think about it, Alec. No one would integrate better there than me. I just need a bit of pocket money.

Davies: Go work for your bloody pocket money. Besides, you have a girlfriend, don't you?

Nike: Maybe… maybe not. I don't want anything from Mable. She's just not my type. But there's another one I have my eye on…

Alec: Out. (Looks at Caleb and London) All of you!

London: Wow, the British king is really unlikeable. Were we like this too?

Caleb: Twin kings would definitely be really cool.

Alec: Out!

***

When I got the inspiration for kiss, marry, kill

Me: We should play a round of kiss, marry, kill!

Jaxon: Because the bikers from Sara Rivers with their tiny dicks did that the other day?

Me: Uh. Yes, exactly. And because it's hot! Mable, you start!

Mable (thinks for a while): That's too easy. Marry Reece, Kiss Sylvian, Kill Jaxon. (She shrugs.) Far too easy.

Me: Yes. Only you won't be able to kiss Sylvian if you kill Jaxon. He'd never forgive you. And you can't marry Reece without… you know.

Mable: Fine, then I won't kiss Sylvian. The main thing is that I get to kill Jaxon.

Jaxon (rolls his eyes): You could never do that anyway, Belle. You'd sooner stab Sylvian in the heart and shoot Reece in the heat of the moment than harm a hair on my head.

Mable (snorts): As if!

Jaxon (grinning smugly): It's the truth, little butterfly. It just takes you a while to realize it.

Bonusmaterial

INTERVIEW
VERY BAD ELITE

Interview with Jaxon Tyrell

Be honest, have you fallen in love with Mable?
And if I say yes, how could you believe me? Didn't you learn anything from last semester?

Will we still get to know your family? Or will you do everything you can to prevent that?
Depends on whether you count my father's whores as part of my family. Because I keep forgetting their names. Rude of me, isn't it?

How would you describe yourself in 3 words?
Suck me hard.

What are you going to do to Mable the next time you see her?
After fucking her little heart last time, I'm going to go for

her head this time. She'll feel me in every single brain cell and unfortunately she won't be able to do anything about it. Who suffers with her?

What three things would you still like to experience?
What do you mean?
I'm not exactly on my deathbed.
The whole universe is open to me and I won't let anyone stop me from living exactly the life I want to live.

Which King's hands on Mable's body bothers you the most?
You haven't understood that yet.
I am the Kings.
I am all five of us.
Nobody touches them except those who share everything physical with me anyway. I'd be surprised if Romeo suddenly touched women, but bothered? What the hell?
You really need to read better. It's not about who fucks her. It's about who gets her.
But that's a different story. We'll see who's bothered by what.

Why are you such an ass, but so cute at the same time?
Counter question: why are you so clever and yet so weak?
It's too easy to win you over. That's why I act shitty something, so you don't immediately give yourself to me and I have a challenge, but even that rarely works.

What went wrong with you?
It's just boring to follow a straight path and only work for people who drain the life from you. But you'll never understand what I mean by that, and that's okay. There are billions

of people, but only 47 of them have become president of the USA so far. Which of the two groups do you belong to? And which one do I belong to?

Why on earth are you such an asshole? And don't give me excuses now!
I just don't try to pretend and be good like ninety-nine per cent of people. That's it.

Do you actually like driving Jane crazy?
We love each other. So far, we've agreed on everything. The one who constantly crosses the line is Zayn. Or fucking Vance Buchanan. Or Mable herself. She never actually does what she's told. But I'll get that out of her.

Have you ever had your heart broken?
Which heart?

What will you do if Sylvian or one of the others wants to keep Mable for themselves without sharing?
Let's go through them.
Sylvian: pretends to, but he can't exist without me by his side.
Romeo: will kill her rather than claim her.
Reece: always shares.
Zayn: doesn't know how to leave girls whole at all.
Does that answer the question?

Are you jealous that the others had Mable before you?
Sometimes I wonder what you think I'm doing.
All the strings are in my hands. Everyone who touches them was controlled by me. There is no "Jaxon mustn't find out", no "He doesn't know". Everything, fucking everything, even

every look, is controlled by me. I just pretend otherwise sometimes. But that's a game, like everything else.

When are you going to tell your Mable why you pull all that crap on campus?
She has known it for a long time. She just doesn't want to admit it.

Which of the Kings could you most easily go without?
Myself. Sometimes I enjoy through the others. Poetic, isn't it?

Describe Mable in 3 words.
Easy to have.
No, I'm joking. How about: "Disturbed like me"? After all, you have to have a proper moral dysfunction to fall for all of us. And she is addicted to us.

What do you like most and least about Mable?
When one of the Kings (including me) touches her or is about to touch her, her blood seems to change color. Red becomes tainted. Salty becomes sweet. Her heartbeat becomes a pounding. The only thing I don't like about her is that I unfortunately have to destroy her. But sometimes a higher purpose gets in the way.

What is your darkest secret?
That I sit down when I pee.

What fascinates you about Mable? Why is she different and special to you?
She sees the good in all of us. It's not there, but hey, I'm still fascinated by such brain errors.

Your favorite position?
Watch.
Well, you wouldn't have thought that now, would you? But no, I'm not a loser. As I just said, I like to enjoy myself through others. So maybe I'm not all cold and heartless after all. Or maybe it's just a psychosis.

Would it bother you if Mable chose Sylvian?
Yes. Poor Sy would probably shoot her because all his warnings were a pointless waste of breath.

What would you do if Sy, Reece, Zayn and Romeo betrayed you?
I would forgive them. If they go that far, they have a good reason. I trust them to do what's right.
Of course I would say something else if they asked me. So only you know that now.

What did you feel at that moment in the limo when Mable was sitting on your lap?
I thought to myself: Seriously, girl. Don't even think of falling for me. Don't be so predictable. Don't be so boring. Come on, show me what you're really made of. You're more than your body. Show me your will.
And that's what she did. It just didn't end well for her. But I have to stay true to my image.

Are you, deep deep down, a softie?
Yeah, I'm a bit of a softie. I cried when all of Nemo's siblings died. That kind of thing really gets to me.

Did you know that Sylvian had Mable first? Or did you lose control over the strings…

Ah yes, someone has been paying attention. I thought so. No, I was even sure. After all, that was my plan. What I wouldn't have believed was that he would actually lie to me to protect her. But the fact that he seems to have found someone, he would even betrays me for, almost moves me to tears.

Such a cute little destructive fucker. If I were Mable, I'd castrate him after everything he's done. But thank God I'm not her.

Do you believe in love?

Of course. It is the beginning and the end of all problems. Without love and without the fear of not being loved, we would still be sitting in the middle of paradise and would never have doubted God.

How can you be so repulsive and so attractive at the same time?

Pure physics. It's called magnetism. #smartassmode

Honestly, does Jane really have all the power with her red pen or are you just letting her do it?

Sure, she does. But as I said, we're in agreement. Didn't you think so?

Where does your sexist image of women come from?

Sex. Woman. Image. Done.

Do you really think Mable is as beautiful as you told her?
You're desperate to get me to talk about my feelings, eh?
It will be a while before you can tell the difference between
my masks. Until then, you can fall in love with the version
of me that told Mable just that.

Who did you have sex with for the first time?
With Amabelle.
Hahaha.
That would be a great plot twist, wouldn't it?

317